A Whisper in the Trees

by

Susan Dalessandro

Cover Art by *Teddi Black*

The Wild Rose Press, Inc.
PO Box 708
Adams Basin, NY 14410-0708
Visit us at www.thewildrosepress.com

Publishing History
First Edition, 2025
Trade Paperback ISBN 978-1-5092-6116-1
Digital ISBN 978-1-5092-6117-8

Published in the United States of America

Chapter One

A cold sweat drenches my skin as I slowly open my eyes. The earthy scent of grass and dirt flood my senses. I reach my hand out and sharp blades of grass prick my fingers.

What just happened?

I start to lift my head when someone touches my arm.

"Don't get up too quickly," a woman says. My cross-country coach, Caroline Wilson. "You passed out, Gabby. You sprinted into the park like it was the last kilometer of a race and collapsed." Coach leans over me, her gaze darting around my face. "Are you hurt?"

"No." I draw myself into a sitting position and tug my tank top over my running shorts. "Omigod, I passed out?"

How? I've been doing so well. I'm down to 107. Almost to 105, the perfect weight. Well, for someone who's a five-foot-eleven giant.

She nods, then hands me a bottle of water. "Here, drink. Thank goodness you didn't hit your head." She narrows her gaze. "You didn't, did you?"

"No, I don't think so. My head feels fine." A little fuzzy, but fine.

"The humidity is high today, but you finished in forty-nine minutes. No one else is back yet." She leans forward on her knees, tucks a lock of blonde hair into her visor and scans the road. "Here they come." She sighs. "Maybe I should've cut back today's mileage."

Soon there's a cacophony of voices filling the air, one higher than the rest and distinctly belonging to my best friend.

"Oh, my gosh, Gabs! What happened?" Asha Shah, my best friend, drops to the grass on her knees, sweat trickling down her face. She flings her long dark ponytail behind her. "You're really pale. Are you okay?"

"Mm hmm. Thanks."

"Give her some space, girls," Coach says.

"What the heck, Gabs? It's supposed to be our long *slow* day. Eight miles at an *easy* pace. Not *race* pace." Asha chugs her water. "I saw you and Breanna up ahead and then like that, boom, you were gone."

"I don't know. I felt pretty good and started picking it up and...I don't remember passing out, but Coach said that's what happened."

"Wait, you passed out?" Her gaze flits over my face. "You ate breakfast this morning, right?"

"Here you go, Gabby, Asha." My coach pulls two bananas from the bunch she's distributing, and hands each of us one, her timing exquisite. "There's more water by your gear, protein bars, too." She rests her hand on my shoulder. "Are you sure you're okay? Do you have a ride home?"

"Um, yeah, my dad."

Asha screws up her face but stays silent.

"Okay, good. I would drive you if you didn't. I don't want to see you walking after you passed out."

"Thanks, Coach. Plus, I feel fine."

And I am fine. Asha and I have a short walk. Well,

not exactly a *short* walk, even with the shortcut through the woods, but my coach shouldn't think she needs to drive me home. That's ridiculous. I'm fine.

Asha nudges me. "What are you waiting for? Eat that now. You'll feel better."

Ugh, I love Ash, but why doesn't she, or anyone else, trust me to make my own choices? It's my body. I know what it needs. And it's not food.

"I'll get us two more bottles of water and some of those bars. They're the good ones, too, with dark chocolate pieces." Asha smiles and dashes off. "And I'll get your bag."

"Thanks." I slowly get to my feet, brushing grass off my legs, and stretch my arms overhead.

Over by our gear, my coach pulls Asha aside. Asha nods, like four times. Great, she's giving me up, telling her I don't have a ride.

"Hey, sit down. We don't have to leave yet," Asha says, when she runs back to me. She hands me my drawstring bag.

"I'm fine. I needed water. I left my bottle of electrolyte solution home today. So, you told Coach I didn't have a ride? Seriously, Ash. I'm fine. I don't want Coach driving me...*us*, home and I—"

"Chill. I didn't say a word. I didn't give you up, Gabby Patterson. But I will be calling 911 if you pass out on our walk home."

I level a steely glare at her.

"Kidding," she says. "Kidding."

But from Asha's tone and her using my full name, she's serious.

"Hey, Gabby, you okay?" Breanna Pozzi approaches, shielding her eyes from the sun.

3

I ball my hands into fists and swallow around the dryness in my throat. All I can do is nod. Why is everyone obsessed with if I'm okay? I didn't drink enough and got a little dizzy. Case closed.

"Cool. It's crazy hot out here. When you took off at Cherry Street, I tried to keep up, but there was no way. Go home and take a cool shower. And eat something. My mom's picking up pizza on the way home for lunch. I'm gonna inhale about four slices as soon as I get in the door."

My gaze glides over her tiny little perfect body. *Hmph, lucky you.*

"Yeah, thanks." I turn to Asha. "Ready?"

She swallows a piece of banana. "What did you do with that banana I gave you?"

"I'll wait until I get home." I drop it into my drawstring bag, which I shrug onto my shoulders. "I don't want my hands to get sticky."

Asha lifts a brow. "Right. Come on, Coach is talking to Natalie. I think she's going to have her run Varsity with us. But now's a good time to make our escape."

"Funny. Ha ha."

****

A block from school, we duck into the woods and find some much-needed shade. The paltry breeze offers little relief. As we walk along the narrow dirt path, I uncap my water bottle and slurp the last drop of tepid liquid.

That's when it hits. A bone-rattling chill that skitters down my spine and settles in my gut.

Are you kidding me? As if passing out at practice wasn't enough.

I shake it off and pick up the pace. I need to get home.

"Hey, what's the rush, Gabs?" Asha asks, jogging to catch up. She drags her arm across her glistening forehead. "You don't want to pass out again."

"I'm fine." I wipe my palms on my running shorts.

What if I'm coming down with something? That would explain passing out at the end of our eight-miler. Getting sick is *not* an option. Not now, right before the season starts.

Beneath the leafy canopy, we navigate a path through the overgrown shrubs and bushes, following the slight descent of the hill, my throat dry, sweat trickling down my back. The overly sweet aroma of honeysuckle chokes my senses and sours my empty stomach.

"Remind me why we're walking home and not sitting in an air-conditioned car?" Asha asks, pushing sopping strands of hair off her face.

"Because one, I'm fine and didn't want coach to think I *needed* a ride home from her and two, you told Liam we didn't *mind* walking when he offered yesterday to pick us up. Remember?"

Asha sighs. "Right. I didn't want it to seem like he's our personal taxi. He gave us a ride yesterday and he's picking us up later for the movie."

"Do you think he'd mind? For us?" I say, although I really mean "for you".

Liam's always had a soft spot for Asha. *Crush* may be too strong of a word. Then again, maybe not.

"I know. Still."

The path starts to widen, giving way to a large circular clearing, a thousand beams of sunlight

5

streaming through the treetops like satiny white threads, dappling the forest floor with bursts of light. As I step into the clearing, I'm again gripped by shivering chills. Like I've stepped into a walk-in freezer. An all-out arctic blast halts me in my tracks. A blistering August day suddenly feels like the dead of winter.

I glance skyward, expecting…what, I don't know. But there's only a thatched canopy of leaves fluttering in the breeze. The *hot*, sticky breeze.

Asha places her hand on my arm. "Gabs, you okay? Geez, you have goosebumps all over. Do you want me to text Liam? I'm sure he wouldn't mind picking us up."

I stand there, hugging myself, uncontrollable chills shaking me from head to toe. Panic roots me to the spot as my heart tries to pound its way out of my chest.

What is wrong with me?

"Gabs?"

"Huh? No, we're not far from my house. Let's keep walking."

"Okay, but maybe we should forget the movie today. If you have heatstroke or heat exhaustion, you should stay home. I'm sure we could convince Liam to come over and watch something at your house. There's a bunch of new movies streaming right now."

"I'm fine." I try to stop my teeth from chattering.

"It's just…you're okay?" It can't just be me. I drag my teeth along my bottom lip and meet her gaze.

"I'm okay, if *okay* means *I'm still wilting*." Her eyes narrow. "Omigod, Gabs, your lips are like, purplish-blue."

Trembling, I lift my fingers to my mouth. "Great." Another spine-tingling shiver races across my skin and

I rub my hands up and down my arms. It's like when I had the flu last year, and no amount of blankets could keep me warm.

"Gabs, why don't you eat that banana or the protein bar? It will probably help."

"How? I'm not hungry, just hot. Well, so hot, apparently, I'm freezing. Ugh, I need to get home."

We reach the other side of the clearing and as quickly as it arrived, the frigid cold leaves me. Sweat oozes from my pores again. I exhale a large breath, but something invisible grazes my shoulder, raising every last hair on my skin. My gaze darts around the woods as a faint tune plays in my head, one I can't decipher, but has a familiar ring to it. It's on my running playlist. I hate it when that happens. Even worse when I can't think of the name of the song.

Asha runs her gaze over me. Her wrinkled brow tells me I'm in for another lecture. "Next time, don't push it so hard. It was just a training run. Supposedly at a *comfortable* pace. Especially in this heat. And I'll text you before our next practice, remind you to bring your electrolyte drink."

"Thanks."

I go to chug a mouthful of water from my water bottle. Empty.

"I'd offer you some of my water, but…"

She shakes her water bottle. Empty, like mine.

"No worries. We'll be at my house in five."

Right. To get ready for the movies with Liam. My stomach churns. This afternoon's movie is his choice. Liam and Ash are both obsessed with horror flicks. Especially those psychological thrillers, the ones that mess with your head. They're not really my thing. Give me a rom-com any time. I don't care if they're sappy or cliché.

I don't know what's playing, but I'm sure he's found something creepy, something that will keep me up at night. Maybe Ash is right. I should stay home. But then Mom will think I'm sick. Keep me home from practice tomorrow. I have to suck it up, go to the movies with my friends.

The path starts to widen, and we walk side by side again. The furious whooshing of the stream below catches my attention as we skirt the edge. I kick a pebble with my sneaker, and it flies over the cliff side and splashes into the creek. I glance sideways and my heart leaps into my throat. It's a long way down. I turn to Asha and force a smile. Everything's fine. Just fine.

Why did I look?

"Come on," Asha says, linking her arm through mine. If we're gonna make that one o'clock movie, we need to get to your house and shower."

"Right."

But all I can think about is the chill, the song, and the eerie feeling that still grips me.

Chapter Two

We manage to make it to my house without any more strange occurrences and an hour later, Liam pulls up to my house in his mom's SUV. We jump in, Asha in front and me in the back. Like always.

"Gabs, I know you're not a horror fan, but this one sounds cool. It's called *Searching for Lisa*." He bites his lip and meets my gaze in the rearview mirror. "Actually, it's not horror, but a thriller. Not gory or anything. I know you're not into that stuff."

A wave of dread courses through me and I clutch my legs. "I'm sure it'll be great," I say with a tight smile.

"Cool," he says. "Oh, did you guys hear they're closing Pine Borough Camp after this summer? My mom saw it in the paper today."

"Really? You mean the place where we crushed Tyler Court and his buddies every summer in dodgeball?" Asha asks, a hint of glee in her voice.

I force out a laugh, but my stomach heaves at the mention of Tyler.

"Sorry, Gabs. I know those guys were awful, especially him," Asha continues.

My chest tightens.

"Such a jerk. What ever happened to him? He doesn't go to West Penn."

"I dunno," I say. I don't care.

"I think he's homeschooled," Liam says. "You're right, though, he was a jerk."

Tyler couldn't resist reminding me every day, 'how *unbelievably* tall' I was. 'Amazon girl' he called me, not to mention, built '*like a boy*.' He'd snicker then elbow his equally noxious buddies until they were all doubled over in mocking laughter. Talk about giving someone a complex.

It was six years ago, and I was eleven years old. What was I supposed to look like? A curvy supermodel? It's not my fault I'm taller than all the girls. Most of the boys. Not my fault I'm built more like my dad than my mom.

"You totally had my back, Liam. For that, I am forever in your debt."

He rakes his hand through his ginger hair and smiles at me in the rearview mirror. "Ah, what are best friends for? Plus, he was a total douche."

My heart swells and I tap his shoulder. "Thanks."

We're still reminiscing about camp as we wait in the concession line, and though our conversation has brought up some bitter memories, it's also pushed my experience at practice, and in the woods today, out of my head. Almost.

We climb to the last row and sink into the plush red seats as the theatre fills. Liam sits between Asha and me.

"Feeling better, Gabs?" Asha asks. She passes the jumbo popcorn to Liam, who naturally offers it to me.

I shake my head. "Thanks, not hungry."

My stomach groans, betraying me, but I smile and tip the bucket back toward Liam. Nothing until dinner.

"None? You usually love this stuff. Last time here,

I couldn't pry it away from you." He screws up his face. "Wait, I take that back. Last time you had nothing either. Must've been the time before that." He snorts. "When you *liked* popcorn, I guess."

I glare at him.

He raises his hands in mock surrender. "Hey, I'm just messing around. You're a little tense today."

"I'm sorry."

"At least you look better than this morning," Asha says.

"Mm," is all I say.

We don't need a full-blown discussion about my non-event today. I was overheated. That's all.

"Wait," Liam says, catching up. "Were you sick at practice?" He tilts his head, flipping his hair off his face. "Was it something you ate at Lucia's last night, you know, before you and Ash brought down the house with your karaoke routine?"

"That was *all* Gabs," Asha says. "I was just background."

"Hah, not true and there was no 'bringing down the house'. The place was empty, or I wouldn't have gotten up there. You know that." I clear my throat. "But it was nothing this morning. Just the heat. The humidity. I'm fine."

It was the heat. That's all. I'll keep telling myself that. I don't want Liam getting all motherly and protective on me. I have Ash for that.

"You should've texted me," Liam says. He stretches his legs out, crossing them at the ankles. "I was at the pool this morning, teaching the tots. Last week of lessons for the summer. I was home by ten-thirty, though. I could've picked you two up."

I smile. "Thanks, but we were fine."

Asha elbows Liam. "It was supposed to be our long, *slow* day." She eyes me. "Then we walked home, and Gabs got the chills. I think she needs to relax and chill—no pun intended."

A soft, lyrical laugh escapes Asha's lips, the kind of laugh that totally beguiles Liam, like it does now. She meets his gaze, and he turns away, his cheeks pinking. He's not very good at hiding his feelings for her.

The look on his face reminds me of the first time we met at summer camp after Asha and Liam moved to Pine Borough weeks apart. Not to mention, next door to one another. We became instant besties, banding together to stand up to Tyler and his gang. We've been inseparable ever since.

"You sure you're okay, Gabby?" Liam asks. "Chills sound serious."

"I'm fine. I forgot my electrolyte solution. I was a little overheated."

"Okay, cool." Liam turns to the screen. "Seriously though, I don't know how you two do it, running an insane number of miles in the heat. Of course, you both *choose* to run cross-country, which means you have to be a little crazy in the head." He makes googly eyes and sticks out his tongue. "But that's what I love about the two of you."

As the lights dim and the eerie music cues, the camera pans from the black, nighttime sky to the woods. Woods that transport me to earlier today. To the uneasiness I felt when that chill hit me. More than being 'overheated'. My hands clammy, my pulse racing, I rise from my seat.

"I'll be right back."

"Gabs, you okay?" Liam asks.

"Fine. I should've gone before we sat down. I'll only be a minute."

They won't miss me.

It's like that the entire movie. Excusing myself to go to the bathroom because I don't have the stomach to be reminded of the woods. Of my eerie experience earlier today.

"Need the bathroom, Gabs?" Liam stifles a laugh, as we walk out of the theatre.

I shoot him a glare. "Funny, not funny."

"Sorry. I couldn't resist."

"Come on," Asha says, smoothing her khaki shorts. "You did spend almost the entire movie there."

I shrug. "It's all that water I drank before we came. No big deal."

Nothing more is said about my weak bladder as we head outside and walk to our usual hangout. Buddy's is a small café nestled between a vintage clothing store and my favorite indie bookshop. A smattering of clouds gather in the sky and a cool breeze picks up, as we round the corner and arrive at Buddy's. It's crowded with patrons, as it usually is, no matter the time of day.

"So, what did you guys think?" Asha lifts her steaming cup of espresso to her lips.

We're seated in our favorite booth in the front, a steady stream of pedestrians filing by our window.

"Come on, you know I'm not big on those kinds of movies. I mean, Liam was right, it wasn't gory, but..."

But I'm still freaked out about the woods.

Liam lowers his spoon. "Aww, I'm sorry, Gabs," he says, talking around a mouthful of vanilla ice cream.

"I thought you'd be okay with it. I thought it was really good. *Crazy* suspenseful. Totally didn't see the ending coming, either." His moss green eyes widen. "But next time when it's my choice, I'll run it by you first. You will have the right of first refusal." He jabs his spoon in the air for emphasis.

"Thanks."

"And what about me?" asks Asha.

"Come on," Liam says, nudging her. "We have the *exact* same taste in movies. We always agree."

"Yeah, I guess you're right." Asha grabs her spoon and plunges it into the thick fudge of her sundae, a dark blush coloring her cheeks. "Gabs, you have no idea what you're missing." She tilts her head. "Have you eaten anything today? I mean, except for your chai tea there." She nods at the cup wrapped in my hands. "You said your stomach was upset earlier at your house when I polished off a turkey sandwich. You didn't have anything at the movies—"

"I'm not hungry."

"Oh, okay." She purses her lips. "If you say so, but—"

"I'm fine," I snap. "Why is everyone worried about what I eat?"

"Hey, chill," Asha says. "Just making sure you're okay. You haven't been eating much lately."

"Stomach off, Gabs?" Liam asks.

I nod. "A little, yeah. Hopefully, it will feel better later."

"Yeah, definitely," he says, smiling at me.

Asha narrows her gaze on me before glancing away and fiddling with her napkin. She mumbles something about 'starving herself', but I don't press her. I don't feel like arguing right now. And she doesn't know what she's talking about.

When we finish, Liam orders another cup of coffee to go, because he can never get enough caffeine. I slide out of the booth and stand. I'm definitely not feeling a chill now, my insides abuzz and happy after my cup of chai tea. Buddy's has the best spicy chai tea.

I follow Asha and Liam to the exit, but halt at the doorway. Cold fingers walk my spine.

Oh. My. God.

The song streaming from the speakers. There was no music playing in Buddy's. There is now. It's *that* song. The one from the woods. The one I couldn't get out of my head. What is it?

And why do I feel like what happened in the woods is following me?

Chapter Three

At dinner, I push my food around my plate with my fork, poking at the chicken I can't finish. Or won't. I ate a few mouthfuls of my baked-potato-sans butter—but it's still a few mouthfuls too many. Almost there, I can't slack off now.

"Not hungry, Gabby?" Mom tilts her head and sets her glass on the table.

Everyone says we look alike, same fine light-colored hair, blue eyes, fair complexion. I don't need to wonder what I'll look like when I'm older. Except that Mom topped out at five-feet-nine. I'm already zooming past her at five-feet-eleven.

At least the guys are finally catching up. Ash can't use her favorite line anymore when I lament my lack of boyfriends, *'Gabs, they're just intimidated by you. Wait till they grow a little.'* Can I blame them? Guys don't want to date an Amazon. I may not be able to do anything about my height, but I can do something about my weight.

I set my fork down and that song weaves its way through my head again. The words sharpen as my brain familiarizes itself with the tune.

Wait—

"Gabby?"

"Huh? Yeah, no. I ate too much junk at the movie. Plus, Ash and I made jumbo sandwiches after practice.

I'm sorry."

My stomach twists from the lie. But Mom worries about me eating enough with 'all the running' I do. Her words, not mine.

She raises a brow. "Too much junk? I doubt that."

"I have to agree with your mom," my dad says. "And you can afford it, all those miles you're putting in."

All those miles. C'mon, Dad, you're supposed to be helping me here.

"I did. I'm sorry, you made this great dinner, and I ruined it. It won't happen tomorrow. Promise." I swallow and drop my gaze to my plate.

If I want to stay ahead of my competition and beat the likes of Katie Watson, Breanna, and look like a serious runner doing it, I can't go soft. Mom doesn't realize how difficult it is, being built like I am, a giant surrounded by petite little waifs. Which is exactly how all the guys see me. Definitely not 'dating' material.

I linger on the leafy romaine lettuce in my salad, and I'm transported to the picnic at our house last summer. My Aunt Kim and cousin Tara sat across from me. Aunt Kim remarked what a 'good eater' I was. *'Such a healthy appetite'*, she said. *'Being an athlete, you must need to keep up your strength, blah, blah, blah.'* Tara, who's my age, but half a foot shorter, picked at the food on her plate, like a grazing bird. I must've looked like a pig at a trough. I don't want to be a 'good eater'. I don't want to have 'a healthy appetite'. Aunt Kim won't be able to say that the next time she sees me.

****

The following day, after practice, Asha's mom

picks her up for a dentist appointment. Which means I'm walking home alone. Through the woods. A shudder rocks me as my experience from yesterday resurfaces. The icy cold. The fever-like chills. The song I can't shake from my brain. But I don't have to walk home yet. I need to stop at the bookstore to pick up a book I pre-ordered. The sequel to the fantasy *Fractured Wings* comes out today. My copy is at the indie bookshop on Main Street.

Tall elms shade the sidewalk, providing some solace from the blistering sun as I make the four-block walk to the center of town. I should go home and shower before I immerse myself in a crowd of people, all gross and sweaty from practice. But I'll only be in there a minute. Two, tops.

I turn the corner onto Main Street and jostle my way through the lunch crowd thronging the sidewalk. That's when Madison Reilly's perfectly waved dark hair, white spaghetti strap tank, and black micro shorts catch my eye.

Ugh.

Why did I have to run into someone from school? And, of all people, Madison. Never a hair out of place and her face always perfectly made up. I should've gone home to shower. Figures.

She gives me a half-hearted wave. "Hey, Gabby."

I dig my fingers into the sides of my legs. "Hey." But she doesn't advance any closer, instead, she pushes into the door of the bagel shop next door and disappears.

Exhaling a sigh of relief, I keep walking when I come upon my favorite music store. I pause and lean my forehead against the display window. Larry's Music carries everything from big band to rock, jazz, R&B, emo, and pop. He has vintage albums, tapes, and CDs. To a music junkie like me, it's pure heaven. Even in the age of music apps, the capacity to download hundreds of songs with the tap of a button, there's something special about getting my hands on a vintage CD or vinyl album. Today, like every day, the store overflows with Larry's loyal customers.

I shouldn't, but curiosity pulls me inside. Like always. The bell jingles as I step through the doorway, into a bygone era of music.

Omigod, I love this place!

A blast of cold air—Larry always cranks the A/C in the dog days of summer and beyond—greets me as I enter the store that transports me back to another time.

"Hey, Gabby, got some new—well, new to the store—eighties and nineties stuff, right over there. I think you'll like it. I know you love your eighties music." Larry tips his cap back, exposing his salt and pepper hair and smiles, a wide friendly grin stretching across his face. He knows me too well.

"Thanks, I'll check it out."

I shoulder my way through the crowd and circle around to the last aisle, perusing the stack of CDs under the 'Just In' banner. A nineties' grunge tune hums from the store's speakers. Leaning against the bins, I draw out a nineties' alternative rock CD—I can't believe Larry got this in—and flip it over in my hand.

Someone starts to hum a familiar tune, but not just a familiar tune, one of my favorite from the sixties and uncharacteristically, I start to sing along. Out loud. I mean, it's one of my favorites. Asha and I have done karaoke to this countless times at Angelo's. In an empty room. Well, if you don't count Liam. But I can't help myself and soon I'm into it.

The person stops humming and starts to sing with me.

My heart pounds. Clamping my lips together, I grip the CD in my hand and peek through my lashes.

Across the table, a guy in a faded blue t-shirt and khaki shorts sings as he nods his head from side to side, his thick mane of blond hair concealing his face. A few inches shorter than me, he lifts his chin and pushes the hair out of his eyes. A smile plays across his lips. "Aww, why'd you stop? You were awesome. We make a great duet."

Heat flushes my neck as two beautiful pale gray eyes connect with mine. I freeze, my fingers in a white-knuckled grip on the CD.

"Sorry, I didn't realize I was singing out loud. Or, *that* loud. I just…" Flames engulf my face.

I just need to get away. Fast. Before I make an even bigger fool of myself.

"You have a beautiful voice." His smile widens, exposing the dimples in his cheeks and quickening my pulse.

"Oh." What do I say? "Thanks, it's one of my favorite songs."

What am I doing? Flirting? I don't flirt. Especially with a total stranger. But a stranger who looks about my age. And *hot*, especially the way his jaw muscle jumps when he smiles. Why don't I recognize him? Everyone around here goes to West Penn. It's not *that* big of a school.

He flashes those light gray eyes at me. I can't move. Or breathe. Seriously, I need to be out of here like, two awkward replies ago.

"Yeah, me too." His gaze darts to the door then back to me. "You, um… run for West Penn?" He examines my tank and running shorts with my school's logo stitched across the bottom. I'm suddenly conscious of my long legs. Being exposed. Judged.

I wrap my arms around me, as if I can somehow shrink into myself and hide all my flaws. Disappear. "Cross-country."

Duh. Obviously, Gabby.

"Do you go to West Penn?" Since I don't recognize him, I doubt he's a junior. Probably a senior.

He rubs the back of his neck. "No."

Damn.

"Oh." I drop my gaze to the CD gripped in my hand. Disappointment sinks in my gut.

I can't resist. He can't be more than a year or two older than me. "Did you graduate last spring?"

"Uh…no." He pauses then with his eyes raking the floor, "I do the homeschool thing. You know, cyber-school?"

"Oh. Right." Cyber-school. Like Tyler Court. I grip the sides of my legs. "Do you like it?"

Do you like it? Silly question, Gabby.

He shrugs. "It's okay. No big deal. I'm CJ, by the way."

My pulse quickens. He's giving me his name. Could he really be interested in me? Nah. Still… Still, he's a total stranger. What's wrong with me?

"Gabby. I'm a junior…Well, I'll be a junior in like six days. What grade are you in, you know, if you went to a regular school?" Heat floods my cheeks. "I don't mean a *regular* school," I say, fumbling my words. "I

21

mean—"

Crap, I'm totally butchering this.

CJ laughs. "It's okay. I know what you mean. It works the same for cyber school. I'm a senior." He rakes his hand through his hair and leans against the counter. Narrowing his gaze, he says, "I don't think I've seen you here before." He shakes his head, a smile twitching at the corners of his mouth. "No, I know I haven't. I would've remembered you." A glimmer simmers in the depths of his gray eyes. "Do you live in the borough?"

Now, I'm not only aware of my body which is way too exposed in a tank and shorts, but my grunginess, my hair in a ponytail, loose tendrils hanging in my face and sweat caking my skin. Not a good first impression. And I thought running into Madison was tragic.

His light, wavy hair falls in his eyes, and he pushes it away with his long, slender fingers. Musician's fingers. I definitely would have remembered him.

"Gabby?" CJ arches his brow.

"I'm sorry, what did you say?"

"Do you live around here?"

"Oh yes, on Cherry Street."

"Cool. I'm on the other side of Main."

Sweat soaks my temples. I should go, even though I don't want to. I want to stay and flirt with this guy who's making my pulse race, giving me all the feels, but I desperately need a shower.

My eyes are glued to the 80's CD gripped in my hand, wishing I'd grabbed something from the seventies or better yet, the 60's. "So, you're into 60's music?"

He nods. "Absolutely. Actually, I love all types. Rock, jazz, R&B, even some hard rock, alternative rock. A lot of current stuff." He nods to the CD in my hand. "That's a great CD," he says, before glancing around the store. "This is *the* perfect place for that. Well, for every kind of music."

"Actually, it's the *only* place like it."

CJ laughs. "I know, right? I thought I was the only one into old music... er, *older* music and still bought CDs."

"Nope, guilty as charged." I raise my hand and CJ busts out laughing.

Oh my God, what is going on here?

I drum my fingers on the counter, sweat pouring off me, even in this freezer of a store. The longer I stand here, the worse it'll be and soon, I'll be drowning in a puddle the size of the Atlantic Ocean. But it's like some invisible force is rooting me to the spot.

"I, um... I should get going. Maybe I'll see you around." I swallow the stickiness in my throat, set down the CD and step away from the counter.

"Oh. Yeah, sure." His shoulders drop. "Um..." He purses his lips, like he's about to say something, something maybe to keep me from walking out the door? But then his eyes narrow, his mouth pulls into a tight line, and he nods. "Yeah, I'll see ya."

I give a small wave and walk out, my head spinning, my footsteps quickening. I turn the corner and leave Larry's behind. Leave CJ behind.

My encounter with CJ consumes me as I walk home. Who is he? And why am I suddenly obsessed with him? Well, duh. Why didn't he follow me? He gave me his name. Asked where I lived. We seemed to hit it off. Maybe I turned him off with my sweat. My odor? The fact I have at least two...*three* inches on him? Five pounds? Uh, I'm obsessing over a guy I talked to for ten minutes. A guy I'll never see again. What's wrong with me?

I should turn around and go the long way, but I don't.

These woods aren't haunted. It was hot yesterday, and I was depleted of fluids.

Hitching my bag across my body, I jog along the dirt path. When I reach the clearing, the place I felt the eerie chill, I don't stop, but sprint across the grass. My momentum carries me, like I'm flying, the wind racing through my sweaty hair. Meeting CJ has proven a great distraction to my overarching fear.

At least it is for a few fast, furious seconds.

When I reach the other side, a fierce wind whips through the trees, shaking the branches and fluttering the leaves. It envelops me in its icy grip.

No, not again.

I hug myself tightly and glance around. Nothing but leaves blowing in the dusty, hot breeze. *Hot*, not cold. It doesn't change the fact I'm frozen inside like the last time. And I didn't pass out at practice today. I was totally fine for our mile repeats. In fact, I killed them.

The chill leaves as quickly as it arrived, and I exhale, a dense vapor billowing from my mouth. I take off along the path and the song resonates in my head. Only this time the lyrics are sharper. Stronger.

My stomach clenches and I try to push the song out of my head, but it refuses to be silenced.

It taunts me.

Transfixed, I stumble and fall, landing on my hands and knees. I lift my gaze. The trees, their leaves

24

thatched together like an emerald canopy, hover above me like a lid to a coffin. I can't breathe. I can't move. I don't know what's going on, but I have to get off the ground, get out of here.

I pinch myself. Hard. The pain breaks the grip of the haunted woods. Or whatever has me in its grip. I scramble to my feet and sprint along the narrow path out of the woods, faster and faster with each stride.

I run the rest of the way home and don't stop until I've slammed my front door behind me. Thankfully, Mom and Dad are at work. I'm sure the look on my face, not to mention, my heart leaping out of my chest, would be cause for alarm.

Taking the steps two at a time, I race upstairs, run into my bedroom and collapse on my bed. What the heck was that?

Lola, my Border Collie, jumps up and licks my face. I pet her head as she nuzzles my neck, her soft black fur tickling my skin. Easing my nerves. The tension begins to leave my body as I sink into my pillows and Lola snuggles into me. I'm able to breathe again.

My phone buzzes, startling me and I jump. It's only Asha.

—*Totally sucks. I have a cavity. Have to go back for a filling in two weeks. How was your afternoon? Did you get your book? Bet u read the entire thing on your way home. I know the way u are...*—

My book? Crap. I totally forgot about it. Obsessing over a cute guy tends to do that, I guess. And freaking out in the woods from...from what, exactly?

—*Don't judge, but I forgot it. Met someone in Larry's*—

—OMG! Who? What's his name?—
—CJ. I don't know his last name—
—What good is that?—
—Doesn't matter. I won't see him again—
—Don't say that. You're always in Larry's—

The sequel I waited for all summer. But I was so infatuated with CJ, I forgot to stop at the bookstore. Asha probably thinks I've lost it. Or, I was so distracted by a hot stranger with hypnotic pale gray eyes and a contagious smile, that reading was the last thing on my mind. Yeah, that's about it.

I'll hit up the bookstore after dinner.

****

"This is good, Mom. Too good." I scarf down the last morsel of rice from the chicken stir fry on my plate and wipe my hands on my napkin. Tomorrow I'll slip in an extra half-mile in warm-ups, another half after practice. I have to. I can feel my entire dinner sinking like a massive weight in my stomach. Why didn't I stop myself?

"Glad to hear it, though you barely ate, Gabriela. You only took a spoonful of everything." She meets my gaze. "Are you sure you don't want any more? You're running so much at practice, you need to be eating more not less. I can tell you've already lost weight since the beginning of the summer." Her brows pull down. "I'm starting to worry about you."

"I'm fine, Mom. Really. And stuffed from tonight's dinner. Thanks." I hit 105 on the scale today. I can't risk erasing the progress I'm making. Well, once I make up for tonight's dinner tomorrow. I can't believe I finished what was on my plate. I smile at my mom.

As soon as the dinner dishes are cleared, I'm out

the door for the second time today. Only this time I'm really buying the sequel to *Fractured Wings*. I've had this day circled on my calendar for months. I let silly flirting with a complete stranger interfere with a good story.

Damn. The woods.

It hits me as I reach the end of my driveway and turn onto the sidewalk. I have to go through the woods. Well, I don't have to, but if I want to get my book tonight, I do. Tonight's the one night where the bookshop closes early, at seven. After what happened to me this afternoon, though... Should I chance it? I could turn back and take one of the cars, but Mom will think something's up if I do that.

No, it's all in my head. I'm freaking myself out for no reason. I've been hanging out with Asha and Liam too long. All their ghost stories are getting to me.

I will my legs to move and moments later, stand at the entrance to the woods. Tall oaks loom over me, the faint light of the fading sun peeking through the leaves and gnarled tree branches. I close my eyes and pull in a deep breath. It's no use. My heart pounds, the vibrations echoing in my ears, making me dizzy. I do what I know best.

Run.

Daylight wanes as I maintain a steady pace along the narrow path. When I reach the clearing, I tense, clenching my hands by my sides, but nothing happens. My body temp doesn't plummet, but instead, my eyes are drawn to a guy in a faded blue t-shirt, sitting against a tree on the opposite side. He's bent over a book, his hair concealing his eyes. My heart thumps.

CJ?

"Hey."

He lifts his head and closes his book. "Gabby?" He scrutinizes me with his gaze. "You look...*different*. Didn't recognize you with your hair down."

"It wasn't the clean clothes and no odor?" I ask.

He laughs. "No, not at all." He narrows his gaze. "You okay? You look like you've seen a ghost." He stands and steps closer.

"Oh, no, it's just..." Heat creeps up my neck. I smooth my khaki shorts with my hands. I'm obviously not out for a run. At least I wasn't supposed to be.

"Gabby?" CJ's voice pulls me from my thoughts.

"Sorry. It's nothing. I need to get to the bookstore before it closes, and the shortest way is through here. All I can think about is the stuff my friend, Asha, said yesterday. Kinda freaked me out."

"Sorry?" CJ asks.

Am I really going to tell a stranger what happened? Even if he is hot?

"Oh, um, when we walked home yesterday from practice, I felt...*cold*, like, teeth-chattering cold. Here in this spot."

CJ swallows. "Right here, in the clearing?"

I nod. "Asha didn't feel a thing, so I was kinda freaked out, thinking something strange was happening to me and..."

I probably shouldn't have said that out loud. CJ's gaze lingers on my face, his pale gray eyes hanging on my every word. Damn, I can't take my eyes off them. They're freaking hypnotic.

"I guess it got to me. She and Liam are all into the paranormal." I stifle a giggle. "Don't judge. I'm a little skittish when it comes to that stuff."

CJ smiles. "Not judging, but...*the bookstore*? Weren't you there—?" He lifts a brow.

Heat flushes my cheeks. "Earlier today? Yeah. I completely forgot about it." That sounds stupid. I bite my lower lip and look away. "Sooo, what are you doing here?" I say, hitting the damage control button. "Don't you live on the other side of Main?"

"I do, but I kinda like this spot." CJ jams his hands into his jeans' pockets. "It's quiet. Especially at night. Which is when I'm usually here. No one bothers you."

He meets my gaze, then looks away. Okay, it's a little strange to be hanging out in the woods at night—a *lot* strange— but I won't judge.

"You live somewhere around here, right?"

Do I live somewhere around here? Is he stalking me? He said, 'no one bothers you.' Is he doing something he doesn't want people to know about? Or *planning* to?

Ugh, I have to stop.

Earlier today I would've given anything to talk to CJ longer, for him to follow me out of the store. Now I have my chance and I'm freaking out. "Yes, I do," I finally say.

He tilts his head, as if to prod me to keep going.

"On the other side of these woods. Second house from the corner." Did I really tell him that? I only met him today, but I want to get to know him better. A lot better. That's crazy. But there's something about him.

"Cool, I'm glad we bumped into one another again. You seemed like you were in a hurry today and we didn't get to talk too much."

My heart thrums. He thought *I* was in a hurry. I guess I was the one who left.

"Sorry about that. I needed a shower." I stifle a giggle. "In case you didn't notice."

"Nope." He steps closer. "Can I walk with you to the bookstore?" A spark lights his eyes as they catch the last bit of sunlight filtering through the trees. "I need to walk that way, anyway."

"Sure."

He has to walk this way, that's all. My jackhammering heart says otherwise.

The wind picks up and starts to swirl around me. And CJ. He shudders and looks me in the face, as if to ask what's going on?

"You feel that, don't you?" I ask, my heart beating faster.

He raises his gaze to the treetops then back to me. He nods. "Is that what you felt yesterday? The wind and all, like it came out of nowhere?"

"Mm hmm. Only it was stronger, colder, and Asha didn't feel it." I tilt my head. "But you did." Why is that?

CJ rubs the back of his neck and with an amused look, laughs. "Maybe we have more in common than we know."

A chill races along my spine. "Maybe."

"So, are you ready?"

That's it? He's not going to talk about it? Just brush me off with some flirtatious banter?

"Gabby?"

"Huh?"

"The bookstore?"

"Oh, right. Let's go."

We shoulder our way around a tangle of bushes and head for the other side of the woods. The air carries

CJ's clean, fresh-from-the-shower scent. Damn, he smells good.

As we walk along the sidewalk, the sun sinks lower in the rainbow sherbet sky, shades of lavender and dusty rose interspersed with orange. A group of screaming kids zoom past on their bikes, enjoying the last, waning days of summertime freedom.

"You go back to school Tuesday?" CJ asks me.

"Uh-huh, you? How does the whole home-school thing work?"

"Same as in the district, just that all my work is done at home, on-line. Instead of sitting in a classroom, I sit in my bedroom with my laptop and my sweats on." A smile tugs at his lips but then his eyes darken. "It's no big deal."

I tuck my hair behind my ear and steal a glance at him, lingering longer than necessary. As if I can glean something by staring at him. "That's good. So, you said you're in Larry's a lot. Me too. Seriously though, I've never seen you there before."

"I'm usually there at night, near closing time. Less crowds." He laughs. "I used to hang out there, like, every night with..." He inhales a sharp breath. "Friends, friends who were into the same kind of music. Now, it's just me." He rakes his hand through his hair. "Anyway, I definitely would've remembered if I'd seen you there."

Adrenaline spikes in my chest, like a thousand butterflies beating their tiny wings in unison. "So, you like all kinds of music, you said?"

"Yeah, I have a special spot for music from the sixties, but I'm also a fan of eighties' music." He turns and flashes a grin. "Don't judge."

I laugh a little too loudly—and stop. "What. Are. You. Talking. About? You didn't see the CD I was checking out today? I love the eighties. Nineties. Ash teases me all the time about it. *Way* too much time in the car with my parents, listening to *their kind* of music. It kinda got in my head and I never got it out. There's so much stuff from that era, so many different artists."

CJ's gaze lingers on my face until he shakes himself out of his trance. "Um, absolutely. I've got a ton of eighties' stuff from Larry's."

We continue talking and walking until we reach the bookstore. Time to let CJ go.

"I guess we're here." CJ rakes the ground with his gaze. "Would you be totally offended if I asked for your number?"

My heart pounds like a drum. I can't get air in my lungs. For real? "No. Why would I be offended?"

"Because we just met today. But you're obviously a loyal Larry's customer. Like me," he says, grinning. "And…" He shakes his head, his grin widening. "Honestly, I'd love to get together some time, hang out, listen to music?"

"Oh," I say, fumbling around the dryness in my throat. "Yeah, that'd be great." Talk much, Gabby?

I recite my number and CJ punches it into his phone. "Cool. Enjoy your book. I'll text you, let you know if I spot new eighties' CDs or any others I think you'd like."

"Awesome, thanks. And I want to hear all about cyber-school."

He smiles. "Absolutely. Oh hey, I just realized, you have to walk home. It's starting to get dark. Do you want me to wait and walk you back?"

Right, I didn't think of that. I probably should've taken the car, but then I wouldn't have run into CJ. "Thanks, but I'll only be a minute in there and then I'll get going." The long way. I'm not going through the woods. Not by myself. "It's not dark yet. I'll be okay."

"Are you sure? I don't mind."

I don't mind either, but I should take things slow. "Thanks, I appreciate the offer, but I'm fine."

"Okay." As he turns to walk away, he starts to hum, not the sixties' tune he was humming this morning in Larry's, but the one from the woods today.

And yesterday.

Chapter Four

The last few days of summer flash by in a blur and before I know it, it's the first day of school. I sink into the passenger seat and smooth my jeans with my hands. Asha pulls away from my house, an alt-rock song blaring from the speakers, my hair swirling about my face in the warm breeze.

"Thanks for waiting. I don't know what was wrong with me this morning. I hit the snooze like four times. I can't believe I did that on the first day of school. I'm usually wide awake, up before my alarm."

"No problem. Oh, my mom has to work tomorrow at the hospital. I won't have her car, so we'll have to walk."

"I'll make sure I get up on time."

"Sooo…" Asha keeps her eyes on the road. "What's up with CJ?" She lowers the volume on the radio and gives me a side-eye glance.

"Nothing."

"Nothing? Have you heard from him since that night you conveniently ran into him in the woods and gave him your number?"

I tap my hand on the passenger side door panel. *Was* it convenient or was he there waiting for me? He said he goes there a lot at nighttime to think. Is that weird? Sketchy?

"Gabs?"

"He texted me yesterday, wished me a *fun* first day of school." I chuckle. "Right. He's probably sound asleep right now. With home-schooling, you probably start whenever you want." I snatch a fistful of my hair and twist it in my hand.

"Yeah, but it's gotta get boring after a while." Asha sighs. "So, all you know is he's a senior and into music? Like, all that stuff you like? Not a whole lot, Gabs. What if he's like, a bad boy? You know, he was kicked out of school for some unmentionable offense?" She plucks her coffee mug out of the center console and takes a sip. "Maybe that's why he's homeschooled."

"Nah, he doesn't seem like the type. He's too...*sensitive* for that. He was humming and singing— out loud—in Larry's. What guy that you know does that? And he freely admitted he likes eighties' music. *Eighties'* music, Ash. Or as you call it, *the stuff I like*." I laugh. "I don't know, I could be totally off, but he doesn't strike me as a *bad boy*, as you put it."

Even if I can't figure out what he was doing in the woods at night.

"Sensitive, huh? He could be a good actor. For your sake, I hope he's not."

I fix my gaze out the window at the borough coming to life with people this morning and wonder if I made a huge mistake giving him my number. "Mm, me too."

"I'm not trying to discourage you, I'm just looking at every angle, thinking out loud, I guess." She pauses. "What does CJ stand for, anyway?"

"I don't know. I didn't ask."

"Sounds like you need to find out." She grins and backs the car into a parking spot on the street, under a large oak. "Can't wait until next year when I can get a pass for the student lot. How come they only give them to seniors, anyway?"

"Hey, at least you have a car to drive. I'm completely at your mercy for a ride to school."

"Some days. Who knows, if my mom's schedule changes and she has to work more hours, I'm out of luck. *We're* out of luck."

****

The next few days I don't have time to think about CJ, whether he's a 'bad boy' as Ash put it or a good actor. School and cross-country consume every ounce of my time.

Well, maybe I do think about him a little.

Today, when I step out of the shower, there's a text from CJ asking if I'd like to see a band from Newtown, playing at the Cactus Grille, a Mexican restaurant in town that features local bands on Friday nights. The band is called The Bullpen and they play their own music, as well as covering eighties' songs. Perfect. Is it a date?

Hmm, dinner and a band afterward. Close enough.

I take about two seconds and answer back.

—*Yeah, I'd love to go. What time?* —

—*Seven. I'll stop by, pick u up?* —

—*Sure. My address is 728 Cherry St*—

—*Great. See u then. Oh, and I have some new music I want to listen to with u*—

Oh my gosh. Dinner. I have to eat with CJ. Wait, why am I worried? He's a guy. Liam's a guy. We eat together all the time. I've never given it a second thought. But Liam's one of my best friends. We've known each other for years. I could down an entire

36

plate of pasta and Liam wouldn't flinch. I could also nibble a few bites of a sandwich and call it lunch— something I've mastered—and Liam doesn't even notice. Ash is a different story. I'll be fine.

****

Asha races down the grassy hill behind me toward school, as we finish a four-mile run at practice. "Wait, I thought we were hanging out tonight, you, me and Liam, but you're going out with CJ?" she asks, breathlessly, and bends over, gripping her knees for balance.

"Sorry," I pant. "I didn't think he'd ask me out and when he texted me this morning, I kinda said yes."

"Don't be sorry, Gabs. It's great. So, where are you going?"

"Cactus Grille. There's a band called The Bullpen playing. They cover 80's stuff, but also perform their own material."

"Sounds perfect." Asha waggles her brows. "*He* sounds perfect for you."

"Yeah, he does. Weird, right? I still don't know a whole lot about him, though."

"That's why you're going out with him tonight."

"I guess."

"Wait, are you nervous?" Asha tilts her head, and a grin plays over her lips. "Of course you are. You'll be fine, Gabs. C'mon, it's exciting. My sister's home from Princeton for the weekend. I think we're gonna do some shopping tonight. I really need jeans. It's one of the things I refuse to order online."

"I know what you mean. Hey, how is Neeta? Does she like school?"

"Loves it. Although from what she says, she has a

boatload of work. Every. Single. Day. Well, of course, Neet, you're going pre-med." Asha purses her lips. "What did she expect? Tons of chemistry and biology courses. You know *I* won't be following in her footsteps. I'm barely passing chem this year."

"Barely passing? You're doing better than me. Solid B+. I'm barely scraping by with a B-." I pause. "So, not to change the subject, but if you're going out with Neeta that means you're not hanging out with Liam. Won't he be disappointed?"

"What? It's Liam. Jake's probably around, anyway. He's not with Breanna anymore, so he has a lot more free time."

"Yeah, I still can't figure that one out. Why'd she break up with him?"

Asha screws up her face. "Dunno." Her eyes narrow. "What about Jake, though?"

"What *about* Jake?"

"You two always seem to hit it off, all those training runs you did together this past summer. He always hangs around talking to you after our meets. He's smoking hot, too."

"Uhh, he was seeing *Breanna*?"

"What does she have that you don't?"

Seriously, you need to ask? But I just shrug. "And those training runs were just that. Training runs. They weren't dates."

"Well, if this thing with CJ doesn't work out, I think you and Jake should give it a shot."

I smile at her. "Right."

"Anyway, I'll probably stop at Liam's when I get home tonight. I'll text him later. If he's not doing something with Jake, I'll stop by afterward."

I chuckle. "Living next door has its advantages."

"What does that mean?" she asks, furrowing her brow.

"Come on, Ash. You and Liam. It's bound to happen, one of these days." I mash my lips together, stifling a grin.

"We're friends, nothing more. We've been friends—*all three of us*—since like, forever. Or, the fourth grade, at least." She laughs.

"Yeah, I know, but—"

She gives me a sideways glare, a look that says 'enough'. I clamp my lips shut. "Right. I'll text you tomorrow. Maybe we can hang out after I do the insane amount of chemistry homework Mrs. Swanson gave us over the weekend."

"No kidding. I have a paper for English I need to start too. But tomorrow sounds good. I want to hear every detail about your date with CJ." Asha leans against the wall, stretching her calves. "By the way, what's up with you, lately?"

I drop my hands on my hips. "What do you mean?"

"I mean today, yesterday…it's just practice, Gabs. You're killing it every day on the course, flying to the finish, like it's a race. No one can keep up with you. You're like a superwoman. I don't know." She pauses. "You've always been one of the fastest on the team, even freshman year, but now…" She shakes her head. "Are you doing anything different? Eating some kind of superfood?"

I shake my head. No, just *less* food.

"Well, you're freaking fast. Keep doing what you're doing, I guess. And send some my way." She laughs.

Keep doing what I'm doing. It shouldn't be a problem tonight. I'll be too nervous to eat when I'm with CJ. The nerves are already beginning to churn. I've never been on a *real* date.

"So, you think it'll be okay tonight? CJ picking me up? *In his car.* I'll be alone with him. I'm not experienced at this 'dating' thing."

Asha laughs. "Yeah, you'll be fine. You told me how you didn't get any bad vibes when you were with him, thought he was such a sensitive *soul*. You're a good judge of character. You've always been. You have a real feel for people. I don't know what it is, but you do. It'll be fun. You two can discuss your weird infatuation with the eighties and all that."

"You're the one who said he could be a 'bad boy'."

"I was joking. You'll be fine."

"I guess, but just in case, be ready if I text and ask you to pick me up. Tell Neeta it's an emergency."

Asha chuckles and drapes her arm around me. "Okay."

We head into the locker room and fifteen minutes later I walk out, refreshed from my shower. As usual, I'm done before Asha who insists on blow-drying her hair. I don't know how she does it, twice a day. Her hair takes so long to dry. I'm envious of course, of hair like hers, so glossy and wavy and full of body. She says all the women on her mom's side have hair like that. Whatever, it's beautiful. I don't even bother with my poker-straight, fine hair. By the time I walk home, it'll be completely dry.

"I'll be outside, Ash," I call to her.

As I step out the door, a gust of cool fall air sweeps across my face and I suck in a deep, refreshing breath.

The hot sticky weather is finally gone. I take a seat on the bench and pull out a new book, a recommendation from the sales guy at my favorite bookstore. He said if I liked the *Fractured Wings* series, I'll love this.

I set my bags on the ground and pull my legs onto the bench. Members of the guys' soccer team start to trickle down the hill. They must've ended their practice on the upper field. They march past, a sweaty, noisy mass of testosterone heading for the showers.

Great, here comes one of my favorite people, Madison. Must've been hanging out at soccer practice, watching her guy. Her guy *this* year. Last year it was Drew Marchella, a lacrosse player. Well, before they broke up—a bad one, if I recall—and Madison moved on by dating a junior on the team. She's all about commitment.

Madison leans her hip against the brick wall and plays with her long brown hair, twisting it in her hand before tossing it over her shoulder.

Hmm. Where's Caitlin? Those two are usually joined at the hip.

I draw out my phone and check for texts. Nothing. I tap my foot on the ground. What am I waiting for? CJ to cancel because I'm so nervous about our date? Or wondering if he's thinking about me? After shoving my phone in my pocket, I open my book and start to read. Fantasy is the perfect distraction for anxiety.

That or Madison's drama.

"Come on, I told them we'd take care of the s'mores if they brought the other food." Madison's shrill voice yanks me out of my story before I even have a chance to get into it. Pacing back and forth, she holds her phone to her ear, her voice rising in pitch and volume. "I have speakers to hook up to my phone for music. It'll be fun." She turns and faces the wall, her hand on her hip, phone tight to her ear. "But it's the perfect place for a bonfire." She clucks her tongue. "We've always done it there. Come on." She shakes her head in annoyance.

I turn my head ever so slightly to listen.

Madison sighs and then goes silent, listening to the person on the other end. "The game? No, Nikki will want to come with us. Jase is coming, too." She pauses. "Okay, fine, but if you change your mind…"

She tucks her phone in her pocket and leans against the wall. Her mouth tight, she crosses her arms over her body. Aiden Wilson and Alex D'Amico stroll through the doorway, shaking out their wet hair like two shaggy dogs. Madison pushes off the wall, hooks her arm through Aiden's and the three of them walk toward the student parking lot.

The door flies open again. "Sorry, I took so long." Asha exits and adjusts her bags on her shoulder. "Ready?"

"Yep." I close my book—I read one whole paragraph—and stand. Asha and I walk through the parking lot which is still half-full when Caitlin races out a side door and zips past us through the parked cars, her boots click-clacking on the asphalt.

"Geez, nice of you to wait." She hops in Alex's black car and slams the door before the car screeches out of the parking lot.

Asha shakes her head. "Must be nice to have a ride every day from your soccer player boyfriend."

"No kidding. Madison was out here the whole time on her phone going on about her epic weekend plans."

Asha laughs. "Isn't everything 'epic' with Madison? Biggest drama queen in school. Well, her and Caitlin." She taps me on the sleeve as we cross the street. "You have your own epic plans, missy. I want to hear all about it the second you get home."

I brush past a low hanging oak tree branch. "Right, unless I call for backup." I bite my lip and glance sideways at Asha. "Getting a little nervous, here."

"C'mon, you'll be fine. Truthfully, I'm jealous. CJ sounds great. Plus, he doesn't go to West Penn, so you don't have to worry about school gossip. Ooh, that's right, ask him why he's homeschooled."

"It could be what his parents want. Or what *he* wants. Although it's odd he didn't want to talk about it." I shrug. "Who knows? Maybe he doesn't want to deal with high school drama."

"Do guys even care about that stuff? There's really no drama with them. Anyway, I want to meet him. It'd be cool if we could go out as a foursome but seeing I'm not part of a 'twosome'..." Asha stops and widens her eyes. "I know. See if he'll come to a home meet or maybe he'll want to catch a football game with us."

"First, you could be part of a twosome if you'd give Matt a chance. Or," I lift my gaze skyward and purse my lips. "Admit what's right in front of your face: you and Liam. You can't deny he's always wanted more than a friendship with you. I think you do too," I say, lowering my voice to a whisper. "And second, *maybe* to a football game, a big, fat N-O to our cross-country meet. I don't need any more pressure, worrying about a guy watching me run." Watching me race against Breanna and those tiny, skinny girls. "Plus, what guy would want to watch our meet?"

Asha lifts a brow. "Uh, Liam's come to our meets, the big ones, anyway, like Districts. CJ would want to come. And what are you worried about? Letting him see you smoke the competition?"

"You're too nice, but no, I want to get to know him, before I subject him to that kind of torture. Plus, it may not even work. This is our first time going out." I pause. "Could be the last."

"Stop. You mean, you may not like him beyond the lustful attraction you feel toward each other?"

I fake-punch Asha in the shoulder. "It's not lust." Is it? Why did I agree to go out with a guy I met once? Technically, twice, but still. It's his eclectic taste in music, which perfectly mirrors mine. His quiet, soft-spoken nature. His infectious laugh. The way his wavy blond hair brushes past his ears, falls into his pale gray eyes. Those beautiful pale gray eyes. The incredible, magnetic attraction I have to him. My pulse quickens.

Okay, maybe it's part lust.

"It's okay if it is." Asha laughs. "But he sounds really nice. *Hot.* I hope it works out."

We arrive at the corner, where Asha and I part ways.

"I wanna hear all about it. Soon as you get in." Asha whirls around and walks across the street. "E-v-e-r-y detail."

"Absolutely." I take off in the opposite direction. Asha's words swirl through my head as I shuffle along the sidewalk.

I hope it works out.

I hope so, too, although I won't be able to make that determination until after this date. What am I worried about? We had so much to talk about both times I ran into him. Of course the second time he was hanging out in the woods. He said it was peaceful and no one bothered him. Should I be worried?

I take the long way home, avoiding the woods, and arrive home just as my mom pulls into the driveway.

Chapter Five

"Hey, Mom."

She pulls me into a hug as she kicks the door shut. "How was school? Any big plans this weekend?"

I should tell my mom I'm going out with CJ, but she'll have a million questions and I can't answer any of them. I'll see how tonight goes then I'll tell her about CJ. "School was fine and…no big plans. I think a group of us may hang out tonight. Not sure what we're doing, yet."

"Oh, okay."

An hour later, swinging my legs back and forth, clapping my boot heels together, I pet Lola as she sprawls out on my bed. Flashing her wide amber eyes at me, she rolls onto her back. I pet her belly and she lolls her head back. Chin scratch, please.

I oblige and she responds with a purring sound, which is music to my ears and eases my nerves. Until a beam of light hits my window, growing larger until it fills the entire frame. The sound of an engine shutting off quickens my pulse.

He's here. I race out of my room and down the steps.

"I'll be back later," I call, flinging open the door, making my escape. No need for my parents to give CJ the third degree.

"Eleven, Gabby. Don't be late," my dad calls from

the family room where he and my mom are watching TV.

"Got it." I told them I was going out with friends from school. CJ happens to be one of those friends. Well, the *only* friend. Asha's aware of my *date*. She knows where we're going. You know, in case I disappear.

I close the door behind me and dash out, smacking into CJ as he approaches the porch.

"I'm so sorry." He retreats and grasps my arm, steadying me. "Are you okay?"

"Fine. Sorry, I heard your car and—"

"And I was going to knock on your door like a perfect gentleman."

"I know. My parents can be a bit...inquisitive, that's all."

"No problem. I can handle nervous parents, though." It's dark, his face concealed, but the smile is there in his voice.

CJ opens the passenger door of his older model German car. I slide into the seat. A rich scent of soap envelops me. Fresh from the shower soap. CJ. I breathe it in—breathe him in—and sink into the seat.

"Nice car."

"Thanks. Great deal from a friend of a friend." He meets my gaze as he inserts the key into the ignition and a smile plays across his lips. "Seriously. My part-time job at the hoagie shop pays for gas and insurance."

"No, I believe you. That's great." I rub my hands on my black pants and take a deep breath. So far, so good.

CJ sets his hands on the steering wheel. "Oh, that's right. I wanted to text you, but I figured it would be easier in person. The band that was supposed to play tonight cancelled. They're going to feature some local comics instead." He taps his thumbs on the wheel. "I didn't know if that was your thing."

My heart pounds. Oh my gosh. He has me in his car, alone, under the pretense of seeing a local band and now the plans have changed. Maybe there's more to the woods thing than I realize. Maybe it all ties together. The chill, the reason he goes there, alone. At night... I swallow the thickness in my throat. "Not really. So, where do you want to go instead?"

Calm down, Gabby.

I haven't gotten one creepy vibe from him. Unless CJ's some sort of supernatural being, like a vampire or a shapeshifter. As cool as that would be—Asha would be blown away—that's not what's going on here.

"Is Angelo's okay? It's on Elm and maybe we can walk around afterward, maybe stop in Larry's?" His eyes brighten.

Angelo's is smack in the center of town, not out in the middle of nowhere. Tons of people around.

"That'd be great."

What's wrong with me? I was so psyched to go out with CJ tonight, but... But what? Nothing's changed. CJ's totally normal. Safe. Yes, that's it, he *feels* safe to me.

"Awesome."

CJ parks on the street, feeds the meter a few quarters then circles around to my door. We navigate the sidewalk traffic, the rich, piquant aroma of Angelo's mixing with the charcoal mesquite from the steak house at the end of the block. It's a few minutes after six, so there's only a small crowd inside and the hostess seats us immediately.

I've been to Angelo's hundreds of times, mostly with my parents for lunch or dinner. We've also had our cross-country and track banquets here the last two years. Casual Italian, they have the best tomato pie. Although the way my stomach's flip-flopping inside me, food's the last thing on my mind.

The hostess leads us to a booth by the window. I take my seat and CJ sits across from me. He taps his fingers on the table.

"Sooo, is this okay?" He shrugs off his brown canvas jacket and rakes his fingers through his hair. "I'm really sorry. I thought it would be cool to see The Bullpen, but like I said, they cancelled."

I lower my menu and nod. "Absolutely. This is great. I've been here a lot. No worries."

His gaze lingers on mine before he smiles. "Cool." He grabs his menu. "Guess I better figure out what I'm having."

Tomato pie. That's what I'm having. Lucia's has the best wood-fired pizza, but Angelo's is known for their tomato pie. And tomato pie has fewer calories. No cheese. Wait, maybe I should order a salad. No. CJ will think I'm one of those girls who only eat salads. Even though I could order chicken on it, and it would be *more* than a salad. But I shouldn't—

"Gabby?"

"Huh?"

The waiter, a short, wiry guy in his early twenties with spiky black hair, stands at the end of our table with pad and pen in hand.

"Oh, sorry. Um, I'll have the single-size tomato pie."

"Hey, I was getting the same." CJ taps his menu against my hand resting on the table. "Should we get one regular and share?"

Should we? It'll be obvious to him how much I eat if we share. But I don't want to be difficult. Ugh, I gotta stop this. "Sure, that's fine."

After the waiter leaves, I fold my hands on the table and CJ crosses his arms, reclining in the booth.

Silence.

I bounce my leg and glance around the restaurant. Our first awkward silence since we met. There are so many things I want to ask CJ, but where do I begin?

"So, how's homeschooling going?" I ask, splintering the quiet.

"Eh, okay. My alarm's set for seven every day to make sure I start on time."

CJ starts to laugh but catches himself and presses his lips together, like something's holding him back from letting go. Something preventing him from fully enjoying himself. Is it me? Maybe he regrets his decision asking me out tonight.

"That's good. I thought you could sleep as late as you want, but the sooner you start, the sooner you're done, right?"

"That's the idea, yeah." CJ pushes the sleeves of his gray button-down to his elbows and rests his forearms on the table. "Thanks for coming tonight, Gabby. I wanted to get together sooner, but it didn't work out."

"No problem. Thanks for inviting me." I focus on the basket of spices in the middle of the table. Zeroing in on each tiny grain of salt in the saltshaker. My stomach groans and I hug myself. Did CJ hear that?

"Hungry much?" he asks, laughing.

Yes, he heard that.

"Sorry, I guess I am," I say as flames devour my face. I meet his gaze. "Can I ask you something?"

"Sure."

I lean forward and rest my elbows on the table. Good thing my mom's not here. "Have you always been homeschooled? You don't seem thrilled about the idea, so I was wondering, did something happen in school to make you choose that?" Okay, that's not too nosy.

CJ grasps a fork and twirls it in his hand. "No. It's..." He hesitates, biting the inside of his cheek. "It's not an easy thing to talk about. And so you know, I wasn't expelled or anything." He stifles a grin. "In case you're wondering. It's just...*easier* for me."

"Oh, no, I didn't think that." I pause. "I didn't think that you were expelled." My stomach clenches at the lie. Now, I wish he *had* been expelled because the truth is probably worse. Although, what could possibly be worse?

CJ taps me on the hand, and I flinch. "It's okay. I just don't want to talk about it now. Even if you did think I was some sort of...criminal." There's a flirtatiousness to his voice. His jaw muscle twitches. "Admit it, Gabby Patterson, it crossed your mind." He chuckles. "I won't hold it against you."

"Nope, not at all."

But the fire burns hotter in my face. I'm a terrible liar. My heart sinks a little lower. What did I do? There's something he's not telling me, something that's bothering him, and I made it worse. Even if he joked about it. Awkward silence was better than saying the wrong thing.

Way to go, Gabby. Open mouth, insert foot.

CJ rests his hand on mine. It's warm and soft and jumpstarts my heart. "Gabby please, don't feel bad. It's just something I don't want to talk about. Not yet. You didn't do anything wrong."

The next five minutes we sit and talk in fits and starts around another awkward silence—caused by me, of course—about the band we're not seeing and each other's plans for the rest of the weekend. When our food arrives, the awkward silence becomes chowing-down-food silence.

This has to be the best tomato pie I've ever had.

After devouring the first slice, I grab a second and take a bite. That's when it hits me. I can't eat any more. Even though my stomach is screaming for more, I have a meet this week. I have to be sharp. An image of all those speedy, tiny runners blooms in my head. I'm finished.

The slice slides from my grip, leaving a floury residue on my fingers, and flops to the ceramic plate with a *thunk*. "Oh my God, I'm so full! I can't eat anymore."

CJ's brows jump. "Really, after only one?"

Why does he ask? Do I look like someone who eats 'more than one slice'?

"Don't you need to eat more for training, for cross-country? I'm sure you must run a ton of miles in practice. Plus, you can't eat just one. It's Angelo's. Best tomato pie in town."

Wait, I told him I ran cross-country when we met at Larry's, didn't I? If not, the way I was dressed, and my overall grunginess gave it away.

"Gabby?"

"Oh, right." I wipe my hands on my napkin and toss it on the table.

If I didn't offend him with the homeschool inquisition, now I'm zoning out at dinner. Or maybe he doesn't notice. I peek at his face. He notices.

"What?"

He shakes his head. "It's nothing."

We finish our food—at least CJ does—and after paying, which he insists on paying for me, saying he asked me out, we pull on our coats and head outside. The crisp fall air sweeps across my body and I tug my jacket closed, wrapping my arms around myself. Crowds swell the sidewalk this brisk autumn night and as we navigate the masses, I steal a glance at CJ, at his pale gray eyes, wondering what it is he's hiding. What he won't tell me. Maybe he doesn't trust me yet? How ironic. All I worried about was if *I* could trust him tonight.

"So, when's your next cross-country meet? I'd love to come." He clears his throat. "You know, if you don't mind."

My mouth falls open. "You want to come? There's not much to see, but if you want to be bored for a few hours, our next one is Monday afternoon at three, at home."

"Cool. Yeah, maybe I'll come over, check it out, if it's okay with you." He raises a brow.

"Yeah, absolutely. It's not much to watch, but it would be cool if you wanted to come."

"I do. I've never been to a cross-country meet. Thanks."

We head to the music store and spend about a half

53

hour perusing Larry's newest arrivals. As I grab a nineties' CD, the song floats into my head again, the one from the woods. The one CJ hummed when we parted ways at the bookstore the day we met.

I grip the CD in my hand. Ugh, why can't I get it out of my head?

"Gabby? You okay?" CJ's gaze searches my face. "You look like you saw a ghost."

"I'm fine." No, wait. What's the worst that can happen? It's just a song. "Can I ask you something?" I laugh. "Sorry, I'm bombarding you with questions tonight."

"No worries. What is it?" He sets the CD he's looking at on the counter and twists his body to me.

"The song you were humming that night you walked me back from the woods to the bookstore, does it have some significance?"

CJ furrows his brow. "I don't remember."

I tilt my head. "It's a pop song, pretty catchy tune?" I laugh. "I was going to say it's not 'a guy's song', but you're not exactly 'conventional' when it comes to music." I place my hand, palm up, in front of my face. "No offense."

CJ laughs. "None taken." He looks off into space before he slowly returns his attention to me, his smile gone, his lips parted, and all the color leached from his face. "I remember."

I tilt my head. "Is there anything to it?" C'mon, CJ. Give me something.

"Um, I don't know. Probably heard it on the radio and it got stuck in my head. You know how that is," he says, without meeting my gaze.

Crap, I've done it again. Made him all brooding

and sad. Sucked the life out of our date. For the second time tonight.

"Yes, I do."

But that's not it. That song has been stuck in my head since that day I walked home with Ash, and I couldn't figure it out. The day in Buddy's with Liam and Asha. Every night at the dinner table. Until the night CJ walked me to the bookstore. Right after we both felt the chill.

The lyrics wind through my head until CJ breaks the song's hold on me.

"So, how was your book?" CJ grabs a CD from the bin.

"My book?"

"The one you were supposed to buy but you got sidetracked by a hot guy in the music store?"

"Oh, right. *That* book."

Heat surges into my face. Okay, he's flirting again. Joking around. The uneasiness is gone. At least, outwardly.

"It was good. I finished it last week." I mash my lips together. "I can't believe you remembered that."

"Of course."

I smile at him as lightness fills my chest. Maybe there will be a second date.

The bells jingle as we exit the store and walk out into the brisk night air once again. CJ's been nothing but a perfect gentleman, not to mention, a blast to hang out with. Even if there is something he's hiding, a secret he won't divulge. A connection to the woods. And that song.

We walk around a little longer, even hitting the bookstore to browse, before heading to CJ's car.

He jumps into the driver's seat and turns to me with an expectant look on his face. "Anything else you want to do?"

"No, unless there's something you want to do." I lift my hand to my mouth and stifle a yawn. Geez, not too rude. "Sorry."

CJ suppresses a chuckle and taps me on the arm. "I'll get you home."

"I'm sorry, it's not you, it's just—"

"Nah, no worries. It's getting late, anyway."

Five minutes later, CJ pulls to the curb in front of my house and kills the engine. Silence deadens the air.

"Thanks," I finally croak out. "I had fun. A lot of fun."

Outside of the awkwardness I created at the restaurant and that weird moment in the music store. Will CJ want to go out again? He did ask about my meet, so that's a good sign.

I hop out of the car and CJ walks around to meet me.

"Thanks for coming with me tonight, Gabby. I had a great time." He pauses. "I mean it, I'm really glad we went out. Can I text or call you? I'd love to go out again. Oh and of course, I want to watch you run this week. As long as you're okay with it."

I nod. "Absolutely. I'd love for you to come." I exhale a long sigh of relief. I didn't ruin things. I stand there looking toward the street, my heart hammering. Now what?

"Gabby?" CJ moves closer and places one hand on my waist. "Can I kiss you?"

I nod. "Yes."

I tilt my face to his as he places his hand on the

back of my neck, his soft, gentle fingers sending warm shivers through me. He parts my lips and kisses me. Softly. Slowly. He has the most amazing lips. He slides his other arm around my waist and pulls me against him, against the thrumming of his heart. I wrap my arms around him as he traces his lips over mine, running his thumb across my jaw. I shudder at his feather touch, consumed with his clean scent, the coconut shampoo that clings to the soft locks of his hair. I'm all in, totally submerged in the kiss. Until I break away.

Breathless, my gaze darts to my house, encircled in a soft white glow. It's got to be almost eleven. Curfew. I don't want to try to explain why I'm late to my parents. That I was sucking face with a guy I met at Larry's. I'm supposed to be out with friends. CJ happens to be one of those friends. Maybe *more* after tonight? If I kiss him again, though, I won't make curfew, because I won't be able to stop kissing him.

"Is everything okay?" he whispers.

Way more than okay. "Yeah, but I'd better go."

He bites his bottom lip, while keeping an arm around my waist. "Do you have to?"

"CJ, I don't want to." Obviously, right? "But..." I nod to my house. "I don't want to miss my curfew."

He pulls his phone from his back pocket. "Ten forty-two. We have eighteen minutes."

He waggles his brows, and a giggle escapes my lips. Hmm, we could kiss a lot in eighteen minutes. CJ taps my waist.

"I'm kidding. C'mon, I'll walk you to your door."

At my front porch, he steals one last kiss, this one way too brief.

"I'll call you," he says then turns to head down the path. He takes a few steps before spinning around. "Or you can call me," he says with a grin. "Anytime. Let me know if you spot anything new at Larry's."

"Yep."

My gaze follows him as he approaches his car. He gives me one last wave before jumping inside. That's when the song floats into my head, the words louder and clearer than before. A sour taste fills my mouth.

There's something he's not telling me.

Chapter Six

"So where do you think he'll be?" Asha leans forward, hands on hips, readying herself for the start of our race. "At the finish?"

"I'm not thinking about him now, Ash. Just this muddy course we have to run. I can't believe how much it rained last night." I grasp my leg behind my knee and draw it against my body, stretching my hamstring.

"No kidding. It's gonna be a swamp." Asha shrugs. "We've run in worse, though."

"You're right. Good luck."

"You too. I'll keep an eye out for lover boy."

I fake-punch her in the arm. "He may not even come."

I glance to my left. Breanna Pozzi, one of my teammates, the one runner who challenges me on our team, stretches her arms over her head. Petite and super-skinny, she catches my eye and gives me a thumbs-up.

"Good luck, Gabby."

God, how I wish I looked like her. "Thanks, you too."

The horn sounds and I elbow my way through the crowded field, mashing through the wet, muddy grass. If all 3.1 miles of the course are this messy, I'm in trouble. I can't get my footing, slipping and sinking into the muck with every step. The only consolation is everyone else has to run in the same sloppy mess.

We push across the field and start the long climb to the top of the hill. The hill though, is where I finally get some traction and begin to settle in.

At the two-mile mark, I've found my rhythm and cruise along the path through the woods at a steady pace, trying to shake off a girl from the other team. Suddenly, my name rings out amidst the trees. I swivel my head, but I can't locate the source. Until...

Ahead, dressed in jeans and a burgundy hoodie, a baseball cap pulled low over his eyes, CJ stands by a tree, whistling through his fingers.

Heat blooms in my chest and I give him a small wave. He smiles and flashes two thumbs up as adrenaline surges through my veins, propelling me faster along the path.

I race out of the woods, sticking close to the course markers, never looking back. Zipping along the dirt trail, it's as if I'm flying. And I am.

As I push through the last half mile, I pass Breanna.

"Nice going, Gabby," she calls. "See you at the finish."

"You too," I say over my shoulder, continuing my manic pace.

I sprint through the finishers' chute and cross the finish line first. I fall over my knees and grasp the bottle of water our team trainer hands me.

"Awesome job, Gabby. I don't think Breanna saw you coming."

"Yeah, I had this burst of energy." I don't tell her the burst of energy was named CJ. "I don't know how she got that far ahead in the first place." I laugh and whirl around at the *thunk, thunk* of sneakers smacking against the grass. Breanna halts and rests her hands on her hips.

"Where did you come from?" she asks. "I mean, I was wondering where you were in the first place. We're usually side by side the first mile. Then suddenly out of nowhere…" Breanna laughs and chugs a mouthful of water. "Either way, it's cool. We finished one, two."

"Yeah, I know. I couldn't get any traction at the start. I was slipping all over the place and fell behind. Thankfully, I was able to pick it up once I hit the hill. Great race."

"Yeah, you too." Breanna jerks her chin behind me. "I think someone's trying to get your attention."

"Huh?"

I whirl around. CJ leans against a tall wooden fence, behind a row of trees.

"Oh. Thanks," I say. "Congrats, again. Great race."

"You too."

"You don't have to hang out here by yourself." I advance toward CJ, my feet moving quicker as I near him. "None of us bite."

One corner of his mouth lifts and he tucks his hands into his hoodie pocket. "I know. I didn't want to get in the way. You looked awesome, by the way. You have this mad determination on your face when you run. Just thought I'd let you know." He kicks the grass with his sneaker as a smile spreads across his face.

My face flushes and I dip my chin. "Thanks." I think. I shake off the image of a crazy, possessed runner. A *tall, gangly*, crazy, possessed runner. "You're my good luck charm. I finished first, thanks to you."

"I know you did. I saw the blur at the finish line.

But don't thank me. I'm only here to watch."

"Hey, I was wondering where you got to." Asha runs up to me. Her gaze flits between me and CJ. "Sorry, didn't mean to interrupt, but I had to congratulate the winner. You know, this is becoming a habit, you finishing first."

That means what I'm doing is working. Bowl of cereal and black coffee this morning. Turkey sandwich and water at lunch. Nothing else to slow me down. And a little extra push from the hot guy cheering me on in the woods.

"Just luck. How about you?"

"Eighth. But I dropped my time by fifteen seconds."

"Awe. Some."

"Thanks." Asha glances at CJ then back to me. "So?"

"Oh, sorry. Asha, CJ. CJ, Asha."

"Hey," says CJ.

"Hi." Asha purses her lips and studies CJ's face, like she's trying to place him, figure out how she knows him.

I ball my hands into fists. *Just wait 'til he's gone, Ash. I don't want to embarrass him.*

Asha elbows me. "I'm going to head over to stretch with the team. I'll save you a spot next to me."

"Thanks, be there in a sec."

"Nice meeting you, CJ," she says.

"Same here."

I turn back to CJ. "Thanks so much for coming."

"I told you I would. And I wasn't the least bit bored, like you said. It was exciting and great watching you run."

My stomach performs a little flip. Great watching me run? Is he serious?

"So, now that you've seen what I 'do', what about you?" I think of his long, slender fingers, the ones I first noticed in Larry's Music Store, the ones that caressed my neck on Friday night as he kissed me. Musician's fingers. "Any sports or hobbies I should know about? Any games...*concerts* I can come watch?"

His face pales and he shakes his head. "Nah, I just like music, I guess. All kinds." He grins. "That's all."

The smile lingers. A forced smile. For my sake. Okay, he doesn't want to talk about it. Whatever *it* is. I shouldn't push it. I tried that with the homeschool thing and it backfired.

"Oh, okay." I finger my ponytail. "I'd better get over there with the team. Coach might make me run extra this week in practice if I don't."

His lips ease into a crooked grin, quickening my pulse. "Something tells me you wouldn't mind."

Heat flushes my cheeks. He knows me too well, already. I wish I could say the same about him.

"I'll call you later," he says as he turns to go.

"Okay." I start to walk away.

"Hey, Gabby."

I turn and CJ stands inches from me. "Yeah?"

He takes one hand and places it on the side of my face, the other on my waist before he leans in and kisses me. "I've wanted to do that ever since I left your house Friday. I couldn't stop thinking about you." His smile grows and he draws away. "Later."

Fire blazes in my veins as I jog over to my teammates and settle in with Asha who sits on a mat, in a butterfly stretch, her back straight, chin out. She turns to me and grins.

"Glad you could join us. CJ leave?"

My face must be about ten shades of scarlet. The taste of CJ's kiss, his sweet warm breath, still lingers on my lips. Does it show?

"Yeah, it was nice of him to come. I didn't think he would."

Coach Caroline clears her throat. "Okay, lets stand and do a few lunges to stretch out those hammies. Nice job today, ladies. Every one of you improved your time. That's great progress. You should all be proud of your hard work."

Five minutes later, Asha and I grab our stuff to walk home.

My heart still beats double-time as I step onto the sidewalk and shuffle through the leaves. Whether from my first-place finish or CJ's kiss, I don't know. Of course I know. I'm positively giddy over his kiss.

"So, what do you think? You haven't said anything."

"You mean your new boyfriend? Gabs, he's cute and those eyes. Oh my gosh, they're like…gorgeous." She halts and grabs my arm.

"What? Do you recognize him from somewhere? C'mon, tell me. I'm dying to know."

"No. I don't think so." She puckers her mouth. "I don't know. Maybe? There's something familiar about him. I just don't know what it is."

"Oh."

"He's shorter than you. Not by much, but are you going to be able to work out the whole kissing thing?"

"Really? That's what you're worried about? Not where you might know him from? If you've heard anything bad about him? Most people are shorter than me, anyway, including some guys." Except for Jake. "But there's no issue with his kiss—" I draw in a sharp breath and clamp my lips shut.

"Mm-hmm, you already kissed him. I knew it!" A grin plays across her mouth. "I guess you conveniently left out that little nugget when you told me about your date with him."

That and the one he dazzled me with a few minutes ago. As for his height? I was concentrating on his other attributes. Like his pale gray eyes. Warm, gentle hands. Soft, sensuous lips.

"So, are you coming to Liam's party on Saturday?" Asha asks.

"Of course. Where else would I be when one of my best friends hosts a party with a fire pit?"

"Bringing CJ?"

"I dunno. He may not want to go to a party where he doesn't know anyone. Plus, he probably has plans."

"Wait, where he doesn't know anyone? He knows *you*."

"We'll see. So, what's going on with you? What's the real reason you and Matt aren't going out anymore? He's great."

Asha sighs. "I don't know. It's not him, it's just—"

"Liam."

Asha whirls on me. "What? What does Liam have to do with it?"

"Come on, Ash, don't deny it. Something's changed between you two. You can't hide it from me. We've been friends for too long—you, me *and* Liam." I pause. "It's been obvious for a while he'd like more than that." I arch my brows. "I think you do, too, but

65

you're scared."

Asha's eyes widen. "Not true." She shuffles ahead of me.

"Whatever, but you two already have the *best friends* thing down."

Asha shoots me a menacing glare and I mimic zipping my lip. "Okay, end of conversation."

"Seriously though, invite CJ. If he can't go then no big deal, but at least ask him."

"Maybe. I'll see you tomorrow."

Asha and I part at the corner, but our conversation continues to knock around my head. I can't ask CJ to Liam's party. We went out once. And kissed. My pulse quickens at the memory of his lips on mine, his arms around me. His cheering me on at my meet. Where he kissed me again. Huh, maybe he would want to go to Liam's party with me. I'll figure it out later.

I clench my hands by my sides as I approach the forest. So obsessed with thoughts of CJ, I took the shortcut without thinking. It probably won't happen again. The chill, that is. The chill that CJ also felt. And what about that song? The one that started haunting me the same time as the chill. It's the same song CJ hummed the night he walked me to the bookstore.

Gripping the strap on my bag, I keep my focus forward and push onward. The late afternoon sunlight filters through the treetops, dappling the forest floor with tiny petals of light, the leaves fluttering in the breeze around me. I reach the clearing when the song lyrics drift into my head. I close my eyes as the music intensifies, rushing through my veins. As if on cue, the wind picks up and swirls around me, zeroing in on me, clutching me in its chilly grip.

I hug myself tightly before I open my eyes and scream at the top of my lungs, "What do you want from me? Why can't you leave me alone?"

And who are you?

Tears spring to my eyes. My whole body shakes before the wind subsides. But the lyrics of the song crystallize in my head, the words burning into my consciousness as the melody continues to move through me. And that's when it clicks. The song has meaning. The words have meaning.

Part of me wants to ascribe it to a prank played by Liam and Ash. But it would be pretty elaborate, even for them. And cruel. My friends aren't cruel. So, what the heck is happening?

"Why me? I'm fine. I'm not trying to be anything else. Anyone else."

I look skyward, like I expect an ethereal form to float from the trees and give me an answer. Right. The lush green canopy of the trees is all that's there.

But then I see a butterfly, a bright orange monarch butterfly that flits through the air and perches on a hollowed-out tree stump. Captivated by its beauty, I walk to where it rests and my gaze darts to something blue beneath the layers of earth-toned leaves and twigs that fill the stump.

I draw out a small, faded blue notebook, the pages dog-eared and worn, the entire book waterlogged. I thumb through the densely written book that appears to be a journal of some sort. There's no name, but the entries are neatly written in black ink. Or were. The writing is smudged and faded from rain and snow. Still, curiosity tugs at me and I brush it off and leave the clearing with the book gripped in my hand. With one last backward glance, I head along the narrow path which leads out of the woods.

The tinkling of the stream below the cliff is like soft background music. Until I glance to my left and my breath catches. I move away, my heart pounding, and almost trip. There really should be a fence there. Someone could get seriously hurt—or worse.

****

Once home, away from the woods, I take a long hot shower then settle in and attempt to make sense of the notebook. The first page is legible:

Today was a good day. That new tune was knocking around my head, the music flowing freely, the words, not so much. There's always tomorrow. I wonder what they would think if they knew? Would they be more likely to be my friends or not?

And that's it. The next clump of pages is stuck together, and the print is faded from the elements. There's more in the middle of the book, but those pages are also stuck together, and I don't have the patience to try and decipher it now. Plus, I have homework. Lots of homework.

I set the notebook on the bottom of my bookshelf. Close enough to my open window to dry it out and inconspicuous enough, if Mom comes in my room that she'll pass it by.

Speaking of Mom, she's making fajitas for dinner. My stomach growls as the rich, piquant aroma of grilled chicken and sautéed onions drifts into my bedroom.

"Gabby," she calls, "Dinner's ready."

"Coming."

As I descend the steps though, the aromatic bouquet of smells pulling me into the kitchen, all I can think is *self-control*. I have to resist the urge to eat more than one tonight. I may have won my race today, but I can't slide into bad habits. Not when I've been doing so well.

"Gabby, I'm sorry I missed your meet today. Thanks for the text, though. I was thrilled to hear you won." Dad enters into the kitchen the same time as I do and pulls me into a hug, his familiar aloe aftershave enveloping me.

"Yeah, awesome, huh? It was like I had this crazy surge of energy with a mile to go and outraced everyone...even Breanna." I wink at him.

"You two still have that rivalry going? Since freshman year?" A grin tugs at his lips.

More than you know.

"Of course. Don't worry, there are plenty of races left. I know you can't make every one. Mom couldn't make today either." I nod to my mom and smile.

"Next one, I promise," Mom says. "I had a late meeting I couldn't miss. I'm sorry."

Dad taps me on the shoulder. "Me too, next one." He takes his seat and grabs a fajita. "Mm, this looks fabulous, Lisa. I'm starving. I'm sure you are too, Gabby."

"Absolutely, Dad." I swallow the guilt as I bite into my fajita crammed with lettuce, tomato and a few strips of chicken.

"Sour cream, Gabby?" My mom lifts the container.

"Already have some. Thanks."

"Oh." Her gaze lingers on my plate before she nibbles at her own fajita. She places her fajita down and clears her throat. Uh oh. Here it comes.

"Gabby, I want to make sure everything's okay

with you."

"Okay? I'm fine."

"But you're not eating. Not as much as you should." My mom clasps her hands in her lap.

"And you've lost weight," my dad chimes in.

Oh no, not you, too.

"I told you before, we're running more at practice. Seriously, it happens every season. We ramp up the miles and I lose a little weight. Once the season is over, I gain it back." Not this time, though. I look at my dad then my mom. "I'm fine. Please, stop worrying."

Something passes between my parents then my mom says, "Okay, but we're both here if you want to talk. We just want you to be smart while you're training. Make sure you're eating enough."

"Yep, I am."

After dinner and thankfully, after no more conversation about my eating habits, I head upstairs to tackle a paper for American Lit and two practice sheets for an upcoming chemistry test. The notebook can wait. What if it's completely unrelated to the weird stuff in the woods? And if it is, do I really want to dig deeper, uncover why some spirit has taken up residence in the woods, with the intention of harassing me?

It's ten o'clock when I finally finish my homework and close my books. Fatigue deadens ever last cell in my body, and I flop on my pillows, grabbing my book off my night table. Only one chapter left. I'm gonna have to stop by the bookstore tomorrow, pick up a new read. Ash says I should buy an e-reader so I can download a book whenever I want it, but what fun would that be? I love browsing the shelves, checking out all the cool covers, reading the blurbs on the back.

Just like in the music store.

As I open my book, my phone buzzes.

—Hey, congrats again on your race today. You were awesome! BTW, what are u doing Saturday? —

This Saturday?

Our kiss from today flutters to the surface, tingling my skin and warming my insides. Saturday? Yes, I'd love to do something. Wait, Liam's party is Saturday. I told him I was coming. And bringing food.

This is my chance to ask CJ. Maybe I can finally get somewhere with this thing in the woods. The song. The chill we both felt. The ghost? My pulse quickens. The heck with all of that, I just want to hang out with him. Kiss him again. Then we can talk about why we both seem to be the object of whatever is haunting the woods.

—Invited to a party. Wanna go? —

I lean into my pillows and drum my fingers on my bed. It was a bad idea. I shouldn't have asked him to a party where he won't know a soul. Even if Asha thought it was okay.

I grab my book. As I read the same line on the page for the fourth time, my phone buzzes.

—Thanks, not too good with crowds. Maybe we can go out another time—

Damn, I blew it.

My heart sinks.

Chapter Seven

"No, I told you, I can't." Caitlin says from the seat next to me. She crosses her arms and sighs.

"Come on, Alex won't go if you don't." Madison's gaze flits to me then to Caitlin.

"Then he doesn't go. We'll do something else, that's all."

This silly exchange has been going on the entire period. I can't believe Mrs. Owens, our English teacher, hasn't told them to shush it.

Caitlin slides her gaze to me as if she reads my mind, but I don't give her the satisfaction and keep my focus on the board. I hate being caught in the middle of their stupid arguments. Literally *in the middle*. Assigned seats since day one of school and I'm stuck between them. Arguing over weekend plans. If history is any guide, Madison will get her way. She always does.

"...chapters four to eight. Now who can tell me what Mr. Orwell was trying to say in these chapters?" Mrs. Owens voice jolts me out of my thoughts, and I sit straight in my chair.

****

Later at lunch, Asha places her tray on the table and takes a seat across from me. "So, lover boy can't make it, huh?"

"Stop calling him that," I grip my fork and glance

72

around the cafeteria. "And you don't need to broadcast it to the whole school. It's no big deal. He said he's not into crowds." I stab my fork into my salad.

"It's like, *eight* people, Gabs. Not really a 'crowd', but that's okay. There will be other parties." She twists the cap off her water bottle and takes a swig.

"Hey." Liam plunks himself down in the seat next to Asha, his green eyes brightening the moment he sees her. "Am I going to get to meet your music store hottie this weekend, Gabs? Bringing him to the party?"

I can't contain the laughter that erupts from me. "*Music store hottie?*"

My gaze darts from Asha to Liam. Is that what she told him? She's right. He *is* hot. But he's not coming with me.

"Hah! Real funny. The answer is no. We've only gone out once. Twice, if you count him coming to our meet last week. I don't want to scare him off by bringing him to a big party."

Liam smacks his palm on the table. "I missed him!" He purses his lips as his gaze bounces from me to Asha. "Wait, I saw both of you finish the race. I don't remember seeing you with anyone afterward. No guys, anyway."

"He was there," I say. "Maybe next time."

"I hope so." Liam turns to Asha. "What about you?" He flips his mop of ginger hair off his face and rubs the back of his neck. "Bringing anyone?"

He looks her in the face, and I can practically see his heart thump in his chest, waiting for her answer. Hoping she says 'no'. Hoping he won't have to compete for her attention at his party.

Liam's so bad at keeping his feelings hidden. If

only Asha wouldn't make him work so hard and go for it. It could be weird between the three of us for a while, since we've all been good friends for so long, but we'd figure it out. I mean, of course we would.

"I don't think so." Asha grabs a half of her sandwich and takes a bite.

"No Matt Kirkman?"

Asha gives Liam a sideways glance and swallows her food. "No."

"Oh, okay."

Liam empties the contents of his lunch bag on the table, his apple rolling across the table to me. I chuck it back into his waiting hands and meet his gaze, silently prodding him to continue, not to give up on Asha. He gives a barely perceptible nod as if to say no, not here.

"Thanks. So why didn't I see Mr. Hottie at your meet?"

"Mr. So-called Hottie has a name, Liam. It's CJ."

"You still don't know what CJ stands for," says Asha, around a mouthful of food.

"No, I never asked." I nod at Liam. "He was on the course then stopped by our tent after the finish, but he had to take off. That's why you didn't see him." I play with the cap on my water bottle. "I know what you're thinking, I'm making him up, my 'pretend' boyfriend. And I definitely get why you'd think that, but Ash met him. He's real."

"I'm just messing with you," Liam says. "So, where'd you go on your date?"

"Angelo's. And yes, he was the perfect gentleman, *Dad*." I roll my eyes as any daughter would.

Liam scrunches up his face the way my dad always does, as if to prove a point. "*Dad*? Just making sure this guy treats you right. I haven't met him, so I can't give my approval yet."

"Is that so? You don't have to worry. You'd like him, I think. But…" I bite my lip and rest my forearms on the table. "Okay, be honest, I mean, brutally honest, do you think I'm crazy for going out with him? I met him in Larry's at the end of the summer. It's kinda not my thing to go out with someone like this, you know, someone I meet once. In a store. He doesn't even go to West Penn."

"You? Crazy?" Liam's mouth tugs to the side and he does this googly thing with his eyes. "No, not at all." He explodes into laughter. "Seriously Gabs, you didn't meet him at just any store, you met him at Larry's. He's obviously into music, especially all that stuff you like. And *only* you like. Plus, he came to a cross-country meet of his *own free will*. He's into you." He smiles. "And I can tell the way you talk about him, you're into him. So, no, you're not crazy."

Hmm, Liam's put thought into this. And made some surprisingly good points. If only I could figure out CJ's connection to the woods, to that song. But I can't share that stuff with these two. Not yet, anyway. And especially not the notebook. Asha knows about the chill—she was there when it first happened—but if I mention the other stuff, both of them will think I've lost it. Maybe I have.

"Okay, thanks. You can meet him another time."

"I plan on it," he says with a grin.

Liam is the brother I don't have. Watching out for me. Making sure any guy I go out with meets his expectations. His lofty expectations. God, I love him.

"We'll do something else, that's all," someone says

in a shrill voice that makes me cringe.

I spin around. Caitlin sits with her back to me at the table behind us. Continuing the silly argument with Madison from English class.

"Like what?" asks Madison. "You're the only one who won't be there." Her gaze darts around Caitlin to Alex who's just arrived. "Well, you and Alex."

Caitlin gets to her feet and shoves in her chair. "It's a stupid bonfire, Madison. We'll live." She tosses her bag on her shoulder and grabs Alex's hand. "C'mon, we'll eat in the atrium."

She starts to stalk away but stops at Liam's chair. "Hey, Liam."

Wait, what? I drop my fork, my gaze zooming to Liam's face. I grip my seat.

"Yeah?" He turns around and rests his arm on his chair.

"What about the party you're having Saturday? I heard you talking about a fire pit in French class. Do you have one in your yard? That sounds really cool. I'd love to see it."

Are you freaking kidding me? She's inviting herself to his party?

"Party's at seven," Liam says. "Coming?"

I kick Asha's foot under the table. "What is he doing?" I mouth. "*Caitlin? For real?*"

Asha shrugs.

"Can I bring snacks?" Caitlin asks.

What alien took over Caitlin's body? She's crashing one of Liam's parties—okay, that part is so Caitlin—but she offers to bring something? The universe has flipped on its head. I mean, outside of her inviting herself.

"Yeah, whatever you want," Liam says. "I'm not picky."

Ugh, you're not, but I am.

"Cool." Caitlin leaves and Alex follows. Like her little puppy dog. Caitlin whirls around, poking her head around Alex.

"You live around the corner from Nick Purcell, right?"

"Right, 405 Beechwood."

"Thanks for the invite," Alex says. He taps Liam on the shoulder and follows Caitlin through the maze of tables to the door.

"*Thanks for the invite?*" Asha's brows creep to her hairline. "Are you crazy? Inviting those two?"

"Technically, he didn't invite them, Ash. Caitlin flat out invited herself. Liam made it less awkward. He's too nice, that's why. And of course, if Caitlin's going somewhere, Alex isn't far behind."

"It's no big deal," Liam says. "They'll stick together and probably won't talk to anyone else, and hey, they're bringing food." A grin tugs at his lips. "I'm not complaining."

"They do know there's no beer, right?" Asha asks. "From what I understand, most of the parties she attends involve copious amounts of beer."

Liam laughs. "Not unless *they're* bringing it."

****

I have no contact with CJ for the next few days. I'm tempted to text him, but I don't. Maybe asking him to a party with my friends—my friends *and Caitlin and Alex*—was too much and this is his way of telling me to ease off. I don't know. It seemed harmless, asking him to a party. As for the woods, I've completely avoided them. It forces me to take the long way to and from school when I don't get a ride with Ash. And that's a bonus. More calories burned.

Finally, Saturday night arrives. I lounge on Asha's bed, my arm behind my head, while she models like, a hundred different outfits. I mean, what's the big deal? It's a party in Liam's backyard. Warmth is the only factor behind my fashion choice tonight. It's been starting to feel like autumn, with temps in the fifties all week.

"So?" Asha asks.

"Yeah, that one's nice." I pick a piece of thread off my sweatshirt.

"You're not even looking. C'mon, Gabs."

I lift my gaze. Asha twirls around, wearing a black mini skirt, purple silk shirt and chunky heeled boots. Her long dark hair is pulled back into a loose knot.

"Whoa! Liam will be very happy to see you tonight if you wear *that* one. Not that he isn't any other time." I arch my brows. "Why are you so concerned with what you're wearing tonight? The party's outside, on his deck around the fire pit. Throw on jeans and a sweatshirt like me."

"I know, but I bought this skirt a month ago and it's too dressy for school, so I thought I'd wear it tonight. Plus, what if we end up inside? Liam said his parents will be upstairs so we can hang out downstairs if it gets too cold." Her gaze slides to her boots. "You think it's too much? I'm not dressing to impress Liam." She screws up her face.

"No?"

Asha sets her hands on her hips. "We're friends. Just like you and him."

I purse my lips. "No, Liam's like a brother to me. I mean, I love him to death, but you two, there's something else. There's always been something else. You have to notice the way he looks at you, blushes around you. The way he touches your arm when he's making a point."

"He's the same way with you."

I shake my head. "No, it's different." I bite my lip and meet her gaze. "So?"

Asha drops onto the bed with me. "So, nothing. Don't get all weird on me, Gabby. Are you ready?" she asks, abruptly changing the subject. "He said seven, right?" She taps the toe of her boot on the floor.

"Yep." I stand and run my gaze over my clothes then glance at Asha. "Well, I feel underdressed."

"Why?"

"Because, look at you. I'm in jeans and a hoodie." I sigh. "At least I changed out of my high tops, put my boots on."

"You look good, Gabs. You always look good, no matter what you wear. I'd offer you something of mine, but nothing would fit. You're like, half a foot taller than me. And skinnier. Way skinnier."

"Not true. The skinnier part, I mean." Unfortunately, I *am* a half a foot taller.

Asha furrows her brow. "Yeah, speaking of 'skinnier'…"

"Nothing to speak of," I clap back and stamp a grin on my face. "I'll be warm. Comfortable." Certainly not trying to impress anyone. No one that will be at the party, anyway. "What about you, are you going to be warm enough?"

"I have a coat. Plus, it should be warm around the

fire pit. I mean, isn't that why Caitlin's coming?" Asha rises from the bed and drops her hand on her hip. *"Ooh, a fire pit? That sounds really cool. I'd love to see it!"* Her imitation of Caitlin's pitch is spot on.

I snort. "She's a piece of work, isn't she? I still can't believe she invited herself."

"I can." She pauses and plays with a ring on her finger. "I'm glad you didn't back out because of her. I know she's irritating, but it's Liam's party. Just ignore her."

"I guess. Even though she's kinda hard to ignore."

Asha nods. "So, have you heard from CJ?"

My stomach clenches. I'd hoped to avoid that subject. "No, not since I made the mistake of asking him to tonight's party." I clasp my hands together. "It's okay. We went out once. Had fun. No big deal." But it is. "I thought there was something between us. Especially when he came to our cross-country meet. Plus, we talked about going to see a concert or two in South Phila in November."

Asha taps me on the arm and meets my eye. "There's definitely something there, Gabs. He probably had plans tonight he couldn't change, that's all."

"How busy do you have to be to text, ask how things are? It's okay. I'm fine."

Asha taps her foot on the floor. "Texting works both ways."

"I know, but I contacted him last when I asked him to the party. I don't want it to look like I'm desperate."

She lifts her brow then wrinkles it. "Desperate? Just shoot him a text, ask what he's up to and tell him he's missing a great party. Include a selfie in front of the firepit. *Wish you were here to keep me warm.*" Asha laughs.

I smack Asha's arm with the back of my hand. "I'm trying to keep him interested, not drive him away. Come on, we should go. I'll text him later."

"Hey Mom, we're leaving for Liam's," Asha says, pulling her coat on, as we walk through her kitchen.

"Hey, Mrs. Shah."

"Hi, Gabby. Asha, didn't you make brownies for the party?" Mrs. Shah asks.

Asha puckers her mouth. "Oh. Right." She slides her glance to me then to her mom. "I took them over earlier this afternoon when I helped Liam set up."

I bite back a smirk. When you helped him set up? Something you forgot to tell me? Oh, you are so busted. Asha shoots me a 'don't say a word' look, but I can't resist.

"You should've told me, Ash. I would've come earlier, help you two set up. I feel bad you had to do it all yourselves."

Okay, I'm laying it on thick, but she had it coming. I guess she didn't want me interfering in their cozy little twosome. Even if she won't admit it.

Asha shrugs. "It wasn't anything. We set up the tables outside, got all the paper products, utensils out. A few other things." She turns to her mom. "Okay, we're outta here."

"Have fun," says Mrs. Shah.

We step out the back door, a bright spotlight casting the Shahs' yard in a pool of light. Asha instantly strides ahead of me. Even in her high-heeled boots. Avoiding me. We have time. Not now, though. Liam lives next door. Like, *right* next door. Whatever I'm gonna say to Asha will have to wait.

The thick smoky aroma of the fire pit permeates the crisp fall air as I follow Asha across the lawn and push open the wooden gate into Liam's backyard.

Tiki torches surround the large rectangular wood deck as smoke billows into the night, obscuring my view of who's here. Laughter and conversation fill the air as we near the deck and the large crowd which spills over its railings. More voices ring out from the group clustered around the fire pit. Music trills from the speakers, blaring through the autumn night.

I catch up to Asha and follow her up the steps to the deck. "I thought you said only eight people."

"That's what Liam said. I guess word spread, people brought guests..." She shrugs. "Maybe Caitlin brought more of her entourage."

My stomach clenches. "Oh joy."

As if on cue, Caitlin's shrill laughter rises from the crowd huddled around the fire pit where she sits with Alex and a few of their friends on a bench. At least I think they're her friends. They're not Liam's friends. *Our* friends.

She catches my eye and waves. "Oh, hey, Gabby. Make sure you try the chocolate chip cookies. Alex and I made them."

Make sure you try the cookies. Alex and I made them. "Oh, absolutely."

"Hey, you made it." Liam emerges through the sliding doors and shoulders through the crowd gathered around the food table. He pushes up the sleeves of his gray hoodie.

"Yeah, you know I live so far, I almost didn't come," Asha says. A grin stretches across her face.

Liam's eyes widen as they flit over Asha's outfit,

before he snaps his jaws shut. "You...you look great," he says. He motions for us to sit on two deck chairs.

"Thanks, you too," Asha says.

"I try my best," he says, his cheeks pinking to match Asha's.

These two belong together. Like, right now. Although I'm starting to wonder if something didn't already happen this afternoon when they set up for the party. Set up *without* me.

"So, where'd the crowd come from?" Asha settles into the chair, crossing her legs at her ankles.

"A bunch of people came with Caitlin and Alex," Liam says. "I guess they're friends of theirs?" He shrugs. "I don't know."

I scope out the back yard. "She seriously invited all these people to your house? Without asking?"

Liam shrugs. "No big deal. She brought chips and salsa. And cookies. It's all good."

I laugh. A little too loud. "Yeah, she told me about her cookies. You're too nice, Liam, letting them all crash here."

"Maybe." Liam kicks Asha's boot with his sneaker. "Not everyone thinks so."

Asha's face flushes and she tucks her legs under her chair. "Sure I do. C'mon, you know I love you."

Now Liam flushes. He rests his elbows on his legs and lowers his chin.

A change in subject is in order.

I nod to the crowd around the fire pit. "So, you think you'll be invited to *her* next party?" Liam laughs. "Hell, no. Doesn't matter. My favorite two people are here. He taps me on the hand and nudges Asha's leg.

I gotta give him points for trying.

"Aww, you only say that because I made brownies," Asha says.

"Right, brownies," Liam replies. He meets Asha's gaze, and she glances away.

For the next hour the three of us hang out on the deck—well, mostly Asha and I as Liam plays dutiful party host—until Jake Rossi, Liam's friend, folds his long, lanky body into the chair next to me.

"Hey, Gabby."

"Hey, how's it going?"

"Can you help me get some more drinks from the kitchen?" Liam says, grasping Asha's hand. "We're getting low." He nods to Jake then me. "You guys need anything?"

"Nope," I say.

Jake runs his hand through his sandy blond hair. "Thanks, I'm good."

Liam and Asha leave and head inside. Leaving me alone. Leaving *us* alone. My opinion of Liam goes from too nice to too sly. How come he didn't mention Jake would be here? I can't get upset, though. It's Liam. Even if he has been trying to get me and Jake together ever since Breanna broke up with him.

I still can't figure that one out. What's not to like about Jake? He's a super nice guy, thoughtful, makes me laugh so hard I snort, which totally embarrasses me. And he's gorgeous.

"Great race last week, Gabby. You totally smoked the competition."

Does that include your ex?

"Probably all those grueling training runs in July with you. How'd you do? I usually get over to the guys' race after ours, but I had to get home." And I had a *guest.*

A smile breaks across his face. "Lowered my time by two seconds."

I tilt my head. "And?"

"Okay, I won. And for the same reason. I had a great training partner this past summer. No, an awesome partner who pushed me, even on those ten-milers."

Heat creeps up my neck and I give him a small smile. "Thanks."

Oh my gosh, why did Breanna break up with you?

He smiles at me, his green eyes glinting under the flickering orange glow of the tiki torches. The warmth of our exchange spreads through me like bubbles fizzing in a shaken soda bottle. Ugh, what am I doing? I don't want to be Jake's fall back. His second choice. The *other* girl on cross-country. But right now, I'm buzzing from head to toe. The way I should be feeling with CJ. But CJ's not here. And who knows what's going to happen between us? Maybe nothing.

This is all Liam's fault. He knows about CJ. Yet he's still trying to get me and Jake together.

It's working.

But I can't give in. Liam probably figures CJ is a passing crush. If only.

Still, Jake and I hang out and talk for a while, mostly about workouts and our next meets. And the fact that Caitlin and her entourage—minus Madison—is here. Suddenly, I can barely keep my eyes open. Only ten o'clock, it might as well be past midnight. Exhaustion tugs at every fiber of my body.

I stand and stretch my arms. "I gotta go," I say with a yawn. "Sorry." I stifle a giggle. "It's not you. I'm exhausted."

Jake stands. "No problem. Do you need a ride? I can take you home. I'm ready to take off, too."

My stomach flip-flops. He wants to drive me home. Crap. I guess we had too much of a good time. That's the thing. There are never any awkward silences with Jake. There's always plenty to talk about. Laugh about. I *do* like him, but I can't get CJ out of my head. Plus, he must be constantly comparing me to Breanna.

"Oh." I fold my arms. "You don't have to do that." Out of the corner of my eye, I notice Asha and Liam sharing the two-seater deck chair behind us. I hadn't realized they were there because they were so quiet. It's obvious why. About time.

"Hey, I'm gonna get going." I'm intruding on a private moment, but I can't leave without saying goodbye to my two best friends, one of whom is the party host.

Asha leans against Liam, her head in the hollow of his shoulder, his arm wrapped around her. Seems I missed a lot while I was engrossed in conversation with Jake. Maybe that's all Ash and Liam needed. To be left alone. To be given their space. Right now there's not an ounce of space between them.

Asha untangles herself from Liam and swipes the hair out of her eyes. "Gabby, wait. Let me get my keys. I'll drive you." She fishes around in her coat pocket.

"Seriously, I can take you home." Jake steps around from behind me. "I don't mind at all."

"Neither one of you have to drive me. I'll walk. It's not that late, plus it's a nice night."

As long as I don't walk through the woods. How can I separate Asha and Liam when something's finally happening with them? My mind wanders to CJ. I'm not ready to give up on him. Ash is right. I should text him, tell him he missed a great party, ask if he wants to get together again. I don't have to wait for him to contact me. Right?

Asha rests her hand on her hip. "Don't be ridiculous. You're not walking home alone. It'll take five minutes to drive you home." She stands and tugs her hair out of her coat, letting it fall down her back.

"Thanks anyway, Jake. It was nice of you to offer," I say.

Jake's face falls and he looks away. "Sure. Maybe next time, Gabby." He steps off the deck and walks out to the fire pit where a few people still gather around a dwindling flame.

An ache pulses in my chest. Great. Now, I've managed to make Jake feel bad. "Liam, thanks again. It was fun."

Liam stretches out his arms and yawns. "No problem. Thanks for coming. You should give him a chance." He jerks his chin to the fire pit where Jake stands with some other guys.

"It's not that. I like Jake. A lot. But, I want to give this thing with CJ a chance." Even if it is just a ride home, I don't want to get too comfortable with Jake. Or be someone's second choice. "Kay?"

"Whatever you say. Always looking out for you."

"I know."

"You're coming back, right?" Liam asks Asha.

"Yeah, for a while then I should go." She covers her mouth, stifling a yawn. "I'm tired too."

Liam reclines in the chair. "Cool. I'll save your seat right here." Smiling, he pats the cushion and Asha blushes.

A small group of people still mill around the fire pit as we walk through the backyard, the shrinking flames of the tiki torches casting their faces in a soft yellow light. Caitlin and her friends took off about a half hour ago. They kept to the fire pit—and the beer they brought—not socializing with anyone else, none of Liam's friends anyway. Typical. Liam didn't seem to mind. He's too nice for his own good. Although I don't think he noticed anyone tonight but Asha.

And for once, the feeling seemed mutual.

Chapter Eight

As soon as we're in the car, I whirl on Asha. "So, you and Liam were awful cozy tonight. And the night's not over. Oh, and nice of you to tell me you helped Liam set up today for the party." I drum my fingers on the door. "Made brownies and brought them over? What's up with that? Why didn't you guys invite me?"

"It was nothing. Thought it'd be fun to make something." She pauses. "And we weren't 'cozy'. Same as always." Asha purses her lips and eyes the rearview mirror as she backs out of her driveway in her mom's car.

"No, he had his arm around you, and you were not in any way, shape, or form, trying to move it or him away. Admit it, Ash. You two are meant to be." I lean against the headrest and sigh. "It's so easy with you two. Comfortable. You've known each other a long time."

"We all have."

"I know and he's the nicest guy in the world."

"You're right." Asha keeps her eyes on the road, her voice low, but steady.

"Then what's holding you back?"

"I don't want things to change. Like you said, it's *comfortable* with him. I don't want to screw up our friendship. Make things weird."

"Things won't get weird. He loved your outfit

tonight." Asha's silent—silently blushing, I'm sure. I glance out the window as we drive through the center of town, the sidewalks still packed with Friday night crowds. "C'mon, you're already good friends. You don't have to act any different, act a certain way to impress him. It would be…easier."

Easier than what I'm doing with CJ. What *am* I doing with CJ?

"I don't know." Asha turns onto my street and slams on the brakes.

A couple of feet ahead of the car, CJ strolls across the street, his hands in his coat pockets and his gaze to the ground.

I power the window down. "Hey, watch where you're going."

"Gabby?" CJ lifts his head and jogs to the car. "Hey." He pokes his head inside. "Hey, Asha."

"Hey, C.J."

Wait, where is he coming from? The hairs stand on my neck. The woods are just ahead of us. The same woods that have freaked me out since the day I walked home with Asha from practice. The woods where a ghost has taken up residence with the intention of spooking me. Harassing me. The woods where I bumped into CJ that night I walked to the bookstore. Where I found the notebook. Why is he walking through there late at night? By himself. He lives on the other side of Main, like Asha. Uneasiness swims in my gut. There's a connection. I just haven't figured it out. Yet.

"So, what are you doing out here?"

He shrugs. "Taking a walk. It's a nice night."

His tone is casual, matter of fact, like it's normal

for a seventeen-year-old to be out for a walk because it's 'a nice night.' *Right.* Does he expect me to believe that? After he blew me off?

"We missed you at the party," says Asha. "Although it was a bigger crowd than planned, with Caitlin and her entourage. Actually, a lot of West Penn people that normally wouldn't be there. You should've come. It was fun."

CJ backs away from the car. "I'm sure it was. Listen, I gotta go. Gabby, I'll talk to you later." He spins around and takes off down the sidewalk in the opposite direction.

"Okay. Be rude," says Asha.

"Yeah, that was rude, right? Not to mention, odd. Especially the part about him being *out for a walk*? When he couldn't take the time to come to the party with me?"

Asha shakes her head. "A little, yeah." She pulls away and continues down my street. "And why did it seem like he couldn't get away fast enough when I mentioned the party?"

"I don't know."

My heart's pounding as I twist in my seat and gaze out the window. CJ's gone. I should forget about him. Forget I ever met him. There is something...*off* about him. But there's also something intriguing and mysterious. And beautiful. The way we share the same unique, quirky musical taste. His laidback nature that puts me at ease. Those eyes. Lips. The way he kisses me. A surge of warmth explodes in my chest. What's wrong with me? He's walking around in the woods on a Friday night then acts like he can't get away fast enough when he sees me.

Forget him, Gabby.

But I can't.

Asha pulls into my driveway and kills the engine. "I'm sorry, Gabs, I know you like him, but there's something…*off* about him."

Okay, is Asha inside my head? Or maybe we think alike. Which in this case, isn't a good thing. It means I should forget about CJ.

She taps me on the arm. "Hey, you and Jake were doing a lot of talking tonight. Anything going on there? He's always been so nice. And hot."

Heat flushes my cheeks. "Yeah, he is. Funny too, but—"

"But he's not CJ," she finishes.

I open my mouth to protest, but Asha silences me with her hand. "I get it, Gabs. I do. Obviously, or you wouldn't have crushed Jake's hopes tonight when you turned down his offer for a ride home." Asha nods. "Mm-mm-mm. He is smokin' hot."

"Yeah, we've established that. We trained together this past summer, remember?"

After Breanna broke up with him. I don't want to be his fall back. And I can't stop thinking about CJ.

"How do you always know exactly what's going on with me?"

"We're best friends. Of course I know what's going on with you. I don't want to see you get hurt though, if CJ doesn't work out."

I pick at a thread on my jeans. *If CJ doesn't work out.* "I won't. Why do you think he acted that way now?"

"I don't know. Maybe he's dealing with something at home." Asha turns to me and places her hand on my arm. "You have to do what your gut says. You like him and it's obvious he likes you. I wouldn't give up on him, yet."

Asha is not making this easy. But she's right. I'm not ready to give up on CJ.

"Yeah, maybe."

"Don't stress over it." She meets my gaze. "Seriously, don't. Alright, I'd better go, or Liam will think I deserted him. I'll talk to you tomorrow, okay?"

"Ooh, that's right." I jump out of the car. "Liam's waiting for you." I wiggle my eyebrows.

"Don't get your hopes up. Nothing's happening."

"Really? Then why didn't you tell me you were over there earlier today helping him prepare for the party?" I purse my lips. "Or how come *he* didn't text me?"

"As I told you before, I live next door," she says, but I shut the door and give her an airy wave.

It's only a matter of time.

****

The following morning, I wake to bright sunlight streaming in through my curtains. I roll onto my side and grab my phone from my nightstand. Two messages. The first is from Asha.

—*OMG. I have to tell you something! Call me ASAP* —

Liam.

That was quicker than I expected, but the way they acted last night, I'm not surprised.

My gaze flits to the second text and my heart beats faster. It's from CJ.

—*Sorry I left abruptly last night. Long story. And sorry I missed the party. Also a long story. Talk to u soon—*

Another apology? Really? It's a long story? We went out once. It's not like we're dating. But that one time went *really* well. Ugh, why does he have this effect on me?

I flop on my pillow and exhale a long, exasperated breath. At least Asha has something to be happy about this morning. I hit her number and she answers on the first ring.

"Hey, I'm dying here. What's the big news?"

"I'll tell you in person. Are you free today?"

I draw myself into a sitting position. "How about a run? Half hour? We can run our usual five-mile course through the borough."

Asha and I have had some of our most heartfelt conversations while running. Today should be no different.

"Perfect. I'll see you in a half hour by the café on Rose."

"Awesome."

But before I get ready, I grab the little blue notebook from my bookshelf. It's dry now, but the pages are brittle and crinkly. Paging to where I left off, the print still barely legible, I read:

What's her problem? What have I ever done to her? She doesn't even know me. I thought we could be friends. Oh well. I probably need to find a new spot. Even if this one is perfect. It's inspirational.

Who's 'her'? It sounds like the person who wrote this was being harassed. Or bullied. She says the spot is 'inspirational'. Is it that spot in the woods? I drop the book in my nightstand drawer. What if none if it is related? I need to get dressed to meet Ash.

I take the long way into town. This way I get an extra mile and a half—each way—in addition to my run with Asha. Burn more calories. And it means I don't have to run through the woods. Genius.

I arrive at the café on Rose just as Asha does and we fall in step with each other and head north. It's a bit sticky as we navigate the narrow sidewalk, sidestepping the outdoor café tables, filled with early diners.

"So, after we cleaned up, we kinda crashed on his sofa in the family room," Asha explains as we run through the center of town, hewing to the narrow road shoulder. "His parents and sister were upstairs."

I tug my cap lower to shade my eyes from the rising sun. "And…"

"I don't know, we chatted about the party and stuff, and I said something about Caitlin being one of his bff's now. We were acting silly, and he picked up my hand, said he wanted me to more than his friend." A blush darkens Asha's cheeks and it's not from the brisk autumn air. "I don't know. It sort of happened. He asked if he could kiss me and…he did."

A smile eases across my face. "About time."

Asha twists her head to me, her ponytail flying over her shoulder. "Gabby!"

"What? It is. We were talking about it last night. I knew something was up the way you two were snuggled together at the party, not to mention you *rudely* excluded me from the party planning."

"Seriously, that was nothing. Plus, it was only a kiss." She pauses. "Okay, maybe a little more." She stifles a laugh. "I mean, it wasn't a full-on make-out session. We were in his family room with his parents upstairs. I felt a little weird, you know. What if Mr. or

Mrs. Abbott came down and caught us?"

I smile. "I'm happy for you. And Liam. You two are my best friends. It's awesome. You can't tell me you never noticed the way he is around you when we're together." I sidestep a woman in a hoodie and yoga pants walking her dog.

"Yeah, I guess. I mean, yes. And no. Hey, any more from CJ?" she asks, redirecting the conversation.

"He texted me this morning. Actually, last night. I didn't see it 'til this morning."

We round the corner where a group of cyclists have stopped for a water break, and we head in the direction of the park. Out in the open, the wind swirls, blowing loose strands of hair around. But I'm warmed up now and the breeze is welcome on my face.

"What did he say?"

"Nothing," I say, tucking the wisps of hair under my cap. Basically, he's sorry he left in a hurry last night and he hoped the party was fun. He said it's *a long story*, the reason why he didn't go." I roll my eyes.

"Do you think he plans on telling you?"

"I don't know. He said he'll talk to me later. It doesn't matter. If he's not feeling me anymore, I'd rather end things now, before I get too invested and then have my heart ripped out."

"Aw, Gabs."

"What? It's true. I don't want to play games. Plus, I gotta work on raising my chemistry grade. And we have two meets next week. I don't have time to worry about him and his moodiness." Or his connection to the eerie stuff in the woods. "Hopefully, he'll come around. If not…" I throw up my hands. "Whatever."

I flirt with telling Asha about the notebook, but like

the music, I keep it to myself. For some reason, it feels personal, something I don't want to share with anyone. Not yet anyway.

"Right. But seriously, what do you have to worry about in chem? You'll pull it out. You always do. And cross-country? Two more *first place* finishes. No pressure, Gabs, but you've been unbeatable so far."

"Thanks, but this week's going to be tough. Katie Watson from South? She's a junior, like us, and she had the fastest time at Regionals last year." I take a long, slow belly breath and blow it out. "That race won't be another 'first place finish'."

"You were sick with the flu at Regionals and still came in fifth overall. You would've kicked her butt if you were healthy. It's only the second time she beat you. You're running great now. Don't sweat it."

But I do. And it's not because I had the flu. I did, but I have at least ten pounds on Katie—maybe eight now—in addition to being at least seven or eight inches taller than her. Those times I beat her, it was luck. Hopefully, I'll run better this week.

When we reach our turnaround point, a small stone church bordered by a white fence, we head back in the direction of Asha's. For the next mile we're silent, the steady shuffle of sneaker tread on asphalt and our even breathing, the only sounds. Of course, inside my head, it's anything but silent. What the heck am I going to do about CJ? Should I even want to go out with him after last night? We turn the corner onto Asha's street.

"Hey, there's Liam," I say.

"What?" Asha swivels her head around, panic coloring her voice. "Where?"

"Jumpy some? Relax. He went in his house. Come

on, Ash, it's Liam. He's still the same guy." I clamp my lips shut when Asha shoots me a glare.

"So, we'll talk later?" I stretch out my hamstrings once we've reached her driveway.

"Text me, we'll figure something out. Or I'll text you. Maybe we can hang out at my house? Find something good streaming on one of the apps or on cable."

"Sounds good." I arch my brow. "Wait, you and Liam don't have plans?"

"No." Asha rests her hands on her hips. "Just because of what happened last night doesn't mean we're suddenly going to hang out together all the time. Not without you, anyway." She grins.

"Aww, thanks. Maybe Liam would want to come over." I scrub my fingers over my chin. "We've turned him onto a few rom coms in the past. Maybe we can find another tonight."

"Yeah, we can do that. Why don't you text him, ask him if he wants to hang out tonight?" She steps away from the garage, clasps her hands together and stretches her arms over her head. "Or maybe Caitlin's having a party and we can crash it, like she did Liam's."

"Can you imagine that?" I laugh. "I'd better get going. I'll talk to you later."

Asha grasps my hand before I take off. "I don't want things to change between us, Gabs because…well, because Liam and I kissed. Okay?"

"Absolutely. But you didn't 'just kiss', you gave in to the sizzling chemistry you two have, that you've always had." I grin. "Text me. We'll do something after my marathon study session."

I take off running but can't ignore the little voice in my head. Will Ash call me later, tell me her plans have changed? That she and Liam are doing something? Without me? Now that they're 'together'…

Nah, it's all good. Nothing can change our friendship. CJ and I are another story.

The Saturday morning rush has doubled since Asha, and I came through here a little while ago. I jog in the street with the wind at my back. Crossing the light on Main, a guy wearing a maroon hoodie and faded jeans catches my eye as he walks in the direction of Larry's.

That walk. The build. The blond hair sticking out of his hoodie. My stomach jumps.

CJ turns as he opens the door, as if he senses my presence. Our gazes meet and he turns away, slipping inside the store. Knots fist my stomach into a tight ball.

What? Not even a wave? Then why the apology text? Jerk.

Asha's right. He's strange. He's been hiding something since I first met him. I need to let it go. Let him go. Jake is a super nice guy. Good looking. Runner. Funny as hell. The perfect gentleman. And I'm his *second* choice.

It doesn't matter. I have to get CJ out of my system. Move on.

I cross the street and pick up the pace, nervous energy propelling me faster down the street. By the time I reach my house, I eye my watch, my heart thrumming at a blistering 182 beats per minute. Drenched in sweat, exhilaration races through my veins.

Sometimes, disillusionment is the best motivator.

Chapter Nine

That afternoon, I recline on my bed, Lola nestled against me, my 'relaxation' playlist streaming into my ears, when my phone buzzes.

—Hey, how about a movie this afternoon? —

— U convinced Asha she'd actually like a rom com?—

— I reminded her about the thriller you endured with us at the end of August. Thought it was time we see something u like—

— Thx. I appreciate it. Congrats, by the way. It's about time it happened with you two—

— Thx —.

— I don't want to get in the middle of your 'date'—

Or the two of you.

— Not really a date, although Jake said he'd go, so it could be. What do u think? —

Hmm, Asha probably filled Liam in on our chance meeting with CJ last night. When he acted so odd. I do like Jake. Still… I'm not quite ready to give up on CJ.

—Thx for the invite. I'm still swamped with homework. Maybe another time? —

—Ok. Jake will be crushed. But I get it. And it wasn't because of me it took so long with Asha—

—LOL! I know—

I've always known.

—*Ok. Asha told me about last night. U ok?*—
—*I'm fine. Have a good time at the movies*—

After dinner, I retreat to my bedroom. I pick up my latest book, a YA fantasy—of course—with the intention of making a serious dent, like *finishing it*. I mean, I have nothing but time on my hands, so I should fly through it. Clenching the book with both hands, I sink into my pillow. My head spins. Ugh, Asha and Liam are off having fun together and I'm here brooding over a guy I should forget about.

But I can't. Because that song from the woods keeps running through my head, linking me to him. Drawing me to him. Which reminds me…

I set my novel down and drawing out the journal, flip to where I left off. There are more water stains in the middle, the words smudged beyond legibility, but I stare at the letters, trying to make some sense of it, but all I can is

pi ce of b ead
app e
chic n

It's like a grocery list, only with three items.
What the heck?

*****

Ugh, what a crappy day. A crappy week. And it's only Tuesday. As I head home from school, I pause when I reach the entrance to the woods. I've avoided going through here for the last week, but today I need to get home quickly. My legs tremble.

C'mon, Gabby.

I can't let a silly fear of spirits haunting the woods prevent me from getting home. I'll run if I have to. I have two big tests to study for.

I plunge into the woods and head along the dirt path. A branch cracks overhead and I almost jump out of my sneakers. I lift my eyes to a squirrel scurrying along a slender branch of a large oak.

Phew! C'mon, Gabby, pull yourself together.

Clenching and unclenching my hands, I move deeper into the forest of trees. Shadows lengthen across the ground, the brush and foliage becoming denser, darkness falling around me. I pick up the pace, keeping my gaze forward, biting my lip harder, until a salty, metallic taste fills my mouth. Dammit.

The air moves around me and my heart leaps into my throat. What the heck was that? Maybe walking through the woods was a bad idea.

I reach the clearing and the hairs on my neck stand on end. Someone's here. Not a ghost. Something real. *Someone* real.

My heart pounds like a drum, but as I focus in, I exhale all the breath in my lungs. CJ sits on the grass beneath a tree on the other side. The same exact spot I encountered him before. I run my tongue over my lip to wipe away any traces of blood. CJ stands as I pad across the grass, drawing close to him.

"Hi," I say.

"Hi."

My cheeks flush. What do I say? Frankly, I have nothing to say. Doesn't he have some apologizing to do? Of course, all I'm trying to do right now is breathe.

"I'm sorry, Gabby." CJ looks me in the face. It's as if he's read my mind. "I didn't mean to take off like that when I saw you and Asha the other night."

"Or ignore me when you saw me the next day?" I fold my arms. "Not even a wave?"

He bites his bottom lip, mirroring my own anxiety, and nods. "Yeah, that was rude. I'm sorry. I wasn't ready to talk, I guess."

You guess?

"Talk about what, CJ? I had a great time when we went out and I thought you did, too." You kissed me at the end of the night. Maybe it didn't mean anything to you, but it did to me. "If I was out of line, asking you to Liam's party, I'm sorry. I thought it would be fun."

CJ takes a step closer to me and a smile softens his face, brightening his pale gray eyes. "What? No, it had nothing to do with that. It's..." He looks up toward the treetops, to the sliver of blue sky poking through the golden and orange leaves. "I'm not ready for the whole party scene, hanging out in a crowd, that's all. I'm sure your friends are great. It had nothing to do with you."

Oh. My body relaxes. "I don't understand. What do you mean you're 'not ready'?"

His gaze falls to the ground, and he blows out a long, slow breath, like he's trying to calm the tension rising in him, the same unease that gripped me a minute ago walking through here. Like maybe these woods *are* haunted.

A chill walks my spine. CJ has something to do with what's happening to me. The cold. The music. I feel it in my gut. But what?

"I know it sounds strange, but I need some time. I really like you." He meets my eyes. "I'd love to go out again, but I guess I ruined it the way I blew you off. I'm sorry. It had nothing to do with you. I'm trying to work some things out."

A thousand tiny wings beat in my chest. He'd love to go out again.

"You didn't ruin it. I was confused, that's all. I wish you would've said something." I nibble at my bottom lip. It's still tender. "I'd love to go out again, too."

Whatever it is he can't tell me, it can't be a bad thing. I've always been a good judge of character, like Asha said. With CJ, it's as if there's a sadness inside him, something that haunts him, dulls the spark in his beautiful gray eyes. I have to be patient.

A grin stretches across his face. "Awesome. Thanks for giving me another chance."

"Sure. So, are you just hanging out here? Field trip for school?" I chuckle and kick the grass with my sneaker. "You seem to like this spot."

"I do. It's quiet. Peaceful. I had a ton of schoolwork today, since I slacked off Friday. I needed to get out, get some air. I always seem to wind up here." He drops his gaze to his feet, his thick blond lashes sweeping his cheeks. "Actually, I hoped to see you on your way home from school, so I could apologize. I didn't want to text or call because I thought you wouldn't respond. Which I totally get. So…"

My brows jump. "So, you stalked me?"

"No." A smile twitches at the corners of his lips. "Maybe. I wanted to talk to you. Apologize. Do you always walk home this way?"

"When I need to get home quickly. Or when I don't feel like walking all the way around the neighborhood." Or when I'm feeling brave and not afraid of the spirit who has made me its personal target. A shudder runs through me. I clear my throat. "I'm swamped with work, too. One test yesterday and two more this week."

"That sucks. Any meets coming up?"

"Two, actually. One tomorrow, away at South. And then Friday at home."

He shakes his head. "Wow, you are busy. I was going to ask if you wanted to do something Friday, but—"

"I'd love to," I say, a little too quickly. Geez, that didn't sound desperate, did it? "Friday, after the meet, I'll be done with everything. That's something to celebrate, right?"

"Absolutely. So, I'll text you?"

"Yes, text me."

"Oh, Gabby?"

I spin around, a weightlessness spreading through me, like I've suddenly sprouted wings. "Yeah?"

"Would it be okay if I came to your meet on Friday to watch you run?"

My pulse quickens. "Sure. As long as you bring me good luck like last time."

CJ laughs. "That wasn't luck. You're crazy fast."

Flames lick my face and I turn to go. "Talk to you later." My heart swells and I practically skip along the path leading out of the woods.

A hint of that song creeps into my consciousness and I quicken my pace.

Chapter Ten

"No, I don't think you're nuts," Asha says as we sit down to lunch the next day. "If you have a good feeling about him, go with it. Like I said when you texted me yesterday, it sounds like whatever he's hiding, his *deep, dark* secret, he wants to tell you about it. Maybe it's a social thing. He doesn't like crowds, being around people? It's no big deal, nothing to be ashamed of. A lot of people are like that."

I arch my brows. "*I'm* like that. But that's not it. He would've come out and said he doesn't like crowds. He said he wasn't *ready* to go to a party, hang out with people. Like, something happened, and he needs time before he can do the whole social scene again." I shrug. "That's what it sounds like, anyway."

"Hello, ladies." Liam takes his seat and playfully leans into Asha.

She shoves him back as a grin plays across her lips, her cheeks pinking. That's about the extent of their PDA since Liam's party. They haven't made their relationship 'official'. Although no one would question their behavior at this moment. They've pretty much always acted this way. Silly. Comfortable with each other. Like best friends.

Liam straightens in his chair and twists off the cap to his water bottle. "So, I'm on the committee for the Brain Tumor Research benefit in November. You know, with Key Club? We need more acts. Do either of you know anyone who sings or plays in a band, does comedy? Any kind of entertainment." He arches his brow. "Gabs, I know you can sing. *Really well.* You kill it at karaoke every time. How about it?"

I screw up my face. "Yeah, karaoke is the *only* time I get on stage. With Ash, in an empty karaoke bar. Not happening. But, can I see that?" I nod to the paper gripped in his hand.

"Sure. Those are the performers from last year. I got the list from Zach Witten, who was in charge last year. Apart from students who graduated, we're hoping everyone from last year will perform again. Oh, and as many new people we can get would be great. Mr. Thompson wants to surpass last year's donation amount."

Asha leans across the table, and I angle the paper to her. She lifts her hand to her mouth and stifles a laugh.

"Ethan Keller. Remember him?" She shakes her head. "I heard his jokes were terrible. No one laughed. Talk about awkward."

"Mm. I guess he won't be back."

"No, he won't," says Liam. "He graduated. Still, it was for a good cause. *Is* for a good cause."

"I know." Asha lowers her hand to the table. "Wait, who's this band, Cal, Hailey and Nate?"

Liam taps the paper. "Hailey Jarvis? The girl who died by suicide? They were good, too. I mean, from my backstage perspective, anyway. Ooh, that's right, you two weren't there. She had an amazing voice. Her brother played guitar." Liam shakes his head. "Shame what happened to her."

"Oh my gosh, you're right. How could I forget?

Wait, she has a brother at this school?" Asha's brow furrows. "Did he graduate or is he younger?"

"Nah, I think he's a senior. Cal, that is. Nate, the drummer, isn't related to them and doesn't go here."

"Okay, you know a little too much about these people," says Asha.

"I have to. If they don't go to this school, they have to provide all this personal information. C'mon, this is my thing, Asha."

"Like a background check?".

Liam nods. "Uh huh. Pretty much."

The words race around my head and our whole conversation blurs. The only thing I'm distinctly aware of is the chill gripping my spine. My gaze is glued to the paper in front of me, to the trio of names, the letters and words that have moved apart then jumbled together. I pitch forward before I catch myself, bracing my hands on the table.

"Gabby, you okay?" Asha grabs onto my arm. "Here," she says, handing me my water bottle. "Drink. You don't look so good."

I take a swig and set the bottle on the table. *Don't make a scene.*

It's probably too late for that.

"I'll be back." I stand, and wrapping my arm around my waist, shuffle away from the table.

"Want me to come with you?" Asha calls after me.

"No, I'm fine." I scoot through the narrow aisle of packed lunch tables, laughter and conversation echoing around me. Pressure squeezes my chest, making it hard to breathe. I pick up the pace until I'm practically running out the cafeteria doors.

The soles of my sneakers screech on the linoleum

floor in the empty hallway as I sprint into the girls' bathroom. I tuck into the last stall, double over and rest my hands on my knees.

The names on the list are seared into my brain. Hailey. Cal. Nate. Hailey Jarvis. Cal Jarvis.

CJ.

CJ plays guitar. Of course. Those long slender fingers have to play some kind of instrument. He's probably amazing, too. But more importantly, it's his sister's death he's keeping from me. His sister's death by suicide. That's what he can't tell me. My heart pounds and I grip my legs, steadying myself. How could I have not known? How could I have forgotten about Hailey Jarvis? I'd never laid eyes on CJ or *Cal*, before I saw him in Larry's that day. He was a junior last year. It's a big enough school I never ran into him.

My heart breaks for him. It's probably why he hangs out in the woods. To be alone. Think about her. What am I going to say to him? He thinks I don't know. And I didn't. Until now.

I tip my head against the wall and breathe. Or I try to. The bathroom door flies open.

"Are you in here? Gabby? That time of the month? You bolted off so quickly." She sighs. "Thankfully, it's not for me. Always sucks when it happens the week we have a meet." She laughs. "Well, we have meets almost every week."

Huh, I haven't had to deal with that nuisance for a few months. I'm not sure why, but I'm not complaining.

"No, it's not that. Be out in a sec."

"What's wrong then? Are you okay?"

I leave the stall and splash water on my face.

"Sorry, I didn't mean to run off like that, but you saw the list?" I dry my hands and face with a paper towel.

Asha nods. "What's the big deal?"

"Hailey and Cal Jarvis?" I lean my hip against the sink.

"Oh, I know. It's terrible. I can't believe I forgot about her. I didn't know her that well. We had American Government together." She bites the inside of her cheek and glances at the ceiling. "French. Yep, she was in my French class the last two years. I didn't know her brother, Cal, but— Asha combs her fingers through her hair.

"*Cal Jarvis*, Ash." I say, crossing my arms and leaning my hip against the sink. "*CJ.* My CJ!"

Asha's eyes pop. "Wait, you're dating Cal Jarvis? Hailey Jarvis' brother?" She leans in and wraps her arms around me. "Oh, Gabs, I'm sorry. And all this time you thought he was a bad boy."

"What? No, I didn't." I draw away. "That was you. I…" I bend over and check under the stalls, making sure we're alone. "I didn't know what to think. I never thought he was like a criminal or anything."

"So, are you going to say something to him?" Her dark eyes widen.

"I don't know. How do I even bring it up?"

Asha squeezes my shoulder. "You'll figure out something, Gabs. Maybe he'll mention it first. You said he wanted to tell you about something when he was ready. That must be it. Give him time."

The door opens and two seniors walk in.

"Come on, let's go back to the table," Asha says.

"Actually, I'm going to my locker, get my books for the afternoon." I toss the paper towel into the trash.

"I don't want to deal with anyone right now." Especially after the way I stormed out of the cafeteria. "Do you mind? Oh, and can you explain to Liam?"

"No, I don't mind and yes, I'll tell Liam, but did you even eat?" Her gaze narrows and she presses her lips together.

"What, are you like the food police now?"

Asha jerks back her head. "Whoa, take it easy. I was just asking."

"Sorry. I'm in shock right now. I didn't mean to snap at you." Even if you are a little too worried about my lunch. "I have a protein bar in my bag. I'll be fine. Honestly, I feel like I'm going to puke."

"Well, stay in here if you're gonna puke. Maybe you should skip today's meet. Go home and rest. Text Coach now. She'll understand. I mean, if you're sick, you're sick."

Our meet. Crap! My stomach clenches. Our away meet. At South. Katie Watson's team.

"No, I'll be fine." I can't miss even though I'm going to totally suck out there today. If I was sluggish earlier, I'm completely useless now. "I'll see you later, in the locker room."

"Okay, don't push yourself." Asha waggles her fingers at me like I'm a child who needs scolding and heads out.

****

I'm sprawled across my bed, my arm resting on my forehead, when my phone buzzes.

My pulse quickens. It's CJ.

—How'd the meet go today?—

Ugh, do I have to tell him? How I totally bombed? Against Katie Watson? And Breanna? Well, we tied, but still. I was doomed before I even stepped to the starting line. Totally dazed and listless since I saw Liam's list of performers. The list with Hailey and CJ's name on it. Nausea roils my insides.

—*Not great. I've had better races, but it's no big deal. How are you?*—

How can I complain about losing a cross-country race when he's lost his sister?

—*Sorry to hear that. You'll make it up on Friday, I'm sure. BTW, I can't wait to see u again*—

Excitement flutters in my chest. That's right, Friday. I can't embarrass myself again. Not with CJ watching.

Sinking into my pillows, I pull my knees to my chest. What am I going to say to him? CJ told me when we first went out, he couldn't talk about something. I have to respect his privacy. Give him time. When he's ready, he'll tell me. In the meantime, I have to try and put it out of my head. Forget he's lost his only sister to suicide.

Right.

Chapter Eleven

Asha approaches as I lie on my mat on the grass, stretching my hamstrings. Our second cross-country meet of the week provides me a chance to redeem myself for my crappy performance in the first one.

I tug off my headphones. "Hey."

She stretches her arms above her head. "Are you ready?"

"I guess. I can't make a fool of myself two races in a row, right?" I sit and cross my legs. "I feel good, so hopefully it'll be a good race."

Asha takes a seat on the grass. "What are you talking about? You didn't make a fool of yourself. You finished fourth. I know that's an *off*-race for you but cut yourself a break. You had a lot on your mind, plus you didn't eat a thing for lunch." She tugs on her braid and arches her neck before looking me in the eye.

"That had nothing to do with it. The eating part, anyway. I did have a lot on my mind., but bottom line, I was terrible. I'll run better today." As long as that turkey and cheese sandwich I inhaled at lunch doesn't weigh me down. I've been doing so well, getting closer to where I should be. But today, I scarfed an entire sandwich, plus an apple. "By the way, I like the braided look. Looks good on you."

Asha fingers her braid. "Thanks. And you'll do fine today." She stands and smooths her tank top with her hands.

"Wait, where are you going?"

A grin tugs at her lips. "Liam's here. I'll see you at the start." She practically bounces away, her braid swinging like a pendulum across her back.

Hmm, Liam never came to our races before unless it was Districts or Regionals. And Asha and I always walk to the start together. I guess it's a small price to pay for my best friends to be happy.

A half hour later I cross the finish line. First. A little winded, my legs fatigued more than usual, and my time a few seconds slower, but still, a win. It's because of lunch. It totally slowed me down. I won't make that mistake again.

I finish sucking down a bottle of water in our team tent when someone calls my name. I whirl around in a circle but can't find the source of the voice. Who the heck is calling me?

"Gabby, over here," he calls again.

My pulse quickens. Where are you, CJ?

I scan the row of waist-high bushes that stretch out along the field behind our tent. Dressed in a gray hoodie and faded jeans, he stands at the end of the shrubs with his hands in his pockets and a huge smile on his face.

My pulse quickens and I walk out of our tent into the bright sunshine. "Hey, you came."

"I told you I would. Congratulations! You were awesome."

He takes a step closer, freeing his hands from his pockets, like he's about to embrace me. Then he looks around the crowded field. He seems to change his mind and stuffs his hands in his hoodie pocket. Too many people? Too soon for PDA?

"Thanks. I didn't see you on the course this time." I definitely looked even though I should've been expending every ounce of energy on my race.

He pushes the hair off his face and his eyes catch the light of the late afternoon sun. "Yeah, I'm sorry. I couldn't get here until the end." A grin twitches at his lips. "Just in time to see you win."

Heat flushes my neck. I'm unable to stop the grin from spreading across my face. Or to stop staring at him, the way his gaze lingers on mine. The way the breeze catches his clean scent and wafts it around me.

"Thanks. Today was better than Tuesday."

He tilts his head.

"Oh, it was a sucky race, that's all." And today could've been better, but I have only myself to blame for eating too much. I shove my hands into my hoodie pocket. "So, where do you want to go tonight?"

"Totally up to you. I picked last time." He takes a step closer and fingers a branch on the bush.

"Um—"

"Hey Gabs. Awesome race. I didn't see you come in, but I know you won," Asha says as she and Liam approach, his arm firmly around her waist.

"Thanks." I glance from Liam to Asha then raise my eyebrows. "You two look awful cozy. Does this mean your relationship is official?"

Liam pulls Asha close and kisses her on the lips. Whoa! It's brief, but still. Am I ready for this? I thought I would be, but the two of them with their arms around each other, kissing, it's…weird. These are my two best friends. Even if Asha told me they already kissed, *seeing* it is another thing.

"Answer your question?" Liam asks with a grin on his face.

Asha flushes and taps his chest in a mock scolding.

"Yup, I didn't need a demo, though." I glance at CJ, whose head is bowed. "Oh, Liam, this is CJ."

"Hey," says Liam.

CJ lifts his chin and smiles. "Hey."

He's smiling. That's cool.

"Are you two doing something tonight?" I ask Asha, keeping an eye on Liam, who scrutinizes CJ like he's my dad.

Asha shrugs. "Maybe a movie. Maybe hanging out at Liam's? I don't know."

"Oh." My stomach squeezes. Maybe my worry about losing my two best friends to coupledom wasn't so far-fetched at all.

"You're welcome to join us," Asha says. "Unless you and CJ have plans."

My body relaxes. "Oh. Well, we were going to do something but…"

I glance at CJ. He's staring at the ground. Will he want to expand our date night to four? It's not like it's a big crowd. Just the four of us. Still, he may not be comfortable enough yet to go out with them.

"What do you think, CJ?"

"Sure, if you want."

"Really?" I struggle to contain the shock in my voice.

CJ smiles and rubs his hand along his jaw. "Yeah, why not?"

"Cool," says Asha. "So, I'll text you later, Gabs?"

"Yeah, sounds good."

"See you guys later," says Liam. He and Asha

leave with their arms around one another.

"We don't have to go to the movies or even hang out with them, you know," I say, once Asha and Liam have left. "It was nice of you to agree, but—"

"No, I want to. It'll be fun." CJ jams his hands in his pockets and toes the grass with his sneaker.

"What's wrong? Seriously, it's no big deal. We can do something ourselves."

"No, it's not that." He looks me in the eyes. "Can I, um, give you a ride home? I don't know if you planned to walk or already have a ride, but I want to talk to you about something."

Chapter Twelve

Crap, what can he want to talk to me about? Realization sinks in and my stomach plummets to my toes. Hailey. He wants to talk about his sister. Her suicide.

I swallow around the dryness in my throat. "Yeah, sure. And no, I don't have a ride."

"Cool. I'm parked on the street."

He offers his hand and I take it. The warmth of his skin is soothing, reassuring, even as I steel myself for what he's about to say. He's silent as we walk along the long line of bushes, across the grass and toward his car.

"I need to tell you something," he says, after we're seated in his car. He lowers his gaze, his thick lashes fanning his cheeks. He balls both hands into fists and rubs them on his jeans. "It's gonna come up at some point and I don't want you to be upset I didn't tell you." He looks me in the eye. "Plus, I should be honest with you."

The torment on his face tugs at my heart. My heart that's trying to pound its way out of my chest. "Are you sure, CJ?" It's clear this is tearing him up inside.

"Yeah, I'm sure."

He takes a deep breath. "Did you know...Hailey Jarvis? She's...she *was* your year."

Pain slices through my gut. I was right, it is about Hailey.

"A little. She was in a few of my classes and—"

"She's my sister. She died last year. It was ruled a suicide. I don't know how much you know, but the official story is she took her own life by jumping off a cliff." He shakes his head. "I still can't believe it. I mean, she had issues, problems, like everybody else, but, ending her life, it made no sense. None."

Without thinking, I place my hand on his arm, and he wraps his hand around mine. "I'm sorry, CJ." My throat is parched. What do I say? But then the truth rushes out. "I actually found out Hailey was your sister two days ago. Liam's head of Key Club, and had a list for the upcoming cancer benefit and both your names were on it from last year's performers. I kinda figured out the CJ, Cal Jarvis connection."

CJ's brows jump. "Oh?"

"I'm so sorry, I didn't know what to say to you when I found out. I figured you'd bring it up when you were ready. Or maybe you'd never be ready. I don't know, but—"

"Gabby, it's okay." CJ squeezes my hand. "It's not an easy thing to talk about. Especially for me. I wanted to tell you, though. I was trying to figure out the right time. I couldn't keep it in any longer."

"You don't have to, CJ, if you're not ready. I don't want to upset you."

"You're not. I haven't talked about it with anyone since she died. Except for the therapist my parents made me see." He runs his thumb across my fingers. "I stopped going after two months. There was *nothing* to talk about. My parents thought it would help, you know, deal with my 'feelings'? It didn't. Just made it worse."

"Oh my God, CJ, I'm so sorry."

"Don't be. I need to talk about it with someone who actually listens." He pauses. "You do. I feel like I can trust you."

My heart swells. "Absolutely. You can, CJ."

"Thanks. I don't know exactly where to begin." Tremors shake his voice. Maybe he's not ready. Maybe he needs a little help.

"You didn't, you know, notice anything, before it happened?" I barely get the words out through the stickiness that's glomming my throat. "Was she depressed?" I stare at my legs. "You don't have to tell me if you don't want to."

"No, it's fine. I want to talk about it. It's, where to begin, you know?"

I nod.

"To answer your question, no. She wasn't depressed—at least not that I could tell. She didn't seem like anything was bothering her. Just the opposite. It was like, things were finally going well for her. And for it to happen *where* it did…" He trails off, shaking his head. "I don't know, it didn't fit."

Cold fingers walk my spine. For it to happen *where* it did. Oh. My. God.

The eerie chill. The music. The clearing in the woods. The same spot where CJ hangs out. It's not just a quiet, peaceful spot, like he said. It's where Hailey died. The nearby cliff and long drop to the ground below. The one that always gives me heart palpitations.

Air races out of my lungs and I close my eyes. Her spirit is there. I don't believe in stuff like that. Spirits aren't real. Ghosts aren't real. That's what I've told myself forever to ease my fears. But it makes sense now in a twisted, freaky sort of way.

"Gabby?" CJ squeezes my hand. "You okay? You're pale and your hand's clammy."

I shake myself from my shock. "Fine."

"What is it? You can tell me." He taps my hand. "It's a lot to take in, I know."

I bite the inside of my cheek. Wait, that's also where I found the notebook. "CJ, I think—"

CJ's eyes widen. "Omigod! Right. You said you felt a chill there, that night I met you on your way to the bookstore. You know exactly where I'm talking about." He tilts his head. "Gabby, how long has it been going on?"

My jaw clenches. I can't keep it in any longer. "Since right before I met you, CJ. Like, the *day* before. I had no idea that's where she died." I pause. "You go there to think about her, don't you?"

CJ nods. "It's where I was coming from the night I bumped into you and Asha. When I was so rude." His voice is low and rough. He rubs the back of his neck, and his mouth tightens. "I go there a lot, mostly at night. It's like I feel her presence there. That's why it doesn't fit. That spot was her happy place, where she went to write music, be inspired. That's what she told me anyway. She wouldn't have ended her life there. I know it. It's not where she was supposed to die."

Heaviness weighs on my chest. "I'm so sorry, CJ. I think you're right, though. I think her spirit is there. I think it's what I feel when I walk through there."

"But your friend, Asha, you said she's never felt anything, right?"

I nod.

He scrutinizes me, probably trying to figure out if

I'm certifiably crazy, before releasing my hand. "Speaking of cold, you're shivering." He starts the car and cranks the heat to high. "Give it a sec, it usually takes a bit to get warm."

"Thanks. That's just it, though, CJ, about the woods? I don't believe in stuff like that, ghosts and the paranormal, strange occurrences that have no explanation." That's Asha and Liam's department. "But what other explanation is there? You actually felt it with me that day. When the cold wind came out of nowhere—on a *hot* day—and swirled around us. Except the last time. It was different. The day *after* I went out with you." The day after I kissed you. "Like, maybe that's what she wants?"

No, that can't be. Can it? A little too dramatic if her aim is to get us together. Like she's some sort of cupid spirit.

CJ gives me a crooked smile. "It's what *I* want."

Warmth spreads across my cheeks. "Thanks, but there must be a reason her spirit lingers there. A reason she communicated with me. You're her brother, but me? Why me?"

Then there's *the song.*

I grip the sides of my legs. What does it mean? Maybe nothing. Maybe CJ will think I've completely lost it. But he's opening up to me. About everything. Shouldn't I do the same?

"Can I ask you something else?"

"Sure."

"The song." I place my other hand on top of his. He said he trusts me. A little reassurance can't hurt. "The one you were humming that night we walked to the bookstore. You said it got 'stuck in your head'. CJ, I hear *that* song in my head when I walk through the woods." I swallow the thickness in my throat. "Other times, too. Tell me what it means. I need to figure out what's going on." Figure out why your sister won't leave me alone.

His eyes widen. "Wait, really? You hear *that* song when you walk through the woods?"

Trembling, I nod. "I wouldn't joke about something like that. I hear it other times, too, but I heard it first there."

"You're not messing with me?"

I yank my hand away from his arm. "CJ, stop. I'm telling you the truth." Was it wrong to tell him about the music? "I want to figure this thing out."

CJ inhales. "I don't know."

"Do you think she's trying to tell us something?"

He lowers his head. Is he hiding something? Still?

"Maybe." He clears his throat.

"C'mon, CJ. I can tell you're keeping something from me. You can trust me. You just said so."

"I know I can." He squeezes my hand. "I dunno." He gives me a tight smile. "Maybe it's like I said, it was her special place and she's still there." He sighs and rakes his fingers through his hair. "You know she hated being on stage, like that cancer research benefit you mentioned. She did it because it was for a good cause. And I begged her to do it." He finally meets my eye and laughs. "She hated attention on her. Absolutely was terrified of performing in front of an audience. When we were in our basement, and it was the two of us and Nate…" A smile lights his face. "She loved it. It was like she was born for that. She played a little guitar, too, but usually when it was the three of us, she sang, Nate was on drums, and I played guitar."

"That's amazing. I'm so sorry, CJ. It must be agony for you." And whatever you're still not saying.

"It is. I don't know, but I've always been skeptical that it was suicide."

"Why, what do you think happened?"

CJ massages my palm with his thumb. "There was a 911 call from her phone right around the time it happened. I was with my parents when the police played the tape for them. It's a girl's voice, but I don't recognize it. It's not Hailey, though." He sighs. "I think it's the key to finding out what happened. If only that person had stayed. Whoever it was, used Hailey's phone to make the call. Which I always thought was strange. But my parents never questioned it; they accepted her death as a suicide. Maybe because..." He draws in a sharp breath.

"What?"

"Nah, I don't know." He shakes his head. "They thought I was in denial, that I couldn't accept it. I couldn't. I can't. There was no suicide note. Not in the woods. Not at home." He swallows the lump in his throat. "Not with her when she was found. And she loved life. She was kinda quiet, had like, one or two close friends, but she was happy." He studies me and a shadow darkens his eyes. "Gabby, she had just—"

"What?"

He searches my face for something to make him continue—trust, maybe—before his lips pull together. "Nothing. She was fine, is what I'm trying to say. Like, really fine. Which is why suicide didn't make sense. But then again, it never does."

Dread churns my insides. What is he keeping from me?

Chapter Thirteen

"CJ, please. You can tell me."

He smiles. "Nah, it's nothing. Seriously, I was thinking how much she loved to sing, write songs. Now she's gone. Music was her passion, Gabby. She went to that spot in the woods because it inspired her. Maybe that's the significance of why you hear the song in your head. She's still there in spirit. Is that crazy?"

An ache throbs in my chest. All this time I wanted to know what held CJ back, why sadness sometimes dulls his eyes. Now, he's told me about Hailey, but there's something he's still not telling me. Something that has a connection to that song.

I finger the strings on my hoodie. "No, it's not crazy and you know what? Maybe I feel her there because she wants me to help you. Figure out the truth."

CJ lays his hand across mine and gives a little squeeze. "Maybe. She couldn't have chosen a better person if that's the case."

I smile. "Thanks. CJ, if you want to forget about tonight, I totally understand." I can't imagine he wants to hang out with me and my friends.

"No, I want to do something with you. I'm glad I finally told you. I'm sorry if I've been distant, if I've acted like a jerk, but now you know why." He shifts closer. "I really like you, Gabby. I want to keep seeing you. If, you know, you're cool with that." It's his turn to blush.

If I'm cool with that? Hell, yeah. "Absolutely."

He leans his head against the seat. "Cool. I'm glad you said that." He brushes his thumb across my hand. "Hailey's death has been really hard on me, especially the way it happened. All the gossip. Why she did it. Nobody knew, but everyone talked about it, speculated what happened, spread rumors. People pity me, Gabby. I can tell, the way they look at me. They don't know what to say. *That's* why I do the homeschool thing. I can't bear to look at everyone's pity."

Pain shreds my heart. "Ugh, I understand, CJ."

"It's also why I've pretty much avoided people since it happened. Except that day, when I met you in Larry's. It felt really good talking to you. You didn't know about Hailey—or at least, had no idea I was her brother—so it was cool, chatting about music and stuff. Not having that weight on me. It was almost normal. I wanted to ask for your number right there, but we'd just met. I didn't want to be a douche." He laughs. "It took a lot not to follow you out the door." He meets my eye and the muscle in his jaw jumps. "A lot."

A grin pulls at my lips, and I look away. Away from his burning gaze, his teasing words. His infectious smile. "Are you serious?" My throat is dry and chalky, my voice like sandpaper.

"Hells, yeah. Then I ran into you that night walking through the woods and I was like, 'damn, this is my lucky day.'" He laughs. "I wasn't going to blow a second chance."

"You mean you weren't freaked out by my singing, my weird obsession for all things music, especially the eighties?" I arch a brow.

CJ snags his bottom lip with his teeth. "Um, same obsession. Plus, I was singing too, much louder, I'll remind you. And I think it's really cool how dedicated you are to running. I can't run a mile to save my life."

"I'm sure you could."

"Yeah well, I think I'll leave the running to you." His gaze flits over my face and he starts to say something but then clamps his lips together.

"What?"

He shakes his head. "Nothing. Hey." He taps his fingers on my hand. "I know it's only junior year, but do you have any place in mind, you know where you want to go to college? You'll probably get a bajillion scholarship offers for running."

Like my top ten list I created freshman year? And consult every day to remind myself why I need to stay focused, so I don't blow it? "I do."

CJ nudges me. "Can you share or is it something you're keeping a secret?"

"Nope, no secrets here." I name my top three and look at his face, trying to gauge his reaction. "There are a few others I'm considering. I know, I'm dreaming, right?"

CJ shakes his head. "Why would you say that?"

"Because they're like, top tier schools, have *the* best running programs in the country, not to mention, the toughest admission standards—"

"And they're really far away. On the opposite side of the country. *That's* what I was going to say. I think you have a good chance at any of them."

"Oh. Well, one of the schools on my list is less than an hour away. Top track and cross-country programs. Pretty good championship basketball teams, too." I wiggle my brow. "I think you know where I'm talking about. Great academics, too."

CJ's face falls.

"What? It's not on the other side of the country."

"No, it's a great school, if I'm guessing correctly. And you're right. It's close to home." He pauses. "It's where Hailey wanted to go."

An ache splinters my chest. "Oh God, I'm sorry."

"Why? Great minds think alike, right? Plus, it's a good school. I think it'd be a great fit for you. So, anyway, it's really cool you didn't punch me in the face when I asked for your number."

"What? You didn't see me turning back as I walked away from Larry's? Hoping you'd follow me?" My cheeks flush. Did I really admit to that? We're sitting here talking about his dead sister sending us messages from beyond the grave. Nothing is off-limits. "I'm sorry I pushed you about being homeschooled. I totally get it now."

"Don't apologize, but right? I couldn't go back to West Penn, Gabby. Well, I did, for a few weeks. I tried, anyway. It was too hard. People came up to me all the time to say how sorry they were, if there was anything they could do. I hated being pitied like that." He rakes his hand through his hair. "They meant well, but it was painful hearing it every day. I couldn't do it anymore." He glances out the window. "Someone out there knows what happened. I wish they'd come forward."

"CJ, that's awful, if someone's keeping that information from the police and your family. And if they were involved?" I squeeze his hand. "I'm sorry. If I can help, if there's anything I can do, please tell me."

"Thanks, I appreciate it."

129

"You can trust me."

He leans in and places his hand on my waist. "I know. It's why I told you. It's probably another reason why you sense her presence in the woods. She trusts you, Gabby. Like I do." Our eyes meet and something stirs low in my stomach. "Right now though, I want to kiss you. If it's okay."

I nod. My heart beats faster as he rests a hand on the back of my neck, leans in and brushes his lips across mine. Electricity races through my veins, making me all tingly inside. He slides his other arm around my waist as I wind my arms around his neck, twining my fingers in the soft locks of his hair. He draws closer—as close as possible with the console between us—and deepens the kiss. His whole body exhales against me. He's gotten something off his chest. He trusts me.

"Thank you for listening," he says, as he draws away.

"Any time. You can talk to me about anything, CJ. What about you, though?"

"What do you mean?"

"What about your college plans? I told you mine. You're a senior."

CJ straightens in his seat, sets his hands on the steering wheel and blows out a breath. "I haven't really thought about it. After Hailey died, it was all about getting through high school, even if it was homeschool. I may start at community college next fall. We'll see. My parents are cool with it. They told me there's no rush, whatever I want to do."

I grasp his hand. "They're right, there's no rush to do anything."

"Yeah, I know. And thanks. I mean it. Thanks for

listening." He smiles as he starts the car and pulls away from the curb.

****

After dinner, as I rinse off the last pan and set it into the strainer, my mom sidles up to me and leans against the counter.

"So, when are we going to meet your new boyfriend, Gabriela?" She crosses her arms, her pointed gaze lingering on my face.

Gabriela? Okay, I'm not getting out of here without giving up some info.

"He's not my boyfriend, Mom, just someone I met in Larry's, who's into music and all. He plays guitar, too." And he has the softest, most amazing lips and beautiful light gray eyes. Eyes that reflect the pain of his sister's suicide. "I'll invite him in so you can meet him, before we go out tonight. Okay?"

She arches a brow. "I guess so. You ran out of here last time when you went out with him. When you told me you were going out with a group. We didn't even see what he looks like. I'd at least like to meet the guy you're dating."

Dating? Is that what we're doing? I set the towel on the counter and stuff my hands in my pockets. "Sorry, I didn't do it on purpose. And we're not *dating.* Just hanging out."

"Just hanging out? Gabby, you can admit to me if you're seeing him. You've always made good choices, been a good judge of character. I'm sure I'd like him *if* I met him."

I rest my hands behind me on the counter. "Okay, maybe we are. Dating, that is." I lower my voice. "But Liam and Ash are going with us tonight. It's not just the

Susan Dalessandro

two of us." After our kiss in his car today and the way he confided in me about his sister, we're definitely doing more than 'hanging.' Although there's something he's still keeping from me, something I'm determined to figure out.

"I'm sorry. I didn't think of introducing him to you and Dad because you were watching a movie."

"You know you can always interrupt. So, does he run cross-country?" she asks, her voice rising.

Hoping I say yes. Mom always thought Jake and I were a good match. It's a shame Jake only thought that *after* Breanna dumped him.

"No, he doesn't go to West Penn." I bite my lip. "He's umm…homeschooled, you know; he does on-line learning."

"Oh." My mom nods, the info. I dropped on her ping-ponging around her brain before she determines if she likes what she hears. Or, if she'll let me go out with him again.

"You can meet him tonight. He's picking me up." I stamp a big grin on my face.

"Okay, call me when he gets here."

"Right."

Halfway up the stairs, there's a knock at the door. No! It can't be. He's too early.

I turn on my heel, but my mom's hand is already on the doorknob.

Crap, no avoiding the parent introduction if it is CJ. Guys are never early, though. Right?

"I have it Gabby. Go finish getting dressed."

I grind my teeth. I can't let my parents give CJ the third degree without me there to blunt their questions. Of course, the first thing they'll notice is his hair. His perfectly messy, blond hair that falls in waves past his pale gray eyes.

"You must be CJ. Come in," my mom says.

My face flushes. "Hey." I meet his gaze and he smiles. "I have to get my boots. Be right back."

"No rush."

I race into my room and strain to listen to the conversation downstairs. My fingers sweaty and trembling, I fumble with the zipper on my boots as I shove my feet into them.

What are they saying to him? I can't make it out.

I stand, smooth my sweater and check myself in the mirror. Ugh! Static electricity. I run in the bathroom and drag a wet comb through my hair, trying to tame the hot mess. CJ's already seen me in a tank top and shorts, my sweaty hair pulled into a ponytail. And still wants to go out with me. What's a little static? But I want to look nice for our date. Date?

Yes, it's a date.

Dressed in a black button-down shirt and jeans, CJ lifts his gaze to me as I race down the steps. The muscle in his jaw jumps, his mouth easing into a crooked grin.

Ooh, he looks good. *Really* good.

My mom hands me my coat which is hung across the newel post. "Have fun. Do you know what movie you're seeing?"

"Where's Dad?" I ask, ignoring her question.

I don't mean to be rude, but why isn't he here asking CJ a million questions, standard procedure when any of my friends comes to the door. Well, any *guy*, that is. Then again, there's not much of a history there.

"Your dad said hello and then went back to the hockey game," my mom says. "First game of the season."

"Oh, that's right." My dad is a huge hockey fan. I have hockey's opening night to thank for CJ not being interrogated. At least by my dad. I can only imagine what my mom said to him. *Pried* from him. But she's letting me leave with him, so it couldn't have been that bad.

CJ opens the passenger door to his car, and I slide in and buckle my seatbelt. When he closes the driver's door he turns and laughs. "Relax. Your parents are cool. They seem nice."

"You noticed?"

"You mean, how nervous you are? Gabby, you sprinted out the door like it was the last kilometer of one of your races and you're still shaking." He places his hand on top of mine, sparking a different kind of heat. "Seriously, they were fine. It's all good."

"You weren't grilled, then?"

"Nah," he says with a chuckle. "But I'd totally understand. I mean, they want to know who's going out with their daughter. I get it." He wiggles his eyebrows. "I won't disappoint." He grips the steering wheel and gives me a sideways glance. "Especially if I get to kiss you again."

My stomach does this little flip-flop thing as I fidget in the seat and power down the window. It must be a thousand degrees in here.

"Kidding." His gaze lingers, saying otherwise.

"O-okay, so—"

My phone buzzes. A well-needed distraction or we may never leave the driveway. It's a text from Asha.

"Ash and Liam are going to the game tonight. Liam's friend, Marcus, is starting at left tackle because

David Reagan is out with a strained calf," I read aloud. "She wants to know if we want to meet them there." I slide my gaze to CJ. "Do you want to stop by the game? We don't have to stay for the whole thing."

After what CJ told me this afternoon, I doubt he'll want to go somewhere surrounded by West Penn students. People who knew his sister. People who will recognize him. Gawk at him. My heart aches. Another one of my stupid, thoughtless ideas. Why didn't I keep quiet and text Asha back with 'no, thanks'?

"Sure, we can go." He looks at me and nods, almost imperceptibly. "Gabby, I have to face people at some point. People who knew my sister. People that *I* know." He rests his hands on the steering wheel. "I still keep in touch with some of the guys from school— texts, mostly—but we haven't hung out since before Hailey died. Kyle was my closest friend, and he keeps asking me to do something with them. One of these times I'll say yes."

I twist in my seat. "So, you really want to go? We don't have to stay long."

"Sure. Maybe we can cut out at half-time, get something to eat?" He turns the key and backs out of the driveway.

"Absolutely. Let me text Asha and tell her we'll meet them there."

As usual for a Friday night game, both the stadium and the school lot are full, so we have to park a few blocks away. It gives me more time alone with CJ before we jump into the noisy, chaotic scene of Friday night football.

The bright lights from the stadium cut through the autumn night as we stroll along the leaf-strewn sidewalk in the brisk air, my hand securely in CJ's. A buzz resonates from the stadium, looming in front of us. Kids stand around their cars talking, as we walk across the parking lot and climb the ramp to the front gate. We push through the crowd thronging the entrance. Liam and Asha must've already gone in.

We purchase our tickets and shoulder our way onto the packed concourse, trying to make our way to the bleachers. Worry sinks in my gut. This is going to be torture for CJ. We should turn around now and leave.

"Hey, you two," calls a familiar voice. Asha.

Amidst a cloud of perfume and greasy food smells, I whirl around and gaze to the top of the bleachers. Asha and Liam, their arms around each another, sit at the end of a packed row.

There goes my idea for leaving. And there's no denying my best friends' relationship, now. They're a couple. A really cute couple. Although it would've be nice if they saved us seats.

"There's nowhere to sit," I mouth, but Liam points to the row below them where there's space for exactly two people. Perfect.

I look to CJ. "Whaddya think?"

He doesn't say a word but grasps my hand and leads me up the steps. Okay.

"Did we miss much?" I ask, when we reach Liam and Asha. Other than the PDA between you two.

"Nah, West Penn drove down the field but had to settle for a field goal. Northern's at our twenty right now," Liam says. "So cool that Marcus is getting to start tonight. Not so good for David being injured, but at least Marcus gets a chance to play."

"Yeah, that's great," I say. "He must be excited."

"Hey Liam, awesome party last week."

Caitlin scoots past us, her auburn hair pulled into a high ponytail, her arm hooked through Alex's. They squeeze into a sliver of empty space at the end of our row. Wonderful.

"Let me know when you're having another one," she says, her voice dripping with goo.

Can I rip that grin off her face? Now?

I nestle in against CJ—one advantage of the stands being packed—but he stiffens, his gaze drifting into the distance. He presses his lips to my ear. "I'm sorry, Gabby. I need to get out of here. I lied. I'm not ready. Text me when you want to leave, and I'll meet you at the gate."

An ache throbs in my chest. I was right. It's too much for him.

"No way, I'll come with you." I slide a backward glance to Asha and Liam, huddled together and oblivious to everyone else. They won't miss me. I clear my throat and stand. "I think we're gonna get going."

"What? You just got here. It's only the first quarter." Asha looks me in the eye. "Is everything okay? Tell me."

"Everything's fine. We're gonna get something to eat. See you, Liam."

Liam's brow furrows. "Gabs, what gives?"

"Nothing. Sorry to cut out on you. Have fun."

We shuffle down the steps and push through the crowd that still throngs the concourse. Minutes later, cool, dark silence surrounds us as we walk through the parking lot, beneath the star-filled navy sky. The cold air nips my cheek and sends a wave of goosebumps across my skin. CJ must sense it. He releases my hand, wraps his arm around me and pulls me to him.

"Better?"

"Definitely." I place my hand on his chest. "Are you okay? You seemed almost...spooked back there. Was it too hard, going back with everyone around?"

"Not exactly." CJ takes a deep breath. "Yes, I'm sorry. Sorry I made you leave so soon. I would've waited and picked you up when you were ready. You didn't have to leave with me. You could've stayed with your friends."

"No way. Plus, I don't think they'll miss me. You saw those two."

CJ snorts. "Yeah, I did. Still..."

"No, I'm sorry. I shouldn't have put you through that."

"It's not your fault. I wanted to go, thought I could handle it. I guess I'm not ready yet."

"Can I ask you something?"

"Sure."

"Do you think the person on the 911 tape, the one who called the night your sister died," I swallow the thickness in my throat. "Do you think they go to West Penn?"

We both stop walking.

"Probably. I mean, all the kids around here go to West Penn. Unless they go to private school." A hint of a smile ghosts across his lips. "Or they're homeschooled."

"Right." I place my hand on his sleeve. "Then let me help, CJ. You said I could. I can ask around in school. If the person goes to West Penn, maybe I can find out something. C'mon, I'm there every day."

"Gabby, I appreciate the offer, but..." He purses

his lips. "People aren't just going to open up and talk to you. The few people Hailey was friends with, they already spoke to the police. Those that weren't aren't going to be very talkative." He blows out a long breath. "I need to let it go. Like my mom's always telling me. Even if you think that's why Hailey came to you. To find out the truth."

CJ's talking, but I'm barely listening. My mind is on the notebook. Maybe there's a clue in there. That is, if it belonged to Hailey. CJ said she went there to write songs. I haven't found any song lyrics yet, but then I haven't decoded most of the notebook due to its waterlogged condition.

I try and keep up with the conversation. "Were her friends with her that night?"

"No, at least that's what they told the police. And I doubt they lied. They were her friends. The police asked them whether Hailey seemed depressed or if she ever talked about suicide. They said no." CJ taps my waist. "C'mon, you need to let it go."

But I can't. "What if someone other than her friends know something, CJ? Someone that's kept quiet all this time, maybe afraid to say something. Don't you think that's what Hailey wants? Why she came to me? She wants me to help you. She doesn't want you to 'just forget about it'."

CJ shakes his head. "Jesus, Gabby, leave it alone. I don't want to talk about it anymore."

Chapter Fourteen

We walk the rest of the way to his car in silence, CJ's hand held stiffly in mine. I had to push him, didn't I?

CJ stops and turns to me. "I'm sorry. I didn't mean to yell at you. It's not your fault. I appreciate you trying to help. It's just, sometimes it freakin suffocates me thinking so much about it." He pauses. "Because, no matter what happens, no matter what I find out, she's never coming back." His gaze falls to the ground. "And what if it turns out I'm wrong? That it *was* suicide?" He shakes his head. "Then I screwed up. It means I could've helped her, and I didn't," he says, his voice breaking.

The anguish in his voice splinters my heart in two. I release his hand and wrap my arms around him. "Don't say that. Even if that's what happened, it's not your fault. You're her brother. You were her best friend. You were always there for her. But you weren't inside her head, CJ."

"I know, still."

"You have absolutely nothing to be sorry about. But I do. I need to let you deal with this the way you want. If you want my help I'm here, if not I won't bug you anymore." Even if it drives me crazy not to do anything. Especially, since Hailey came to me, too. I rub his shoulder. "Are you going to be okay?"

"Yeah."

"You can take me home if you want. I've ruined the night."

CJ's eyes widen. "Don't be ridiculous. You didn't ruin anything."

"You're too nice."

"No, I'm not. Just honest." He slides his arms around my waist. "So, where do you want to go? I'm starving. You must be, too."

Guilt churns my stomach. How can I think of food? Contrary to what CJ said, I *have* ruined the evening. Ruined our date. First, by bringing him to a football game where almost the entire school is there and then I push to help him when he doesn't want help. I'm 0 for 2 and in serious jeopardy of striking out.

Once we're in his car, CJ inserts the key and turns to me, clasping his hands in front of him. "So, where to? What are you up for?"

"Are you sure?"

"You better stop asking or I may change my mind. Do something like this." He leans close, cups my face with his hands and kisses me. Drawing away, he laughs this low, throaty laugh. "Yeah, I have definitely changed my mind." The muscle in his jaw pops. He leans in again and parts my lips with his, taking his time, a slow, deep kiss that sets fire to my insides.

I wind my arms around his neck and pull myself closer to him. Or try to. If only that wretched console wasn't in the way.

"Glad you changed your mind," I whisper.

He smiles against my lips. "Uh-huh."

He trails his mouth across my jaw and down my neck, setting fire to my veins. The silky locks of his hair tickle my neck as he brings his lips to mine again, hungry and urgent, his clean scent flooding my senses. He lightly grasps my hips and tugs me closer me when loud rapping of knuckles on the glass jolts me. I whirl around in my seat, my heart thumping.

Asha stands there with Liam, both smirking. We are so busted.

I disentangle myself from CJ and exhale. "Hey," I say, as the window slides down at the push of my fingertips. Flames devour my face. I'm never going to hear the end of this.

"I see why you two left the game early." Asha chuckles and leans her hands on the car door. "Hey CJ," she says, a little too much spunk in her voice.

"Hey." His face crimson, he glances away, unable to stop the grin forming on his lips.

"We're going to get something to eat at Lucia's. Wanna join us?" asks Liam. "Or do you two have 'other' plans?" He stifles a laugh.

I swallow my embarrassment and ignore his question. "What happened? I thought you wanted to see Marcus play? Not to mention, Caitlin will be disappointed if you're not there."

"Caitlin?" asks Asha. "Yeah, no. She's our new best friend." She rolls her eyes. "Seriously, it was too cold sitting on those metal bleachers and I'm starving. Liam too." She leans into him. "Satisfying his stomach means more to him right now than seeing Marcus play. Right?"

"Damn straight."

"How'd you know we were here?" I ask.

"We didn't, but I'm parked about three cars in front of you," Asha says. "There was no room in the lot when we got here."

I turn to CJ and arch my brows, silently asking his opinion. We were going to get something to eat. Eventually. After our little make out session.

"Sure. Do you guys want to jump in? I can drive then bring you back for your car when we're done."

Asha opens the back door and slides in. Liam follows. I guess we're having dinner together.

Lucia's is casual Italian. The best wood-fired pizza around. Once the football game ends it will be packed to the gills with students. If we go now, we'll have no problem getting a table.

"I need to use the restroom," says Asha after the hostess has seated us in a booth and we've ordered. "Gabs?"

She stands and catches my eye. Understanding passes between us.

"We'll be right back."

CJ can find some guy stuff to talk about with Liam while I'm gone. *If* he gets the chance. Liam will probably use his time away from Asha—all ten minutes of it—to grill CJ like he's my dad. Ensuring he's a 'suitable' guy for me, a gentleman. Although there's nothing to worry about with CJ. I realized that on our first date.

"So, I see things are going well with CJ," Asha says, the moment the restroom door closes behind us. "Sorry we interrupted."

I lean against the counter. Heat flushes my neck. "It's okay. What about you two, though? You guys seemed pretty oblivious to everyone at the game. You had your own little private thing going on there."

Asha tilts her head. "What do you mean?"

"Nothing, just that it didn't take long to get the whole 'couple' thing down."

Asha chuckles. "C'mon, Gabs. Isn't that what you said the night of Liam's party? That it would be easy with him? I mean, it still feels weird sitting on the bleachers with his arm around me. In front of everyone. But it also feels...right." Asha folds her arms and looks down at her boots. "You're not jealous, are you? You know, of us spending time together? I mean, it's just a football game. We haven't even been on a 'real date' yet."

"Of course not," I say, around the stickiness in my throat. "No, absolutely not," I add for emphasis.

"Nothing's changed between the three of us, Gabs." Asha puckers her lips. "Right?"

"Yeah, I know. Well, between you two, it has. In a good way. I'm not jealous, Ash. I'm the one who always said you should be together. And I'm incredibly happy for you." I give her a small smile. "Don't forget about me, okay?"

Asha takes two steps and throws her arms around me in a giant hug. "Not a chance. You're my best friend."

"Thanks."

"So, what happened; why'd you leave the game early?" She giggles. "I mean, other than to totally make out in his car. CJ seemed uncomfortable at the game." She leans against the divider and folds her arms. "Oh, and you know you're going to hear about your little make out session from Liam."

I chew on my lip. "Yeah, I'm expecting it. But CJ? It was difficult for him being there. Being around everyone from school. I should've known, especially after he told me about his sister this afternoon."

"Wait, what?"

I nod. "Yep, he finally told me, Ash. I had to tell him I'd seen the charity benefit list. I said I didn't know how to bring it up, which is the truth, but…" I clasp my hands together. "I feel so bad for him. You can tell how much it weighs on him. But here's the thing, he thinks Hailey's death may not have been a suicide. And that someone who goes to West Penn knows what really happened."

Asha wrinkles her brow. "She didn't die by suicide? Then, what?"

I lower my voice to a whisper. "He's not sure, but it was a girl's voice on the 911 tape."

"Wait, how—"

The door opens and a mom and her two young daughters walk in.

"We'll talk later," I say and slip into the first stall.

Our food arrives a few minutes after Ash and I return to the booth. I'm thankful for the plates of steaming food everyone focuses on rather than the embarrassment I still feel, after being caught sucking face in CJ's car. Although, every time I glance up from my plate, a smirk adorns Liam's face.

"Geez, Gabs, I thought you loved the pizza here," Asha says after everybody finishes and I push my plate away, with half of my single-serving pizza still left. "Aren't you going to finish?"

Ugh, can't Asha give it a rest for once? Shouldn't she be focused on her 'new' boyfriend and not what I'm eating?

"I do. I can't finish tonight, that's all."

Asha slides her gaze to CJ then to me. "Right," she

mouths.

As if, being out with a new guy means not eating in front of him. It's not that, but I need every advantage if I'm going to kill it at Districts in a few weeks. I can't be carrying any excess weight. And no, I don't want to look like a porker when I'm out with him.

"Guess I'm not as hungry as I thought. I'll take the rest home."

"You said you were starving earlier," says CJ.

Huh? I whip my head around. Where did that come from? He was busy scarfing down a cheesesteak with the works. "Guess I thought I was hungry. No big deal."

"It's not, don't worry about it." He taps my hand and stands. "I'll be right back." He heads in the direction of the restroom.

"You okay?" Asha asks.

"Yeah, why wouldn't I be?"

"No reason. You seem a little jumpy." She pauses then bites back a grin. "What about it?" She nods to the small room adjacent to the dining room. "It's Friday. Karaoke," she says in a sing-song manner. "The stage is empty. Come on, let's go find something." Asha wiggles her brow. "Liam can come if he wants. CJ too, when he gets back from the restroom."

"Nah, I think I'll let you girls have fun on your own," Liam says. "You roped me into that last time. Taking a pass tonight. You two go. I'll wait here for CJ."

Asha's always had a thing for karaoke. I used to watch with Liam, until she pulled me on stage one night last summer when the place was empty. I figured I couldn't embarrass myself too much if no one was around. Big mistake. It was like I found my inner rock star. The high I got belting out my favorite songs was like the adrenaline rush I get from running a cross-country race. Now, every time we're here, Asha can't resist. Usually, I'm game. Not tonight. I can't make a fool of myself with CJ here. Well, a bigger fool than usual.

"Come on, Gabs."

Asha pulls on my hand. Sure, why should she worry? Liam's used to our karaoke routine. I don't want to scare CJ.

"Come on, one song. If you're worried about CJ, he just walked outside. Probably to get some air. And really, you have an awesome voice."

"CJ left?"

My heart beats faster. I whirl around as Lucia's front door closes with a thud. Maybe he's had enough of me and my friends. Even before karaoke. CJ drove us here from the field. He wouldn't just take off, would he?

Asha taps me on the hand. "Come on, let's go find a song."

"I should check on CJ. What if he's sick?"

Asha tilts her head. "He's fine. Like I said, he probably needed air."

"Right." Everything's fine. I pinch the rubber bracelets on my wrist as my gaze ping-pongs around the restaurant, which has started to fill up. "Okay, let's go." My stomach churns as we walk into the other room where the bartender stacks glasses in the rack on the back wall. I follow Asha up the steps to the small stage.

No, it's not fine. I'm not fine. After what CJ told me today, all I can think about is the enormous burden he carries with him. Is he thinking about Hailey now? Maybe that's why he left. He needed space. Fresh air. He's not ditching us. I don't know. I'm over-thinking things as usual.

I lean over Asha's shoulder as she scrolls through the list on the monitor when a certain song title catches my eye. Cold fingers walk my spine. No, it can't be.

It's *that* song.

I'm yanked from my stupor when two warm hands land on my waist from behind. The smell of coconut envelops me, and the hairs rise on my neck from his warm breath and the feel of his body close to mine. My stomach does a little flip-flop and I lean into CJ. "Hey."

"Hey. Karaoke? I bet you're good. I heard you in Larry's—"

"Uh, no," Asha interrupts, "She's awesome. Gabby's a great singer. She doesn't like to sing in front of anyone."

CJ leans his chin on my shoulder and pulls me against him. "You're shivering."

Shock does that sometimes. But it's not shock. It's a chill that's blasted me out of nowhere, drilled down into my bones, shaking me to my core. A cold like I've never felt before. I turn to CJ and his face pales.

"You okay?"

"Yeah, fine." I grasp his hand and squeeze. "I...I was going back to the table," I say, my teeth chattering. No karaoke. "Where'd you go, anyway? Out for a walk?" I ask, swiftly changing the subject.

"Kinda." His face flushes and he glances sideways, biting back a grin.

"What? What do you mean 'kinda'?"

"I left my wallet in my car. How would it look

when the check came and I'd be like 'damn, it's in the car', when it's time to pay for us." He snorts. "Real smooth, CJ."

"Uh, no. You're not paying for 'us'; we're splitting." I grasp his hand and lead him into the other room.

"Wait, where are you going, Gabs?" Asha calls after me.

"I changed my mind. Sorry. Plus, there's other people here now."

"Right," she mumbles.

I slide into the booth and CJ scoots in, wrapping his arm around me. "Are you warm yet?" he asks.

"Yeah. It was freezing in that room."

Asha drops into the seat and clears her throat. "You two done?"

Ouch! Okay, she's pissed. But does she have to embarrass us like that? I get it. She wanted to do karaoke and I bailed. I couldn't tell her I lost interest when I saw *that* song on the playlist. And started shivering like I'd stepped into a walk-in freezer. Asha doesn't know about the music—because I haven't told her—but now, with CJ here, it's not the right time. He's brushed me off both times I've brought that song up. There's been enough tension for one night.

"Sorry."

"No big deal, Gabs." Liam intercepts, as he always does, when tension arises. Even now, when he and Ash are dating, he still plays it cool, totally neutral, Mr. peacemaker. "Right, Asha?" He nudges her shoulder.

Asha grits her teeth and levels a steely glare at me. "Right."

"Thanks, Liam," I mumble.

The check comes and I practically rip it out of the waiter's hand. CJ is not paying for me. Not this time. He got the check at Angelo's.

It doesn't stop him from trying. He leans in, trying to eye the bill, but I keep it away, until I place my money in Liam's hand. "Here's my portion." I hand the check to him, cross my arms and sink into the booth, fixing a large grin on my face.

"Sneak." CJ shakes his head and hands Liam some money out of his wallet. Something passes between them before Liam stands, counts the money and walks to the front desk to pay the check.

I'm alone again with CJ when Asha and Liam climb out of CJ's car ten minutes later. "Thanks." I rest my hand on his sleeve. "For going tonight. You didn't have to. And I'm sorry for what happened at the table. Ash was ticked off I didn't do karaoke with her. I'll talk to her later."

"Don't apologize. And don't worry about Asha. I had fun. Seriously, Gabby, your friends are great." He smiles at my raised brows. "Yes, fun. Even if I didn't get to hear you do karaoke."

"Really?"

"Absolutely." He rests his head on the seat and closes his eyes.

"Are you okay?"

He places his hand over mine. "Yeah." He opens his eyes. "It happened again, didn't it?"

"What are you talking about?"

"The Karaoke room. You felt that chill there tonight."

My pulse quickens. How did he know? "No, it was just plain freezing in there, CJ. You were there."

"Gabby, it was stuffy and hot." He pauses. "And I saw that song on the play list."

I swallow the boulder in my throat. "What? Why didn't you say anything?"

He squeezes my hand and meets my gaze. "Because I don't know what it means. I'm trying to figure it out, too."

I sink into the seat and stare out into the night, the sidewalks crammed with people. "Oh."

"Hey, look what time it is," he says, starting the car. "Let me get you home."

I shake myself out of my stupor and whirl on him. "There's something you're not telling me. What is it? C'mon, you can tell me anything."

CJ's face goes slack, and he rests his hands on his legs, like all the life has gone out of him. His eyes search my face. "It's nothing, seriously."

"Nothing?"

"Nah, I'm tired."

"Okay."

Even if it isn't.

Chapter Fifteen

Monday morning, my mom races around the kitchen, mug clenched in hand, gulping her coffee, grabbing things for her lunch. "Gabby, I need to go in early today. Do you want a ride?"

Pulling on my boots at the kitchen table, I shake my head. "Thanks, but I need to talk to Ash before school. I'll walk."

My mom grabs a folder full of papers from the island and shoves it in her bag. "Okay, I gotta run. I'll see you after school." She kisses me on the forehead and flies out of the kitchen, her boot heels clacking on the hardwood floor.

"Bye."

After Lucia's on Friday night, I spent the whole weekend studying for my chemistry test and working on my essay for history. Well, after wracking my brain, trying to figure out CJ's connection to that song. I didn't figure it out, but I did manage to escape Saturday morning for an eight-mile tempo run. I barely talked to Asha, except for a few texts—one where she apologized for embarrassing CJ and me at Lucia's. And for overreacting.

I tried to decipher more of that notebook, the one I was certain belonged to Hailey, but now I'm not so sure. I lost patience trying to read the smudged writing and tossed it aside.

****

The air has a decidedly autumn feel this morning when I step out the door. The brisk chill, the leaves, the late September air. Summer is officially over. Which means perfect running weather has arrived.

I tug my sleeves over my hands as I walk along the sidewalk and breathe it in. Stray leaves swirl in the wind, past my swiftly moving feet. Until I halt at the entrance to the woods. I can do this. I have to get to school.

I jog along the path that overlooks the stream below, the stream where Hailey was found. My backpack, weighed down by books, thumps against my back, but I keep running. Ducking beneath the low hanging branches, I run faster until I land in the clearing. That's when it hits.

A blast of air, but it's cool and breezy like last time. Not icy and frigid like the first few times. It's like, it has my attention and doesn't need to be so forceful and dramatic. That's my interpretation, anyway.

Whirling around, I lift my gaze skyward then back to the ground. Like I expect something to be there. A spirit or ghost hovering. Hailey's ghost. But I'm alone. Like always. But then those powerful song lyrics play in my head and I race out of the clearing, sprinting through the rest of the woods.

"Hey, what's the rush?" Asha says as I jog up to her at the corner of Center and Bridge. She glances at her phone. "You're early. Why are you running?"

Do I tell her? I stop and drag my sleeve across my forehead. "I guess I thought I was late." I pause. "Wait, where's Liam? Sleeping in this morning?"

"He texted me last night, said he had a Key Club

meeting before school. They're organizing the fall coat drive. His mom took him in earlier."

"Oh."

"You're not upset we hung out Saturday night, are you?"

"No, why would you think that?"

Asha rests her hand on her hip. "Because you replied, '*have fun*', when I texted what we were doing on Saturday. You could've come over and hung out with us."

Like old times? The way it used to be before you two became a couple? "You know I don't like horror movies. It's no big deal. I had a ton of homework. Plus, a chem test today."

Asha purses her lips. "Okay, because I don't want this 'thing' with Liam to come between us. And you know I wasn't really upset on Friday night, right? I was in the mood for karaoke and when you bailed on me—"

"Ash, it's fine. We discussed it yesterday."

Asha screws up her face. "By text, we did. I'm sorry, though. I didn't mean to get all huffy at the table."

"It's okay. Really. The same goes for Saturday night. You two should do stuff together. Plus, CJ asked me to come over and watch the game, but I had too much homework. Seriously, it's all good."

It is and Asha's right; nothing can come between us, which is why if I don't say something now, I'm going to explode. Not about our friendship, but what's going on in the woods. Asha's my best friend. Even if she and Liam stiffed me Saturday night. If I can't confide in her, who can I?

"Can I talk to you about something?" I say.

"Of course. What is it?"

"It's about what CJ told me. About him not believing Hailey's death was suicide. You know it happened right there in the woods, where we take the shortcut to my house." I pause. "Unless I'm lucky enough to get a ride from you or Liam."

"Seriously? Where, off that steep drop, along the path?"

I nod.

Asha shudders. "God, that's awful."

"I know, but Ash, I think that's why I feel a chill when I walk through there." Should I mention the music? The notebook? Maybe I should take it slow, one thing at a time.

Asha whirls on me. "Wait, what?" Her eyes slowly widen. "Omigod, you mean that day after practice when you had the chills? Gabs, that's freaky. Like her ghost is there."

I swallow the dryness in my throat and nod. "It's happened more than once since that day. When I wrote it off as me being overheated." I step off the curb and start walking.

"I remember that day," she says, catching up with me. "You were acting loopy, like the heat had gotten to you. You said you felt cold all the sudden, even though it was like, eighty-five degrees. Wait," she taps my arm. "It's happened since then?"

"*Every* time I walk through the woods."

"Gabs, why haven't you said anything?"

Hurt colors her voice. Like I didn't trust her enough to tell her. Asha, my best friend. She looks at me, waiting for my response.

"Because I thought I was losing it. I mean, what

would you think if it happened to you? You joked about the woods being haunted. You and Liam are totally into that scary, paranormal stuff, but it weirds me out. When CJ told me about his sister, how she died in that spot, it was like it was the only explanation. As crazy as it sounds."

Asha stares at me, unblinking, unmoving. Finally, she opens her mouth. "I was just messing with you when I said the woods were haunted."

"Apparently you're on to something."

"Who knew? When I said that to you, I wasn't thinking that's where Hailey died. I'd forgotten about her suicide until we saw Liam's benefit list. So, it happened right along the path, over that steep cliff?"

"Uh huh. Ash, I could never look over the side when I walked past before, you know me and heights, but now... CJ says he feels her spirit there and that's why he goes there." I stop and Asha runs into me.

"Sorry. So, if it is Hailey's spirit, which is totally wild, what do you think she wants from you?"

I shake my head. "No idea." My stomach squeezes as the faint sounds of that song plays in my head. "Except, maybe she wants me to help CJ figure out what really happened."

Asha's eyes go wide. "That must be it. If he's convinced she didn't die by suicide, then maybe she thinks you can help him."

"The strange thing is, I hadn't even met CJ when I first felt the chill, so..." I shrug, throwing my hands outward.

"Maybe she thinks you two should be together. She's like a matchmaker ghost." Asha snorts but stops when I glare at her. She draws in a sharp breath.

"Sorry."

"Don't worry about it. It's all so weird."

"Well, I'm not sure what's going on with Hailey's spirit, but *he's* totally into you." She elbows me. "And I know you're totally into him."

My cheeks flush. "Maybe."

Asha snorts. "*Maybe?* Good one. But seriously, Hailey probably wants you to help her brother uncover the truth. Like a crack detective team. Although," Asha squishes her mouth sideways. "Why doesn't she tell you herself?"

"Right, Ash. This isn't a movie. I don't think spirits just come out and tell you what they want."

Although maybe that's what that notebook is about. If only I could make sense of the smudged writing. Maybe once it dries out.

"Well, it would make things easier." She chuckles. "Is that why CJ was coming from the woods the night of Liam's party? Does he hang out there like, to be closer to her?" She shudders. "Kind of morbid, if he does."

I nod. "But it's not just where she died, it's where she wrote her music." And whatever she was writing in that notebook. Where I've bumped into CJ, twice. "He says it's peaceful. Especially at night." I shake my head. "And to think I suspected him of doing something, you know, *wrong.*"

Asha rests her hand on my shoulder. "You had no idea. Although, it's weird you never ran into him before, if he's there a lot."

"He goes at night, Ash. I do everything in my power to avoid the woods at night."

"True. So, if he doesn't think it was suicide then

what?"

I shrug. "He's not sure, but he thinks someone else was there that night. I asked him if he thought it was someone from school and he said, yes. Ash, he thinks someone in our class was there the night Hailey died and knows what happened. Someone who's kept quiet all this time."

Asha shudders. "That's horrible. Although it could be someone who graduated."

"Yeah, that's true. CJ said there was no note, and his sister wasn't depressed or dealing with anything serious. He said he would've known if something was going on with her. He was pretty close with her. Plus, the 911 call. It was made by a female. Obviously, *someone* saw what happened and called the police, but didn't stick around til the EMT's got there."

"Seriously? I never heard that, you know, about the 911 call. Why wouldn't the police have followed up then, if someone else made the call? Why would they conclude it was suicide?"

"Maybe they thought someone saw what happened and called 911 but didn't want to stick around to be questioned." I exhale an exasperated breath. "I don't know. CJ said his parents accepted her death as a suicide and never asked any more questions." I shove my hands in my pockets. "It sucks, right? But what if I can help CJ figure out the truth?"

Asha lifts her shoulders. "But, how? Like I said, what if the person who made that 911 call, who has any knowledge of what happened, graduated?"

"I don't know, but I have to at least try, hope that's not the case and the person's still in school. I'll fish around, see if anyone knows anything." I kick at leaves on the sidewalk. "It's a long shot, but still. CJ was initially on board with it, but then he did a one-eighty, told me to leave it alone. He doesn't want me poking around." I exhale. "I should help him, though. Right? I mean, it's gotta be why I can 'feel' her there in the woods."

"Maybe. But if someone knows something—or worse, *was* involved—and they've kept quiet this long, what makes you think they're suddenly going to tell you? If I were you, I'd take his advice, leave it alone. I think Hailey wants you two together. *That's* why you sense her presence in the woods. You two make a great couple."

"Yeah, no. There's gotta be more." The song? The notebook? "Something *I* can investigate, even if CJ doesn't want me to."

"Gabs, like you said to me, this is real life. Clues aren't gonna pop up out of the blue. Unfortunately, the most likely explanation is suicide. Not to mention, it happened like, ten months ago. Any evidence is long gone. You need to let it go. Have fun with CJ, see where the relationship goes." She meets my gaze. "Right, you're not gonna let this go."

I should tell her about the notebook, tell her the name of the song I hear. Not yet. Not until I figure it out for myself. If I ever do.

"Sorry, I can't help it, Ash."

We turn onto the narrow walkway into school.

"I know, Gabs. And I know how much you like him. *Really* like him. But you should forget about it. I know how difficult that is for you. But this is one time you should let it go."

We pass a few students sitting on the low wall that

borders the school's front lawn as we head for the front door. Ash is right. I need to leave it alone.

But I can't.

Chapter Sixteen

"Have fun at the game?" Caitlin asks when I take my seat for first period English.

Huh? Is she talking to me? Her BFF, Madison, isn't here yet, so she's making small talk. No, Caitlin doesn't do small talk. Not with me. Normally, her face is in her phone until class begins. Or she's gossiping with Madison. What does she want?

"You were with some guy I've never seen before. Does he go to West Penn?"

Gossip.

"No."

I grip my pen and tap it on the desk. Caitlin can't stand not knowing his name, unable to obtain every juicy tidbit to report to Madison. And ultimately, the whole junior class.

"Oh, okay."

Wait, what? That's it, 'okay'? I open my notebook and uncap my pen. She may have Liam fooled, but not me.

I pull out my phone. No texts from CJ.

"Hey, was that Cal Jarvis I saw you with at the game?" someone says.

Cal Jarvis?

I whirl around. Drew Marchella sits one seat behind me in the next row, his arms folded on his desk, an expectant look on his face. All these people who never speak to me suddenly want to chat?

"Um, yeah. Do you know him?" I pause. "Or were you friends with Hailey?"

Wait, Madison's ex, friends with Hailey?

"Um, no, not well anyway. Except that he performed at last year's cancer benefit with Hailey. They were good. I mean, *really* good." His mouth pulls into a tight line, his bright blue eyes dimming. "And yeah, I knew Hailey a little," he says, his voice breaking. He clears his throat. "So, how's Cal? I haven't seen him around school. Is he doing okay?"

"He's okay. And you won't see him. He doesn't go here anymore."

"Oh, he transferred?"

Huh, what's with all the questions? But for some reason, I answer him. Truthfully. He seems sincere, even if he's one of Madison's exes.

"Sorta, he's doing the online school thing."

Drew nods. "Oh, that's cool. Glad to hear he's doing okay." He sinks into in his chair before pulling out his phone.

"Yeah, any time."

I turn around. Caitlin glances past me, her focus on Drew.

"So that's who you were with at the game, Cal Jarvis?" asks Caitlin, jarring me from my thoughts.

Ugh. I sigh and fold my arms. "Maybe."

"Maybe?" She twists a fistful of her auburn hair in her hands and emits this shrill high-pitched laugh that blisters my ears.

I turn to face her, balling my hands into fists, but Madison blows through the door as the second bell rings. She drops into the seat in front of me, a flurry of long, dark hair, exaggerated sighs, and a cloud of gag-worthy perfume.

"Hey," Madison says to Caitlin.

"Hey." Caitlin lowers her gaze to her desk.

Madison's gaze ping-pongs from me to Caitlin. She puckers her mouth and taps her boot toe on the floor. "Am I interrupting?"

"Nope," says Caitlin. She glances one last time at Drew, before twisting in her seat to face forward.

****

At the end of the day, after an exceptionally grueling cross-country practice—Districts are only a week away—I shuffle along the periphery of the baseball field to head home.

"Hey Gabs, sure you don't want a ride?" Liam pulls alongside me, with Asha in the passenger seat. It's become a thing, Liam giving us rides from practice.

"Thanks, but I feel like walking today. My quads are a little tight. Walking will loosen them up. Maybe tomorrow?" I don't need to ask if Liam will be here again.

"Absolutely. See you later."

Asha waves as Liam pulls away. I head through the parking lot and pass by the front of the school when a flash of red hair catches my eye. Suddenly, Caitlin's next to me, her bag swinging back and forth on her shoulders.

"Hey." She exhales a giant breath, like she sprinted to catch me. "Walking home?" Okay, twice in one day. What gives?

"Uh, yeah. Why are you still here?" It comes out snarky and I should care, but I don't. We're not friends. The few words in English class today were more than she's spoken to me the whole time I've known her. Since first grade. "Don't you take the bus? Like, a bus that left an hour and a half ago?"

Her lips curl into a sneer. "Geez, someone's in a pissy mood. And no, normally Alex gives me a ride, but I had to make up a test."

"Oh." I stuff my hands in my hoodie pockets and keep walking. Whatever.

"So, you're really seeing Hailey's brother? Must be weird, after what happened to her. How'd you meet him, anyway? If he's a senior—although I don't know him and I know most of the seniors."

Of course you do.

"He *is* a senior. He just doesn't go to our school anymore." And it's not weird I'm seeing him. Is it?

The moment in his car after the game crashes my thoughts, enveloping me in a warm tingly blanket. The way we kissed, the way he liquefied my insides, the way those pale gray eyes stir something deep inside when they connect with mine. Every. Single. Time.

"So, how'd you meet, then?"

The girl craves gossip. It's the only reason she talks to me. Still, "Over the summer, at Larry's," I blurt out.

"The music store?"

Ugh, she's dancing on my last nerve. "Yeah, so?"

"No need to get all huffy." She gasps. "Oh, this is where I turn off. See ya."

And like that, she's gone.

Yeah, see ya.

I continue walking, the silence a salve to my ears after Caitlin's incessant blathering. I pause when the entrance to the woods looms ahead. What am I afraid of? It's Hailey. The only question is why? Or, *why me*? Is it really about helping CJ learn the truth? Getting us together? Laughter animates my insides. Getting us together. Right. Maybe it's something more…subtle. My stomach groans and I brace my hand on the trunk of a small tree, a sudden bout of dizziness overwhelming me.

I can't stand here all day, so I proceed into the woods, beneath the canopy of tall, sturdy oaks and sheltering pine trees. Fallen leaves crunch underfoot as I follow the dirt path, narrowing as it skirts the edge of the cliff. Hurrying, I push deeper into the heart of the forest before I steel myself and take the plunge into the clearing, the place that's caused me such angst these last few weeks.

I pause as a breeze splays loose strands of my ponytail across my face. The cool air refreshes as it passes through my nose and my mouth, filling my lungs. Okay, this isn't so bad. But as I shuffle to the other side, a fog descends upon me like damp, heavy drapes. Dizziness slams me and I lose my balance, my vision blurring. I slump to the ground, fatigue sinking into my bones. That's when the music cues and the song streams through me. An ache throbs in my head. My empty stomach groans as I rise off the grass and brush myself off.

Just leave me alone.

Chapter Seventeen

The following Friday after school, CJ texts me and asks if I want to go out, get something to eat. As much as I want to hang out with him, talk music, laugh…*kiss*, I'm exhausted. I was dying the whole five-mile loop at practice today. Probably because I stayed up late studying for two tests. I should've been light as a feather, after I skipped lunch. My fingers hover over my phone, indecision wracking my brain. Finally, I type,

—*Thx for asking, but I'm exhausted. I'm gonna stay put tonight*—

—*Even if we hang out at my house, order pizza? My parents are going out. It will be u and me*—

It's followed by a smile emoji.

Him and me. Alone in his house. Pizza. Heat blooms inside me, sparking life where there was none a minute ago. How can I say no? And if we do hang out, maybe I can get him to open up about that song.

—*What time? Text me your address and I'll come over.*—

—*As soon as u want. I can pick u up.*—

—*Don't be silly. I can take one of the cars.*—

—*U said you're exhausted. It's no problem. I can come get u.*—

—*I'm not too tired to drive two whole miles to your house. LOL. See you in a few.*—

CJ lives on the same side of town as Liam and Asha, who happen to be hanging out at Liam's tonight. No horror movie this time, but when Liam texted to invite me, I said I was exhausted from practice, from a long week of tests and papers. Plus, I've been kinda rough on Asha about those two spending so much time together. They need their time alone. Time as a couple.

I turn down a wide street, the numbers on the mailboxes barely visible in the dark, until I arrive in front of number 716 and kill the engine. A stately federal-blue Victorian house with pewter shutters sits back from the street, illuminated by a single spotlight. Two giant oaks rise into the indigo sky, their network of branches reaching out into the street. CJ stands at the front door, in a gray flannel shirt and jeans, his hands tucked in his pockets.

He jogs out of the house in socks and opens the driver's door before my seatbelt is off. "I'm so glad you came." He smiles and I inhale his clean soapy scent.

"Me too."

A rich garlicky aroma envelops me as I step into the house. CJ leads me through the family room, where a college basketball game plays on TV and into the adjacent, brightly lit kitchen. Steam emanates from a large pizza box on the island in the center. Pizza from Lucia's. Wood-fired pizza. My favorite. CJ remembered.

"Pizza just came. Grab what you want." He hands me a plate from the cabinet. "We can sit inside. Plain cheese, right?"

"Yeah. What do I owe you?" I reach into my bag and CJ grasps my other hand, making my skin tingle.

"You're hilarious, Gabby. I invited you. You're my

guest and it's on me."

"You mean this one *and* last weekend with Ash and Liam? When you conveniently slipped money into my bag when I wasn't looking?" I arch my brow.

CJ's eyes go wide. "I have no idea what you're talking about." A smirk tugs at his mouth.

"Right. I'll figure a way to pay you back, Jarvis."

He meets my gaze, and something passes between us, something that flutters deep in my gut. My face flushes and I look at the floor.

"Thanks." I clear the stickiness from my throat. "You know this is my favorite." I set my bag on the chair and when I lift my gaze, CJ's looking right at me.

"What?"

His jaw muscle pops, and he grins. "Nothing. Something to drink?"

"Water's fine."

I follow CJ into the family room, and he shuts off the TV. "You don't have to turn that off on my account. I love college basketball. That's what I would've been doing at home with my dad. That or watching something on one of the streaming channels."

He taps his phone and music streams through the speakers. "Okay, we can turn the game on when we're finished. You're okay with music, right?" He gives me a lopsided grin.

"Uh, isn't music what started this?"

He laughs. "And here I thought it was me and my irresistibility."

I smile. "Well, that too. Hey, did you hear there's a nineties' music festival in South Philadelphia in two weeks?"

"No, but it sounds like something we need to check

out."

We?

"Yes, we do."

"It's really cool that we like the same bands, a lot of the same music. Pretty awesome, really."

Heat floods my face. "Yeah, well, great minds think alike, right?"

CJ gives an emphatic nod. "Absolutely. Speaking of the music festival in two weeks," He clears his throat. "I *may* have two tickets to the Winter Jam in Philadelphia in November."

My eyes widen. "Get out! Really? I'm so jealous. I've tried to win tickets to that every year."

CJ laughs. "Gabby, I want *you* to go with me." He grins and nods, as if to say, 'please say yes'. "How about it?"

"Oh my God. CJ, I'd love to go, but shouldn't you ask a friend? I mean—"

"I want to go with *you*."

How can I say no? "Yes, absolutely. Thank you so much."

"You're welcome. It should be awesome." CJ sits on the sofa as I take a seat on the large chair with the ottoman across from him. He pats the sofa cushion. "I don't bite."

"I know." I round the table and drop onto the wide burgundy sofa cushion, falling back before righting myself. I grab my slice of pizza, but set it on the plate again, calculating the calories in my head.

I can afford one piece. It's my favorite. Plus, it's dinner. I have to eat something. But Districts are next weekend. I've been doing so well, even if my times have fallen off a bit. I drum my fingers on my leg. I have to beat Katie. And Breanna.

CJ taps me on the knee. "What's wrong?" His worried gaze searches my face.

"Nothing. It's hot. I'll give it a minute."

I can't not eat in front of him. Especially when he ordered it special for me. How rude would that be?

I'm about to grab my slice again when a stray thought distracts me. "I have to tell you about my two bizarre encounters today." I pause. "Well, three, actually." My brief conversation with Drew was anything but typical.

CJ sets his plate on the table and crosses his arms behind his head. "I'm all ears."

I fold my right leg onto the sofa and lean forward. "Okay, so they were both with Liam's new bestie, Caitlin."

CJ pales. His arms fall to his sides. "Wait, you two are friends?"

I wrinkle my nose. "What? Hell, no. She's in first period English with me and for some reason, decided to talk to me today. Well, her and Drew Marchella." I shake my head. "Weird."

"Who's Drew and why is it weird?"

"Because they're both friends with my least favorite person, Madison—or at least Drew *was* until they broke up last year." I tilt my head. "Do you know him?" I swallow around the thickness in my throat. "Or was he friends with Hailey?" I lower my gaze to the floor. "I didn't think she was friends with Caitlin or Madison. I mean, I never saw her hanging around with them, but…"

"No, she wasn't friends with them, at least I never heard her mention their names, but Drew? I don't know him, and I never heard Hailey mention him."

"Oh, because he asked me if you and me were...*dating*." I study CJ's reaction, but his expression doesn't change. "He said he saw us at the game, and he knew who you were from last year's benefit. He mentioned how good you guys were."

"Oh? That's cool."

I tap him on the knee. "He also said he was *sorta* friends with Hailey. That's why I thought you might know him, but if Hailey never mentioned him..." I lift my shoulders. "Of course, Caitlin was listening to us the whole time and threw in her two cents. She cornered me when I was walking home from practice, too. I think she's jealous. Because she saw me with this *totally* hot guy."

I bite my bottom lip, but CJ's expression is unreadable. Not even a smirk? My attempt at flirting has fallen flat.

I clear my throat. "Bottom line, she wanted gossip. She doesn't talk to me otherwise."

CJ leans forward, resting his elbows on his knees. "Why does she care who you go out with?"

"She doesn't. Like I said, she's looking for gossip. C'mon, it doesn't matter."

"She's looking for gossip being she knows I'm Hailey's brother, the guy who couldn't hack staying in school after she died. Who left to be homeschooled." He lowers his head. "It's okay. You said you're not friends, right?"

"Absolutely not. Which is why I can't believe Liam let her come to his party a few weeks ago when she so rudely invited herself."

CJ grasps my hand and scoots closer, his leg

brushing mine. "He probably didn't want to offend her."

I nod. "I'm sure. Liam's too nice for his own good."

"Nah, but it's cool you have a friend like that. He and Asha, are they like, a thing? They looked like they were together at your meet."

"Yeah, which is kind of a new thing. It only took forever to happen." Now they're inseparable.

CJ leans into me and rests his head on the sofa, his hair brushing my neck. The scent of his freshly laundered flannel shirt and his coconut shampoo envelop me. I breathe it in as I twist to him.

"CJ, I care about you. I'm here if you want to talk about anything." Maybe what that song means to you. "I wish you'd let me ask around about that night. I feel like I should be able to do something. I'm sure that's what Hailey wants."

"Hey." He lifts his head from my shoulder and furrows his brow. "Where's this coming from?"

"I want to help you. However I can."

CJ smiles and rests his head on my shoulder again. "You have. And I care about you too, Gabby." He pauses. "A lot." His body shifts against mine and he inhales a deep breath. "But I don't want you poking around for me. Asking about Hailey. Promise me you won't." He turns to me and grasps my hands, searching my face.

That's when a guitar propped in the far corner of the room catches my attention.

"What?" His eyes widen.

"Is that yours?"

"What?"

"The guitar." I nod at the guitar propped against the far wall. "I've never heard you play. I wasn't at the benefit. Drew said you guys were really good. Can you play something?"

He laughs. "That was nice of him. And yeah, it's *one* of mine. The other two are in my room. My mom's been on me to put it away. That or get back to playing. I haven't picked it up in months."

"I'd love to hear you play."

CJ considers the guitar, a shadow dimming his eyes, before he slumps into the sofa cushion and lowers his head. "No."

"I'm sorry, I didn't mean to upset you."

I finger the seam on my jeans. My stomach rolls. How insensitive of me. Playing the guitar reminds him of his sister. Happy times with his sister.

"Hey," CJ leans close and brushes a strand of hair off my face with his thumb. He trails his fingers along my jaw, triggering a wave of warm shivers across my skin. "It's okay, I don't want to play right now or talk about it. Maybe another time?"

"Sure." I lift my chin and our gazes lock.

The music changes, the rhythmic, sensual beat filling my head, making my body go slack. CJ swallows hard, never taking his eyes off mine. He places his hand on the nape of my neck and brushes his lips across mine, slow and gentle. His other hand winds around my waist, guiding me back against the cushion. I wrap my arms around his neck, the soft locks of his hair tickling my fingers.

It's the first time we're alone, like, *really alone*. Not outside his car in front of my house or in his car with a console between us…and my friends knocking on the window. I'm aware of my racing heartbeat, the blood pumping through my veins like a raging river, my breaths coming fast, breaths that taste sweet and warm. Like CJ.

He hooks his leg over mine and I trail my hands down his back, his sinewy muscles flexing beneath my fingers. He pulls me closer as his mouth become more urgent, greedy. "Is this okay?" he breathes against my lips.

"Uh huh."

Fire blazes in my veins as the space between us collapses to nothing. Until my stomach groans and CJ pulls away. Breathing hard, he stifles a laugh.

"You must be starving. Sorry, we should finish eating." A crimson blush shadows his cheeks. "Then we can...you know." The muscle in his jaw pulses, a glimmer simmering in his eye.

"I'm fine." Food is the *last* thing on my mind.

"Seriously, Gabby, your stomach's moaning. Literally screaming, *give me food.*"

He grasps his plate from the table and bites into his pizza. He's worried about eating? My stomach *was* loud, but still. We were kinda in the middle of something. I wasn't thinking about food. I didn't think he was either.

His gaze narrows. "Come on, you haven't touched yours yet."

"You're worried about me eating?"

I grab my plate. He did get Lucia's for me. I can't be rude and not eat.

"Hells, yeah. You run all those miles for cross-country. Come on, you have to eat."

You run all those miles. Where have I heard that

before?

"We have plenty of time for other stuff, once we're done." His mouth eases into a crooked grin.

"Okay, *Mom*. But I'll make you happy and finish, okay?"

CJ's face falls. He swallows his food and sets his plate on the table. "Hey." He grasps my hand. "I'm sorry. I'm not trying to be your mom. I figured you must be starving after hearing your stomach growl. That's all." He bites back a grin. "I want to keep kissing you. C'mon, hurry up," he says, laughing.

Heat floods my face. He's right. I am hungry. Starving, like he said. But I can't shake the fact that he's aware of what I eat. Isn't he a guy? Isn't he worried about his own stomach? I swallow my irritation, lift the piece to my mouth and sink my teeth into the rich, piquant sauce, creamy mozzarella and flaky, thin crust.

Oh my gosh, this is good. Really good.

Of course, it's Lucia's famous wood-fired pizza. Maybe I *can* eat this one piece. Just one. Then we can get back to what we were doing. Did I really think that?

"It's okay," I say around a mouthful of food. I ran six miles today. I'll tack on an extra two to my scheduled run tomorrow, burn it all off.

"Cool."

We sit there and eat until CJ finishes his slice. "Ready for another?" He stands, a smile tugging at his lips. "Sorry, guess I didn't realize how hungry I was either. That first piece didn't have a chance." He looks at me expectantly.

I swallow my food and wipe my hands on a napkin. Another?

"I'm good. Still working on this one."

"You sure?"

"Absolutely."

I glance at my plate. Only a piece of thin crust remains. I could easily polish off two more.

"Here," CJ sets the box on the table. "Now we don't have to run back and forth." He exhales, settles onto the sofa and bites into another piece. His gaze ping-pongs back and forth from his pizza to me.

I fold my arms. "What? Out with it?"

"Nothing. I thought you were hungry and…" Shadows darken his eyes. He places his plate on the table. "Okay, I don't want to seem like I'm prying, but—"

"Then don't!"

CJ's face pales. He drops his slice to the plate.

I draw in a sharp breath. "CJ, I'm sorry. I didn't mean to snap at you."

But I did. Because this conversation is going in the wrong direction. Liam doesn't care what I eat. At least he never says anything. Why does CJ? I don't want to ruin things, get into a big argument about nothing. Because that's what it is. Nothing. I stand and wipe my hands on my napkin before walking into the kitchen and placing my plate on the counter.

"I should go."

CJ catapults off the sofa. "What? No. Gabby, you just got here. I'm sorry. You don't even know what I was going to say."

I grab my keys from the table and go to the door. "Yes, I do. And we're not having this conversation. Thanks for the pizza. I'll talk to you later."

An ache throbs in my chest. My heart trying to

pound its way out.

"No, don't go. I'm sorry. I don't want to screw up things between us." He lowers his chin. "I'm falling for you, Gabby. Hard. And I tend to be overprotective of people I care about."

My chest squeezes. *I'm falling for you, too.*

That's why I have to leave. I don't want him to worry. To try to fix something that doesn't need fixing. He wouldn't understand, anyway. I grasp the door handle.

"Don't be sorry. But I need to go."

CJ closes the distance between us in two strides and wraps his arms around me. He gently pries my fingers from the handle. "C'mon, I want you to stay," he whispers. "I care about you so much. It just seems that you're too hard on yourself with...*food.* Depriving yourself. And then driving yourself so hard with cross-country. Like, you should be eating twice as much as me." He laughs, his chest rumbling next to mine.

I can't contain the laughter that erupts from me. "Good one."

"No, I'm serious. "You run *so* much. You need to eat, girl. Not starve yourself."

"It's not that much."

"It is and I care about you and don't want to see you exhausted and drained."

My heart swells. "I care about you, too—*so much*—but you don't have to worry about me."

"But I do," he says, turning me around. "I've gotten to know you so well since that day in Larry's—I noticed you right away," he adds. A smile plays across his lips. "I couldn't help *but* notice you." He pauses and touches his forehead to mine. "I was in a bad place after

Hailey died. I couldn't accept what happened, that she'd taken her own life. And I didn't want people talking to me about it, trying to explain or figure out the unexplainable. My mom made me get out of the house that day, told me I couldn't hole up in my room forever. So of course, I went to Larry's. I used to always go there at night. Monday nights, especially when he got the new stuff in."

"You mean, new 'old' stuff?"

CJ laughs. "Exactly. But that's why I'd never seen you before. We were there at different times. And that day, when you started singing along with me, it was like…" He draws away and smiles. "I don't know, this warm feeling, in here," he says, tapping his chest. You reminded me how much I missed music, playing it, singing…everything. And you had such a beautiful voice." He pauses, squeezing my waist. "I had a great time talking to you." He flushes. "Flirting with you. *Major* flirting," he says. "I wanted to follow you when you left, but I stopped myself, like 'what the hell am I doing?'"

"Mm, I wanted you to follow me, too." Heat floods my face and I snort. "I can't believe I admitted that."

"Why? Gabby, I didn't want to fall for you, because it was too soon to be happy about anything—at least that's what I told myself—but damn, I couldn't help it." He bites his bottom lip. "Plus, I thought you were beautiful. You *are* beautiful." He pulls me against him and kisses my neck, his lips lingering below my ear, setting fire to my skin. "Just don't be so hard on yourself, where you end up," He swallows, then, "you know, *hurting* yourself. Okay?"

I open my mouth to reply but am overcome by my

emotions. "CJ, I—"

"You don't have to say anything. Just enjoy things, don't think so much."

I draw away and look him in the eye. "Okay, but I do want to say something. In case you haven't noticed, I feel the same way about you." I pause, my gaze darting about the room. "When I saw you in the woods, I couldn't believe it was you. I mean, I was so happy I forgot to buy that book and had to go back for it. It gave me a chance to talk to you again. Please don't worry about me, though. I'm fine. And you shouldn't feel bad for being happy. You'll never be *over* Hailey's death. She was your sister, your friend. She died way too young. I'm sure she'd want you to be happy. I'm here for you if you want to talk. Anytime."

"Thank you." He rests his head on my shoulder. "You know if you hadn't forgotten your book, I may have had to go back to Larry's every day at the same time, hoping you'd show up again."

"Not too stalkerish."

"Nah, not at all. But I don't have to worry about that, do I?" He lifts his head and meets my gaze.

My heart trips in my chest as CJ leans in and brushes his lips across mine before taking my hand and leading me to the sofa, picking up where we left off a few minutes ago.

Before my noisy stomach so rudely interrupted.

Chapter Eighteen

Gym is one of those classes which, depending on the day—and Mrs. Allen's mood—I either love or hate. After two straight classes of basketball—just because I'm five-foot-eleven doesn't make me good at it or even adequate—we're doing one of my favorite things: yoga. Outside of running, which for some reason, Mrs. Allen rarely has us do, it's one of the classes I look forward to. Yoga is perfect for both mind and body. Ideal after a grueling cross-country practice or a few days before a big meet.

Our big meet, Districts, is only two days away and I've finally reached my goal weight. Exceeded it. I'm so pumped for Districts, I've barely slept this week. Why does CJ think I have to eat *more* to run? Less is better and I plan on showing that to everyone in my race Saturday. As long as I shake off this fog I've been in the last few days. Maybe it's all the excitement for Saturday.

"In and out, breathe deeply," Mrs. Allen says.

I straighten from my downward dog and segue into the tree pose. A wave of dizziness passes through me, but I shake it off and manage to hold the pose.

"Slowly lift the right leg and cross it over your left knee." Mrs. Allen turns her back to us and demonstrates, her long chestnut ponytail reaching to the middle of her back. Her ease of movement and flexibility is testament to her own daily yoga routine. She's like a human pretzel.

I follow her lead, although I'm nowhere near as graceful as she is.

"Oh, and to anyone here in the class running Districts on Saturday—Gabby, Ella, Brandon, Sophia—good luck to all of you," she calls over her shoulder.

Amazing. Somehow in the middle of meditation she manages to think of the cross-country team. In the hierarchy of high school sports, cross-country is one of the lowest rungs. Far below football, basketball or baseball. So, it's cool when a teacher, especially the gym teacher, who doubles as the girls' soccer coach, recognizes our team and its efforts.

"Districts?" Caitlin asks

Ugh, how did I miss her on the adjacent mat? Why isn't she with Madison in the last row?

"Yep. Coming out to support us?" I ask.

She snorts. "Uh, no. I've got plans. Like, sleeping in." She loses her balance, falls out of her tree pose and has to start over. It's my turn to laugh. "I'm sure your boyfriend will be there." She tucks a strand of her auburn hair behind her ear.

I clench my jaw. Boyfriend? What does she have a thing for CJ? "Maybe."

"Things must be serious with you two."

I lower my leg before I'm done the pose and turn to her. "Don't you have your own boyfriend to worry about?"

She laughs. "Alex? Nothing to worry about. Everything's great with us."

I roll my eyes. "Of course it is."

I take a deep breath and close my eyes, try to push

181

Caitlin out of my mind. Like Mrs. Allen says, clear our minds of all distractions. Then it's time to switch legs, but as I do, a massive wave of heat and dizziness slams me. Everything's fuzzy, then black before—

"Gabby? Are you okay?"

The voice echoes around me. I open my eyes. Mrs. Allen hovers, her face lined with concern. She kneels on the floor and places her hand on my forehead. My butt's sore. My pride—what little I have left—is crushed.

"What happened?" A cold sweat clings to my face. My heart's like a speeding train, trying to smash out of my chest. My gaze darts around at everyone staring. Crap.

"Here." Jasmine Thompson runs up to me with a bottle of water and twists the cap off.

I pull myself into a sitting position. "Thanks." I gulp down a mouthful and glance at Mrs. Allen. "I was a little dizzy, but I'm fine now."

"Mm." Mrs. Allen presses her lips together and surveys the gym. "Why don't you take a walk with someone? Caitlin, would you mind walking Gabby to Nurse Jones? I'll call ahead, tell her you're coming. I want to make sure you're okay. You're probably overheated, but just to be sure."

Caitlin? Really?

I'm grateful for Caitlin's silence as we walk down the hallway. She keeps the snide comments to herself, probably because she's worried I'll pass out again and then I'll be her problem. Good thing, because an ache throbs in my head, like someone's stabbing me with a knife. Still, I thank her when she delivers me to the nurse.

Nurse Jones goes through all the standard stuff, takes my temperature then checks for signs of a concussion—I fell on my butt, not my head.

"No," I say when she asks if I'm nauseous or dizzy. "Yes, I do have a headache."

Then the last one, "What did you eat for lunch? Or, *did* you eat lunch?" She studies me with accusing eyes as I squirm in the chair.

I swallow the lump in my throat. "Umm, a sandwich."

I don't offer it was a half of sandwich. She wouldn't understand. Not about keeping up with Breanna or posting a fast time on Saturday at Districts. Not about beating impossibly skinny Katie Watson. Not about attaining 'that look', the one where I can finally see my hip bones jutting out through my shorts, my stomach flat as a pancake. If I'd looked this way last year, maybe I would've been Jake's *first* choice for his girlfriend instead of Breanna.

"Is that all you've had today?" She rests her hand on my shoulder, scrutinizing me from head to toe.

"Since breakfast, yeah."

"Gabby, you need to eat more. Aren't you on cross-country?"

How does she know?

I nod.

"I think your blood sugar is low. It's probably why you also have a headache. Trying to hold those yoga poses exacerbated the problem. But Gabby, you need to eat. Here." She hands me a banana from a basket on her desk along with a bottle of juice from her mini-fridge. "What is it with you girls? Especially if you're participating in sports, you need to eat. I remember that one girl, all that talent. Beautiful voice. What a shame…"

"I'm sorry?"

She shakes her head. "Nothing. Sorry." She looks me in the eye. "Eat. You'll feel better once you've had something."

Ugh. She's not letting me out of here until I do. At least she's not making me get on the scale. How embarrassing would that be? Finally, the dismissal bell rings, and I'm sprung from my lockdown with Nurse Jones.

"Gabby," someone calls.

I whirl around amidst the crowd surging for their lockers and the exits. What now?

My jaw clenches. Madison. What does she want? I'm sure it's not to see if I'm okay.

"What were you and Caitlin talking about during gym?" She tilts her head. "You guys didn't shut up the entire time. Well, before you face planted on the floor." She snickers and waggles her phone. "Now *that* would've made a great social media post. Shame I didn't have my phone out."

I ball my hands into fists. "Not funny." I turn and keep walking as Madison's cackling laugh rents the air. Talk about throwing salt in the wound.

Asha is leaning against her locker with her backpack on her shoulder when I walk up to her. Finally, a friendly face. "So, are you ready for Saturday?" she asks. "We have to be here like at 6, right?" She winces, likes she's in pain. "Why do Districts have to start so darn early?"

"I know, it's ridiculously early, but we're in the second group. The first race goes off at eight and we're right after that."

We exit the front doors of school and turn onto the sidewalk, past the buses waiting at the curb.

"Yeah, I know. I'm griping. I've gotta get to bed early on Friday."

"Liam coming over?" I lift a brow and grin.

"Probably. Not like he has far to go, right?" She laughs. "I told him he doesn't have to come Saturday—he's not a fan of early wake-ups—but he insists on watching his two favorite people run." She nudges me.

"That's sweet of him." I clench my hands at my sides.

"And…"

I turn to Asha and shield my eyes from the sun. "And what?"

"What about CJ? I'm sure he wants to see you run. It's Districts, Gabby. Kind of a big deal."

"Yeah, no. I didn't tell him." How could I? School-related events are difficult for him. This would be no different. "We're getting together Saturday night, anyway."

Asha sets her hands on her hips. "What do you mean, 'you didn't tell him'? He's gonna be ticked off if he misses our race on Saturday. You *winning* on Saturday."

I shake my head and continue weaving through the cars in the student lot. A guy jumps into a car and starts the engine. I circle around the car, keeping up my manic pace. Frustrating Ash, by the way she's sighing.

"He'll be fine."

A clap, clap of footsteps makes me spin around, as Asha and I are about to cross the street.

"Hey, Gabby. Asha. Gabby, you okay? You went

down pretty hard in gym." Sophia Clemens stands in front of us and raises her arm to shade her eyes from the sun.

"Fine." I glance at Ash then back to Sophia. "Just a little dizzy. Nurse Jones said it was probably from holding that pose too long. But thanks for asking."

"Wait, you passed out in gym, Gabs? Why didn't you say something?" She examines my face, her eyes growing wider with concern.

"It was nothing. I'm fine." I cross my arms. "Really."

"Glad you're okay," says Sophia. She glances to the bus line. "I gotta go. See ya."

My stomach tenses and I start to walk again.

Asha puts her hand on my shoulder, halting my escape. "Gabby, seriously, are you okay? Can you run on Saturday?"

Damn, she's not letting it go.

"Of course. Why wouldn't I? Like you said, it's Districts, it's a big deal. No way I'm missing. I got dizzy, that's all. You know how those yoga poses can be, trying to stand on one leg for an eternity. Of course, Mrs. Allen sent me to the nurse. She had to do that. But I'm fine."

Asha scrutinizes me with her judgey eyes. "Are you sure? I don't want to see you pass out while running Saturday."

She says *I* don't let things go?

"I won't. C'mon, I have to get home."

"Gabs, seriously, though, you're not doing anything crazy are you? You're already the fastest on the team. Yes," she says, when I throw her a skeptical glance. "Faster than Breanna. Not to mention, one of the fastest in the league. You're not doing anything I wouldn't approve of." She arches a brow. "Hmm?"

I ball my hands into fists, unable to keep my irritation in check. "What, are you my mom? *Anything you wouldn't approve of?* And I'm not *doing* anything."

Asha doesn't relent.

"You sure?" Her gaze lingers on mine, before I look away. She lets out a long, exaggerated sigh. "Okay, I'm gonna say it. You've gotten skinny. Way too skinny. Ever since this summer. I don't want to sound judgey, but—"

I slam on the brakes. "Then don't *be* judgey. There's nothing to talk about it. Okay?"

Asha presses her lips together. "I'm sorry, but I care about you. And I don't want you to get hurt because you're starving yourself."

"I'm not, Ash. I've just been running more. We all have. Trying to get ready for Districts. Hopefully, Regionals."

Asha rests her hand on her hip and tilts her head. "No, you've definitely been running more than me. Training harder. C'mon, you don't want to pass out again. You need to eat if you're going to smoke Katie at districts."

"I do eat and I'm fine."

"I hope so." She scrutinizes my face, like she's waiting for me to crack, like she's not convinced but then we start walking again. We get about ten feet when she says, "So, do you think CJ would want to ride up with Liam on Saturday?"

"What?" Where did that come from?

"Just thought it would make sense for the guys to go together."

"I told you, CJ isn't going. He doesn't even know about it. He'll be uncomfortable, with people from school there. I learned my lesson from the football game."

"Gabby, it's a cross-country race. Only family and diehard friends—and boyfriends—come to cheer us on. CJ will be fine. But he won't be if he finds out you didn't tell him. You better text him ASAP." She taps me on the hand, like it's supposed to change my mind. "And tell him he can ride up with Liam. He already told me to ask you."

We reach the corner where we go our separate ways. But Asha grabs my hand and looks me in the eye.

"Gabby, be smart. Please. You're already fast— and really skinny. Any skinnier and you'll disappear. I'm not sure why you have this thing with Breanna or Katie Watson, but you don't need any more of an 'edge' to run fast. To beat them. You already have it. You've always had it, that motivation and drive to be the best." She places her arm around me. "And if it's something more than competition, you don't need to look any different than you do. You're gorgeous the way you are."

"You're too kind. And how long have you been holding that in?"

Giggling, she pulls me into a tight hug. "C'mon, I care about you. You're my best friend, Gabs."

"I know and I appreciate you saying that, but I'm fine. Seriously."

She draws away and smiles. "Okay. Text me and let me know if CJ's going Saturday. I'll let Liam know. Or text Liam. He's your friend too."

"But he's not my *boyfriend*." I ease my mouth into

a lopsided grin.

"Oh, shut it. He's still one of your best friends."

"Is he?"

Asha rests her hands on her hips. "Why wouldn't he be? You two have an argument or something?"

"Nope." I pause. "But I'm sure you'd know if we did."

Asha narrows her gaze. "See, this is what I didn't want to happen. I didn't want things to change between us, just because Liam and I are dating. We're all still friends. *Best friends*, last time I checked."

"I know. I'm not upset. I'm happy for you guys." But things have changed, and I have to accept it. "Don't forget about me, okay?"

"No way, Gabs. Best Friends Forever."

"Thanks."

"Don't forget to ask CJ, okay?" She pauses then touches her hand to her face. "Ooh, are you going to be okay walking through the woods? Do you want to come to my house with me and I'll drive you home?"

I snort. "Nah, I'm used to it. But to be on the safe side, I think I'm going to go the long way." Try to brainstorm how I can help CJ.

"Okay, but if you need me, text."

My phone buzzes as I enter my house. Ash?

—When were you going to tell me Districts are this Saturday? Like, after they were over? —

Ouch! How did he find out? Asha wouldn't have told him. Liam? No, neither one of them has his number.

—Sorry, didn't think you'd want to go. It's not like it's around the corner. It's at the university—

—No kidding. There is something called a

189

SCHOOL website. Although I shouldn't have to find out there. Or the newspaper.—

His text is followed by a sad face emoji.

My stomach squeezes. I was only trying to save him grief.

—I'm sorry. If you want to go, Liam's driving up. Ash and I have to take the team bus, but I'll see u there if you decide to go.—

—Of course I'm going, but I'll drive up myself if that's okay.—

— Sure. Gonna give me a ride home? We don't have to go home on the bus... I'm sure my parents won't mind.—

—Really? Cool, it's a date.—

A date? It's like a thousand hummingbirds take flight inside me.

Yeah, a date.

Chapter Nineteen

I huddle with Asha and the rest of my teammates amidst a sea of runners, bracing against the chill. Nerves bind my stomach in knots. The first race of the day has finished and it's our turn to run the course. The schools in our division are poised in the wide-open field at the start, the bright sun providing a smidgen of warmth in the chilly morning air.

Rubbing my hands on my shorts, I focus my gaze ahead and away from where Katie Watson and her South teammates are gathered to my left. No need to stress any more than necessary.

Murmurs roll through the sea of girls, the air thick with anticipation. I've run this 5000-meter course so many times. The hills and straightaways. The narrow, rocky path snaking through the woods. The finish line.

Relax, you've got this. I have to run my own race today.

Asha hops from leg to leg, running her hands up and down her sleeves as the wind swirls around us. "Good luck," she says. "I'll see you at the finish."

I give her a thumbs up. "Yeah, you too." I rub my gloved hands on my tights and take a deep breath.

Breanna Pozzi jogs up to me and stretches her arms over her head. "Good luck, Gabby."

I give her a tight smile. "Thanks. You, too."

Craning my neck, I scan the crowd for Jake. He

must be here somewhere. The boys' races aren't until later, but if Breanna's racing, he's watching. Even if they aren't dating anymore. Ugh, I gotta stop.

The horn sounds and I flash Asha a thumbs up before lunging into the wind.

Starts are not my forte and today is no different, especially with the blustery conditions. I hang with the main pack while a handful of girls bolt to the front. Katie Watson is one of them, her tiny, muscular legs powering her across the wide-open field toward the first hill on the course.

My strength is in the second half of the race, so if I stay with the main pack 'til then, I should be in good position. I'm feeling strong today. Only a cup of black coffee and a spoonful of dried cereal. Nothing more to weigh me down.

About a half mile in, the frontrunners still in sight, I break away from the pack, scaling the hill and powering my legs faster. With the woods looming ahead, someone calls my name. I whip my head around. My parents stand across the field with other spectators, waving.

Two other girls stay with me as I crest the hill and sprint into the woods, leaves and twigs snapping beneath my sneakers. I've been consumed with catching Katie and the two others who bolted to an early lead, I forgot to worry about anyone else.

Once in the woods, without the harassing wind, my breathing steadies and I settle into a comfortable pace, gaining speed and pulling away from the two girls behind me. I've put a good hundred meters between us when a flash of electric blue catches my eye ahead on the left. The color of South's uniforms. It's Katie

Watson and directly in front of her, two other girls from another team. Time to make my move.

The path narrows and winds through the tall trees. Pushing hard, my concentration focused, I catch Katie and scoot around her on the right. "Hey."

"Hey," she says with a quick glance, but never breaking stride.

I wait for her to speed up, to catch and pass me, as if we're playing a game. But she doesn't.

Don't look, Gabby. Keep running.

It will only cost me valuable seconds.

"Way to go, Gabby!" It's one of my coaches with a timer in hand, as I exit the woods. "You've got this. They look like they're tiring." She nods to the two girls who are about 50 meters in front of me. "Go get 'em."

"Thanks."

Soon, I'm closing in on the last two runners standing between me and the finish line. They shuffle along, their heads bobbing, their arms high and tight. My coach was right. They're tiring. Probably went out too fast.

I pass them and start to descend the hill with only a mile left in the race.

At the bottom, I run along the dirt path that borders the football field and loops around the baseball diamond. This is where I get my proverbial 'second wind', when I turn on the jets, but instead, as I run past the sculpture garden, the opposite happens. Massive fatigue. It slams me, zapping all my energy. What the heck? I was feeling so good.

No, no, no. I can't tire now. There's only a half-mile to go. A half-mile that suddenly seems like a marathon.

193

Susan Dalessandro

I glance behind me. Here comes Katie Watson, confident and strong. No, I can't let her catch me.

"Keep it up, Gabby. Finish strong!" a chorus of voices ring out.

It's too much effort to smile. I have to conserve what little energy I have left. Exhaustion pulls at every cell in my body. My legs are like lead. Bone-tired, I want to get this over with. The debilitating fatigue. Torture. What the heck is wrong with me? I should feel light as a feather. I've been doing so good, barely eating a thing. I'm down another pound since two days ago. I checked the scale this morning.

Movement out of the corner of my eye snags my attention. It's CJ and Liam running parallel with me along the course route, shouting encouragement. CJ's smile falls when he realizes I'm in trouble.

With everything I have, I push through the fatigue and the pain, the pounding ache in my head and sprint across the open field. Cheers ring out through the large crowd surrounding the finish. I break through the tape and collapse. Everything fades to black.

****

A soft voice and gentle hands encourage my eyelids to open. The pale gray eyes that greet me soften the blow of being flat on my back with a crowd hovering around me.

"Gabby, are you okay?"

CJ nudges me into a sitting position. Slowly, I shake off the fogginess and rest my head on my knees. With the assistance of one of my coaches, CJ helps me stand and settle into a chair off to the side of the finishers' chute, where he covers me with a fleece blanket. *His* blanket he brought with him to sit on. It smells like him. Coconut and soap.

"Oh my goodness, Gabby!"

It's my parents and my mom specifically, who shrieks as she elbows her way through the crowd, which parts immediately. Frantic mom coming through. CJ kneels by my side, squeezing my hand.

"I'm fine, Mom."

"What happened, Gabriela?"

"I don't know," I say, between gulps of water from the bottle CJ hands me. "I was cruising along and then...hit a wall. I crashed." Literally. But I beat Katie. Breanna, too. I won. I'm in great position for Regionals in two weeks.

Coach Caroline, her face pinched with concern, extends her hand. "Gabby, we're going to take you to the medical tent, have you checked out. Are you okay to walk?"

"Yeah, of course." Coach acts as if I'm injured or sick. Like someone to be pitied. I won the freakin race. "I'm fine." I got a little dizzy, that's all. Ran too hard the last leg of the course. I stand and tug the blanket around my body. "I'm okay."

"C'mon, I'll walk you over." CJ places his arm around me and squeezes my shoulder. "You're shaking. Where are your sweats? I'll get them for you."

"In the team tent. On my blanket, right corner—"

CJ doesn't wait for me to finish but races off. "I'll find them."

"Hey, are you okay?"

I turn in the direction of a male voice. Jake jogs up to me, breathless.

"Hey, Jake. I'm fine. Just a little dizzy coming into the finish. I'll be—"

"Okay, Mr. Rossi, I need to get Gabby to the med tent. You can see her later."

"Bye, Jake."

"Take it easy, Gabby."

Her hand on my shoulder, my coach walks me the short distance to the medical tent, where she leads me inside and helps me onto a table. My mom hovers, concern creasing her ashen face.

"Mom, I'm fine. Seriously." I smile and she forces one in return, her worried gaze flitting over my face.

"I need to get back to the finish, see the others come in," Coach Caroline says. "You're in good hands here with Dr. Martin. I'll be back shortly to see how you're doing, okay?" She nods to my mom and leaves.

Dressed in jeans and a fleece hoodie, a stethoscope looped around her neck—the only indication she's a doctor—Dr. Martin takes my pulse, blood pressure, all the usual stuff. I guess it's the usual stuff. I've never needed the medical tent before except for blisters, a black toenail once.

CJ pushes into the tent, my sweats draped over his arm. "Here you go."

"Thanks. You're a lifesaver."

I grab my sweats from him and shrug on my hoodie, my fingers trembling as I do. The fuzzy fleece is soft and warm against my skin and calms the chills that have rocked me since I collapsed. I glance at the doctor who's scratching something on her pad.

"Can I go now?"

"Almost. Can I have a moment, folks?" The doctor eyes CJ and my mom.

CJ squeezes my hand. "I'll be outside," he says with a smile.

My mom nods and follows CJ out.

"So, you seem fine," the doctor says, adjusting the wire-rim glasses perched on her nose. "I don't see anything obviously wrong that would cause you to pass out. Your blood pressure is good. Your pulse, normal, for someone who just ran a 5000-meter race. The weather's cool, low humidity. You drank plenty of fluids before?"

I nod.

"Not anemic, are you?"

"No, not that I'm aware of."

She presses her lips together. "You said you had a crushing headache. That can be a sign of anemia. Or if you're depleted of fuel," she adds. "You should probably be checked by your family doctor—for anemia, that is. Just to make sure. I'll mention that to your mom. It's a simple blood test." She pauses her pen. "Not starving yourself, are you?"

She keeps her gaze on her pad, her dark hair falling into her eyes. I can't gauge from her tone if she's serious.

"No."

"I know a lot of you runners, boys *and* girls, do everything to compete—and win—at any cost, but starving yourself isn't the way to do it." She looks me in the face. Okay, she's serious. "It's dangerous. I don't know if that's what you're doing, just that it's not a wise way to train. You need to eat to run. I'm sure your coach stresses that all the time. With all the training you do, you burn through calories like that." She snaps her fingers. "I've been a doctor for over 20 years," she says, crossing her arms and leaning against the medical supplies table. "Be smart, okay?"

197

Haven't I been smart? Doing everything I'm supposed to? "Yep. Can I go now?"

"Here," take these." She hands me two ibuprofen tablets and a cup of water. "And drink. Make sure you drink."

"Thanks." I swallow the last drop of water and pitch the cup into the trash. "I'm good to go, then?"

"Yes. Could you send your mom back in for a minute?"

My stomach clenches. Mom will freak out if she thinks I'm starving myself. Which I'm not. I mean, obviously. Still, she's always on me to eat more because that's what moms do. If the doctor even suggests to her I'm not eating enough...

"Sure."

I push through the flap and exit the tent. My mom and dad are a few feet away, talking with CJ.

Wait, what? What are they possibly talking about?

"Gabby, how are you? What did the doctor say?" My mom takes my hand and squeezes it.

"I'm fine, but she wants to talk to you for a minute."

"Oh, okay." She catches my dad's eye and the two of them head into the medical tent.

"Is everything okay?"

CJ winds his arms around my waist. I breathe in his clean scent, and it makes things all better in an instant.

"Yeah, for now. Until my parents come out."

"Oh, I told them I'd take you home." He looks me in the eye. "If that's okay with you."

If that's okay with me? Like, yeah. "Seriously? And they were okay with that?" I place my hands on his chest.

"Absolutely. I told them we'd stop for lunch then I'd take you home." He smiles. "Do you need to get the rest of your stuff or check in with your coach before you leave?"

"Actually, I want to say bye to Ash and Liam. Do you mind?"

"Nope. I'll wait right here."

On my way, I bump into Katie Watson.

"Congratulations Gabby on the win. Are you okay? I saw you collapse at the finish." Concern darkens her eyes. She seems sincere. It's genuine concern for a fellow runner, a rival. Ugh, why does she have to be so nice? Not only is she super skinny, and a great runner, but she's considerate. Nice. Makes it that much harder to dislike her.

"I'm fine. Thanks. I pushed it too hard the last quarter mile."

"Well, feel better. I'll see you at Regionals in two weeks."

Regionals. I can't have a repeat of today. There'll be a lot more schools at Regionals, even if there'll be fewer runners from each. "Yep, see you there."

I can't figure why my parents are letting CJ drive me home. Don't they want to have this long talk in the car about what's going on with me?

"Hey, how'd you do?" I lower myself to the grass where Asha's stretching on her blanket in our tent.

A grin plays across her lips. "Lowered my time by twenty seconds."

"Awesome!" I pause and bite the inside of my cheek. "Wait, that means you qualified for Regionals. Aaah!"

Asha nods. "Yeah, I can't believe it. Hey, what

about you? I heard there was all this drama at the finish. Someone collapsed. Did you see it?"

I lower my gaze and grip the sides of my sweatpants.

"Gabby, no! I didn't know." Asha grabs my hand and sits up. "You collapsed? What happened? C'mon, you promised me. You've gotta stop this crazy dieting."

I shake her off and stand. "I'm not doing any crazy dieting, Ash." I'm doing what I have to do to win. "Look, I gotta go. CJ's waiting for me. Is Liam going home with your parents?"

"No, he drove separately." Asha rises and pulls me into a hug. "Sorry, I didn't mean to upset you. It's just I think you're going overboard with…stuff. You're so good, already. You don't need to be like someone else, someone you *think* is better. C'mon, we've talked about this."

Asha doesn't understand. I'm not going overboard with anything. I've always had a rivalry with Katie Watson. Her and Breanna. It's nothing more than friendly competition. Both of them with their tiny little bodies and skinny, muscular, legs make them look as if they're flying through the air. Perfect runner physiques. The knots tighten in my stomach. And Breanna was Jake's first choice. Maybe I'm not built like either of them, but with all my training I'm closer than ever. Closer to perfection.

She nods at the med tent. "So, CJ's driving you home?"

"Yes, I can't believe my parents are okay with it."

"Why? You said they like him."

"They do, but I'm surprised they don't want to trap me in their car for an hour and lecture me. You know

I'm right." I lift a brow.

Asha folds her arms. "I'm sorry. I'm sure they're only worried about you."

"I'm fine. I pushed it too hard at the end."

I glance behind me. Hands in his jeans' pockets, CJ stands outside the tent with my parents, engrossed in conversation. Again. When we started going out, I worried they wouldn't like him because he's a senior and doesn't go to West Penn. Now? They're super tight. Like, best friends. What could they be talking about?

CJ jogs over to me. "How are you feeling?" He rubs his hands up and down my sleeves 'before grasping my hands. "Ooh, your hands are cold," he says, squeezing them.

"I'm fine." I smile. "Better now. What were you and my parents talking about? Should I worry? Seemed pretty intense over there."

CJ laughs. "Nah, it was nothing. Just chatting. They told me to take care of you. Get you lunch." He smiles and the muscle ticks in his jaw. "I can handle that."

The glimmer in his eye quickens my pulse and I flush, my irritation with him dissipating. Why does he always do that to me? With one look.

"I'm sure you can." I snatch my bag from the grass. "Let me say goodbye to my parents before we go."

After reassuring them I'm fine, CJ and I say goodbye to Asha and Liam. Asha pulls me into another tight hug.

"Congrats again. Everything's going to be fine."

"Thanks. And congrats to you, too. I'm so psyched

we're going to Regionals together." I waggle my fingers. "See you guys later."

****

Once we're on the road, CJ grasps my hand. "So, are you going to tell me what's going on?"

Not you, too. CJ was supposed to be my out. My escape from the madness after my dramatic finish. At least until I had to face my parents later.

Focused on my lap, I pick at a thread on my sweats. "What do you mean?"

"I mean, what's going on with you?"

"What are you talking about? I got a little dizzy. I pushed to the finish too hard. I'm fine. I'll make up the time at Regionals, I swear."

CJ squeezes my hand. "Your *time*, Gabby? That's not what I'm talking about. I'm talking about *you*. Asha talked to me. She told me you passed out in gym, that you're trying to get to some ridiculous weight to run faster, to beat that girl, Katie. You never said anything to me." He pauses. "Even though you barely eat a thing when we're together and I guess I should've figured that out…"

I yank my hand away from CJ's and fold my arms. "She shouldn't have told you. And I eat plenty when we're together. So there. There's nothing to *figure out*." I clench my jaw and turn my focus to the trees rushing past outside the window.

"Gabby, please. I didn't want to say the wrong thing. I still don't, but I think you're taking your training too far. Going to extremes."

Ugh, if I wanted to be preached to, I could've gone home with my parents. Although why am I surprised?

"Can we please talk about something else?"

CJ pulls onto the shoulder of the road and my stomach tightens. "I think we should talk about it, now."

He kills the engine. Panic grips my chest. I'm not having this conversation. Not with CJ.

I fold my hands in my lap. "Not now. I thought we were getting lunch."

"We are, but you have to promise you'll talk to me, tell me what's going on."

I nod, before closing my eyes and resting my head against the window. We don't speak the rest of the way until CJ pulls into the borough and I straighten in my seat.

"Would you mind dropping me off at home? I'm in desperate need of a shower. In case you haven't noticed. You'll probably need to deodorize your car." I force out a laugh. "I can find something to eat in my kitchen."

CJ pulls to a stoplight, turns and narrows his gaze. "Seriously, Gabby? Don't do this. I thought we were getting lunch *together*."

"I reek. I can't go anywhere smelling like this. *Looking* like this." I consider his face, his eyes which are a stormy gray, his mouth in a tight, frustrated line. "Okay, how about you wait while I take a quick shower, then we can go? Unless you have somewhere you need to be? I don't want to monopolize your time."

CJ eases one hand off the wheel and grasps mine, squeezing tightly. "I'm yours for the whole day. Night?" He waggles his brows. "I can wait for you to shower."

Crap. We're going to have this discussion.

"Okay, I won't be long."

I step inside the foyer and Lola leaps on me with her furry paws, slobbering fat, wet kisses and jumping around like I've been gone for days and not hours.

"I'll be quick. You can hang out in the family room, put the TV on, if you like."

"Thanks. Hey, does she need to go out? I can walk her around outside while I wait."

"Yeah, that'd be great. I don't know when my parents will be home. Knowing them, they probably stopped off for lunch then hit a few stores." I nod to the coat closet. "Her lead is in there. Thanks."

Steam fills the bathroom as I stand in the shower, the hot water washing away the sweat and grime and kneading my tired muscles. If only I could stand here forever under the soothing pulse of the shower. CJ's waiting, though. And I am hungry.

I towel off and dress, pulling on a fresh pair of sweats and a hoodie. As I walk into my room my stomach lurches. Am I really going to have this talk with CJ? It's not his responsibility to help me. Aren't I supposed to be the one helping him with his sister? If he'd let me. He's the one with the problem. Not me.

I drop onto my bed and sink into my pillows, closing my eyes. Exhaustion slams me. I just want to sleep. Forget this day. Wake up and start over. Except for the part of beating Katie Watson and qualifying for Regionals. Even if I felt like crap and collapsed at the finish. Ugh, how can life be so complicated? I'm not even seventeen yet.

A rap on my door startles me.

"Gabby? Are you okay?" CJ pauses. "I hope you don't mind me coming upstairs. I was wondering what happened to you."

My pulse quickens. "No, it's fine, but I'm gonna pass on going out. I'll eat something here. Sorry to make you wait around for nothing. Thanks for bringing me home. I'll text you later." I squeeze my eyes shut and grip the comforter in my hands.

"Text me later? No way. Are you decent? I mean, can I come in?"

I've never had a boy in my room. "Um, sure."

CJ cracks the door and pokes his head in. "Actually, I was hoping you'd say you weren't dressed, but still wanted me to come in." He flashes a toothy grin. "Kidding."

I can't stop the smile that breaks across my face. Always the jokester. "I know. It's not that."

CJ shrugs off his coat and sits on the edge of my bed. "Wanna talk?"

"Not really."

"Too bad. You said we could. Why are you keeping me in the dark? You can tell me if something's up, something that's driving you to starve yourself." He shoots me a pointed look, his steel gray eyes boring into me like lasers. "Why? Because you think you should look like someone else? C'mon, talk to me." He taps me on the leg. "I'm a pretty good listener."

I bite the inside of my cheek and glance sideways. "First, there's nothing going on and second, I'm not starving myself. And third, I'll talk to you, *if* you'll be truthful about something with me. Fair's fair, right?"

CJ nods. "Sure. What do you want to know? I'm an open book." He rakes his fingers through his hair and leans his head back.

I scoot to the wall to make room and my pulse spikes as he slides close, his leg brushing against mine.

My heart thudding, I take a deep breath.

"I want to know who I can talk to in school about the night your sister died. Hailey came to me in the woods so I would help you. I know I'm right, CJ."

"Gabby, I—"

"One or two names, CJ. Like, who was she friends with? I didn't know Hailey well. She was in a few of my classes, but that's it. I want to help you. Please, let me. C'mon, she came to me for a reason. I'm there in school, every day."

CJ scans the room before he meets my gaze. "Maybe. I don't want you digging around, asking questions on my account." He grasps my hand and rests it on his leg. "I don't want you getting involved, Gabby. No need for you to play detective."

"Why not?" I lean into him and rest my head on his shoulder, inhaling his fresh clean scent, his coconut shampoo. "Don't you want to know the truth?"

"Hells, yeah. But not by using you, putting you through crap for me. It's a theory of mine, that's all, that someone else knows what happened, but the police already interviewed her friends. As far as I know they told them everything. Hopefully, the truth. What more are they going to say?" He rests his leg over mine, tugging it toward him. Every nerve buzzes. "I don't know what I hoped to find out. I mean, the truth, obviously. But that might be impossible."

"You're not putting me through anything. If you think someone at school has information about that night, if there's something they didn't tell the police, maybe I can dig around." I nudge him with my shoulder. "I'm sure her friends were nervous talking to the police. Maybe they forgot something, a detail they'd remember if I asked."

"No. I don't want you to worry about it. It's my problem. You have enough other 'stuff' going on." He taps my hand with his fingers and quirks a brow. "Right?"

I wiggle my hands out of his, but he takes them back and wraps his hands around mine. "Don't pull away. You promised. Why are you killing yourself, not eating, risking your health to beat this girl? To win a race. You don't need to do that. You have the fastest times in the league this year." His eyes search my face. "And you already look great. Not great. *Amazing*."

Flames engulf my face. I lift my eyes to the far wall, unable to meet his gaze.

"Asha told me you beat Katie in every race since freshman year except last year's Regionals and that's because you were coming down with the flu." He squeezes my hand. "Right?"

"Maybe. It's not just her, CJ." Even though I envy her tiny little body, the way she seems to defy gravity, zips through the air like a flash of lightning, while I clop along like a horse.

Even if I did beat her today. And Breanna. I don't feel fast. I certainly don't *look* fast.

"I told you some of the schools I want to apply to, hopefully earn a scholarship to. In order to do that, my times need to be fast." My attention is drawn to the window, at the dark clouds gathering in the sky, the way my insides feel right now. "And my grades really good. I can't assume I'll have next year to make up for a bad junior year."

"Bad?" CJ releases my hands and winds his arms around me, pulling me against him. "Gabby, why do you put so much pressure on yourself?" He massages my back, the soothing sensation of his hands triggering a flood of warmth and I collapse into him. "You'll be accepted to a ton of schools. You don't need to starve yourself to do it."

"Maybe."

He draws away and studies me, like he's wondering how he ever wound up with me. His mouth eases into a crooked grin. "Come here."

He doesn't give me a chance, instead leans in and crushes his lips to mine, hungry and urgent. His blistering kiss makes me forget everything but him for a moment. Placing his hands on the sides of my face, he trails his mouth across my chin, down my neck to my collarbone. His mouth lingers in the hollow of my neck, making the blood hum in my veins. "Gabby, he says, breathless, "please, don't starve yourself. You're beautiful the way you are."

"That's sweet of you to say, CJ, but not true. And I'm not starving myself."

We continue kissing until I stop and place my hand on his shirt. "Can you at least give me a name, let me see what I can find out from one of Hailey's friends? You'd be surprised at what people will tell you if you ask nicely. If I find nothing, then fine. But I have to at least try, CJ. Why else would Hailey have come to me in the woods?"

"Ask *nicely*?" CJ bites his bottom lip. A spark glimmers in his eye. "I'll think about it. I don't want you to get into trouble for me."

"What kind of trouble can I get into? And I've been honest with you, CJ. I have no secrets."

His mouth presses into a tight line, his eyes

narrowing. "Have you? Can you honestly say you're not restricting food, counting every calorie because you're trying to be skinnier?" He shakes his head. "Like you can possibly be any skinnier."

I shrug away from him and the faded blue notebook poking out of my nightstand drawer catches my eye. Something about what I read. Pages with only a few words. Food lists. Daily calories. My stomach clenches.

"Gabby?"

"Huh?"

"Be honest with me."

"I am, CJ. I'm not doing anything different than anyone else. I'm doing what it takes to compete. Or at least I'm trying." I linger on the notebook and a chill races down my spine.

"Hey, you okay?" CJ touches my arm.

I shake myself out of my trance. "Yeah, fine."

He winds his arms around me and nestles his face in my neck. "You're cold."

I exhale a long slow breath and relax into him. "We should probably go. Lunch, right?"

Although my body language is saying to stay put right in this spot. No more talk of food or secrets, just him and me wrapped up together.

A smile tugs at his lips. "Absolutely. Lunch." He rests his hands on my hips and scoots closer.

"Wait, I thought we were getting lunch."

"No rush, right?"

Oh. Is he a mind-reader? He takes my leg and hooks it around his. His gaze dark and wanting, he brushes his lips across mine, slow and soft. A thousand tiny wings flutter in my chest as his hands flirt with the waistband of my sweats, his fingers brushing along my bare stomach. Fiery heat races across my skin. I drink in his scent of coconut and soap, winding my arms around his neck and threading my fingers through his hair. His hands explore my stomach, every nerve and muscle jumping beneath his tender, shiver-inducing touch.

"Gabby," he whispers against my lips, "I want to ask *nicely,*" he chuckles. "Is this...okay?" His chest rises and falls against me, his heart thrumming inside. "No, it isn't. You need to eat something. We shouldn't be—"

"No, I'm fine."

But we probably should stop. We're in my bedroom and if my parents come home now, I won't have to worry about applying to college because I'll be grounded for life. Plus, we're wading into unfamiliar territory. At least for me. I don't know if CJ's had other girlfriends or if he's been in serious relationships, but... Wait, of course he has. He's a guy. In a band. What's wrong with me?

He's the first guy I've kissed like this. Who's kissed *me* like this. Touched me this way. I've only kissed two other guys. Brief pecks on the lips.

"Maybe you're right. Can't have my parents coming home to you in my bedroom."

CJ draws away, his face flushed. "Yeah, I wouldn't want them to get the wrong impression." A grin ghosts across his lips. He sits up and stretches his arms. "So, where to? Sandwich shop on Main? Maybe some ice cream afterward?"

"I don't know. We can figure it out in your car."

"Yeah, sure. Whatever you want."

Right now, I want to stay here with CJ, but he stands, reaches for my hand and I let him take it.

We walk out of my room and head downstairs.

Chapter Twenty

CJ relented and gave me the names of two people who were friends with his sister after I'd eaten a whole salad with grilled chicken on Saturday. That was the deal. One salad for two names. The ice cream afterward was a little much, but I did manage a few spoonfuls of chocolate he ordered for us to share. I thought I would burst after lunch, I was so full.

I still don't understand why he welcomed my help when he first told me about Hailey, but then did a complete 180 and changed his mind. I'm glad he finally came around and gave me their names. I don't know either of Haley's friends well, but I have class with both of them. Maybe nothing will come of it, but I have to try. Hailey came to me to help CJ figure out what happened to her. Someone at this school knows something. My job is to find out who and what they know.

I have first period English with both Kelsey and Taylor, Hailey's two friends, but I don't sit near either one. Mrs. Owens made our seats permanent the first day and lucky me, Caitlin sits to my right and Madison, directly in front of me. Today, their non-stop blathering about their dresses and shoes for the upcoming Homecoming Dance induces a splitting headache.

"Are you two finished?" Mrs. Owens finally asks, turning from the board.

Her gaze ping-pongs from Madison to Caitlin who both clam up. Geez, it's about time.

Quiet reigns as Mrs. Owens resumes writing on the board, but my mind's racing in a hundred different directions. Like, scheming for an excuse to talk to Kelsey and Taylor. Besides English, Kelsey shares my lunch. Taylor is in my gym class. Can I wait that long, though?

When the bell rings I jump out of my seat and race out the door.

Breathless, I catch up with Kelsey. "You were friends with Hailey Jarvis, right?" Real smooth, Gabby.

She turns to me, her dark ponytail sweeping her shoulders. At least a half a foot shorter than me, she furrows her brow, and searches my face. "You're dating her brother, aren't you?"

My stomach clenches. I wrap my arm around my waist. "Yeah, sorta. I mean we've gone out a few times." Kissed a few times. Totally made out a few times. "How did you know?"

"Come on, nothing's secret around here. It's not that big of a school."

"Right."

Kelsey laughs. "No, but that's not how I found out. I saw you at the football game with CJ, which was kinda weird, because he never went to games before Hailey..." She halts and glances away. "Before she died."

I take a step closer and cross my arms. "Did you know CJ, too?"

"No, but Friday nights they practiced as a band in the Jarvis' basement or sometimes hung out at Lucia's in the karaoke room. Hailey said it was CJ's way of

213

getting her to sing in front of people, even though the place was usually empty when they went there. At least there was no chance of West Penn students being there, since they were all at the football game. In the fall, anyway." Kelsey chews her lip. "He was always trying to get her out of her comfort zone, you know?" Shadows darken her eyes. "Especially after…"

After what? But Kelsey presses her lips together, like she's already divulged too much. Can I blame her? It's probably painful talking about her best friend after she died by suicide. Here I am bringing it up almost a year later, opening up the wounds again.

Now it makes sense why CJ left Lucia's when we were there with Liam and Ash. He said he'd left his wallet in his car, but it was probably to escape the memories of being there with his sister.

Guilt twists my gut. He should've said something. We didn't need to go there.

"I'm sorry, I don't want to upset you."

We step around a group gathered in the hall and keep walking. I don't know where Kelsey's next period is, but she's still talking to me, so I'll go wherever she's going.

"You didn't. I was saying Hailey never liked to sing in front of a crowd. She had an amazing voice, but that's how she was. She hated being the center of attention."

"Yeah, CJ mentioned that."

"I think her brother had a lot to do with her agreeing to the benefit concert last year. Plus, she said it was for a good cause, so she was going to force herself to get past her stage fright." She nods her head emphatically. "She nailed it, too. They got a standing O for every song."

An ache throbs in my chest. Asha and I didn't go to the benefit concert last year. We had a meet that Saturday, an invitational at Central on their hilly course and we were both wiped out afterwards. We binge-watched TV in my living room. That's why I had no idea who CJ was when I met him in Larry's.

"I'm sure they did. CJ doesn't play anymore." *Won't* play anymore. "I think it's too hard for him." I let out a long sigh.

Kelsey stops. "I'm not surprised. Listen, I gotta go or I'm gonna be late for Spanish."

"Okay, see ya."

Wait, what about that night? I didn't even ask. *You blew it, Gabby.*

I shoulder my bag and trudge off to chemistry. Maybe I'll have the chance to ask her at lunch. Now that we've talked, maybe it won't be as awkward if I ask her about that night.

Right. Like asking someone about the night their close friend died by suicide isn't awkward.

****

"Hey, you hammered everyone on the course today," Asha says as we walk across the grass after practice. "Are you feeling better after last weekend? You seem better."

Translation: are you eating more, Gabby? You haven't passed out lately. She doesn't say that, but I know what she's thinking.

I can't have a repeat of Districts at Regionals. Even though what happened had nothing to do with what I ate. But after the lecture from Mom, I have to at least make it look like I'm eating more. She threatened to pull me out of cross-country if I don't eat. No way that is happening. It just means I have to run more to work off those calories. Run on my own in addition to practice. This morning I slipped out with Lola and put in four miles before anyone was awake. Before I choked down the scrambled eggs and toast my mom cooked for breakfast.

"Yeah, I guess."

"You're going to kick butt at Regionals." She nudges my shoulder. "Just don't come down with the flu." She laughs. "Have you asked CJ about Homecoming on Saturday?"

We reach the gym doors and I stop and lean my hip against the wall. "Homecoming? Nah. It would be too hard for him. Everyone from school will be there. I can't do that to him." Although, he'd go if I really him wanted to. I shrug. "It's no big deal. I think we're gonna hang out at my house. There's gotta be a basketball or hockey game on. Plus, I don't have a dress."

"Seriously, Gabs, we can go shopping this week, pick something out. But did you even ask him? He may surprise you, say he wants to go."

"I don't think so."

Asha tucks a strand of hair into her hairband and crosses her arms. "So, you're not going at all?"

"You mean so I can hang out with you and Liam? You two don't need me. This is your first time going to something as each other's date. You don't want me ruining it."

"Stop. It's not like prom. It's Homecoming. You don't need a date. We'll hang out together, the three of us. Like we've always done. Even so, you should still ask CJ."

"Mm. Hey, I never asked, and I can't believe I haven't, but are your parents cool with you and Liam dating?" I narrow my eyes. "They do know, right?"

A grin plays across Asha's lips. "Of course. And if you mean, are they disappointed I'm not going out with a 'nice Indian boy' instead? No. They're cool with it. They like Liam a lot. We've been friends a long time. They've known him since he was ten and our parents are friends. They're happy for me."

"That's awesome. I'm so glad."

"Yeah, I kinda figured they'd be okay with it. Like I said, they like Liam. They've always told me it's my choice who I date. And it's not like we're getting married. We're dating."

I arch my brows. "For now," I say.

"Right, for now," she says with a chuckle. "But what about you?"

"What do you mean? My parents like CJ." Maybe a little too much.

"No, I mean are *you* okay with us dating?" She puckers her lips and rests her hands on her hips.

"Of course. Don't be ridiculous. I'm the one who said you two belonged together." I cross one foot over the other. "I don't want to lose either of you as a friend."

"What? That's crazy talk." Asha pulls me into a hug. "*That* will never happen. How many times do I have to say it to you?"

"Just making sure, I guess."

Once in the locker room, we pull on our sweats, grab our stuff and head outside.

"Crap, I left my phone in my locker upstairs." Asha

says as she halts outside the door, one hand scrounging around her bag. "Do you mind waiting while I get it? I'll be quick."

"No problem. I'll be right here on the bench."

"Cool. Thanks."

I take a seat on the wooden bench and tilt my chin skyward, the sun warming my face. I'm about to pull out my phone when Taylor Piazza saunters down the hill and takes a seat on the bench.

"Hey." She rifles through her bag and pulls out her phone.

"Hey."

Don't sit there. Say something.

"Were you watching the soccer game?" I'm certain there's a guys' soccer game going on in the upper field. That's normal conversation, right?

Her fingers stop racing across her phone screen, and she lifts her head. "Yeah, my brother's on the team."

"Really? What position?"

"Forward. It's two zip, West Penn. They're playing Caufield. Five minutes 'til half-time." She sets her phone aside and twists her body to me, folding her hands in her lap. "So, you're dating Hailey's brother?"

Again? Talk about being direct. But she brought it up, not me. Convenient. Both of Hailey's friends in one day and I barely had to make an effort. Maybe things are starting to fall into place.

"Um, yeah. How did you know?"

As if I don't know. She's best friends with Kelsey.

"I saw you at one of the football games. I didn't know if you were just friends or if you were seeing each other." She smiles. "He's cute."

Heat floods my face and I look away. Yeah, he is.

"I guess you could say we're dating. We met over the summer and have gone out a few times. He's nice. Into music. Like me, I guess." A smile pulls at my lips, the memory of the day we met, joining CJ singing in Larry's. Something I would never, *ever* do, but for some reason I couldn't help myself. "So um, what was she like, Hailey, I mean? You were friends with her, right?"

Taylor nods. "She was sweet, kind and had a beautiful voice before…" She draws in a sharp breath. "I still can't believe she's gone. The way it happened, it didn't make sense." She shakes her head.

"I know. It was terrible." I take in a shuddering breath. "Wait, what do you mean it didn't make sense? It was suicide, right?" My heart races. Here's my chance.

Taylor pulls her legs onto the bench and hugs them to her chest. "Yes, but I can't believe she'd do that. I know it's the official story, but—"

"But you don't believe it?"

Down, Gabby. You'll scare her away.

"It doesn't fit. Hailey was happy at the time. Healthy, too. I know she could've been hiding something, but…" She bites her lip and shakes her light brown curls off her face, lowering her legs to the ground. "Like I said, she had a beautiful voice. She was a singer, wrote a lot of her own songs for the band she was in with CJ and Nate."

"Yeah, CJ told me about their band."

"Well, right before it happened, she'd been humming a lot, singing way more than usual. Like she was in a really good mood. She liked to go to that spot in the woods to write." She meets my eye. "You know, not far from where they found her," she says, her voice rough.

"Yeah, I know. CJ said she went there a lot." I scoot closer to Taylor. "So, what do you think happened?"

"I don't know, but..." Taylor's gaze volleys around before coming to rest on her lap. "I think she was talking with someone, maybe even *dating* someone. I think that's why she seemed so happy. You know when you first go out with someone, it's like nothing else matters and you walk around with your head in the clouds."

Um, yeah. I may know something about that.

"She never told Kelsey or me, but I think she was meeting someone in the woods when she went to write." She gives a small laugh. "That's probably how she'd tell us they were dating. When she wrote a song about him." She pauses. "Of course, we never got the chance. I asked her one time if there was someone she wasn't telling us about. She smiled and said, 'Maybe. Too soon to tell.'"

My stomach drops. Drew Marchella. What if Hailey was dating Drew? And she didn't say anything because he hadn't broken things off with Madison yet? Total. Scandal. Drew was so interested in hearing about CJ that day in class. His exact words were, *'yeah, I knew Hailey a little.'* Maybe *more* than a little. And maybe he knows a lot more about what happened that night. I tighten my arms around my waist.

"I really miss her. Hey, are you okay?"

"I'm sorry, what?" I fidget on the bench.

"I said I really miss Hailey." She clasps her hands

together in her lap.

"I'm so sorry." What else can I say? I glance toward the soccer field then to Taylor. "Did you tell the police what you told me? That you thought she was meeting someone in the woods?"

Taylor nods. "Kelsey and I were at the station for hours. We told them everything we knew. But if she met someone there we didn't know about..." She shrugs. "That was it after that night. They never contacted us again."

"Did they talk to anyone else? Anyone else from school?"

"I don't know. I only know about me and Kelsey. I never heard anyone else say anything."

"But what about the 911 call?" I tilt my head. "CJ said it's a girl's voice."

Taylor nods, smoothing her jeans with her hands. "Yeah, I heard that rumor."

"It's not a rumor, it's true. CJ listened to the tape. It's a girl's voice."

"Mm, I guess that kinda makes sense. The police seemed to suspect one of us, the way they questioned us at the station that night. They grilled us about our whereabouts. Both our parents had to 'corroborate' our stories. They checked out, I swear. Plus, why would either of us do anything to hurt Hailey? Or try and cover something up."

"Omigod, no! I'm not saying it was you or Kelsey. Just that it was a girl who made the call, so even if Hailey met a guy there, it was a girl who called, who knows something."

"Oh." Taylor laces her fingers together and sets her hands on her lap. "I have no idea who it could've been.

Other than me and Kelsey, Hailey didn't hang out with anyone else. Maybe, whoever called 911 doesn't go to this school. Maybe someone walked through there, saw her there and made the call. I don't know. It must be so hard for her parents. I can't imagine how they're dealing with it. Or CJ. Hailey and he were pretty tight." She pauses and lifts her head. "I hope he's doing okay. Are you bringing him to the Homecoming dance?"

"Homecoming?" says a flinty voice.

I spin around. Wearing high heeled boots, Caitlin gingerly steps down the hill, combing her fingers through her long auburn hair.

"Is that what you're talking about? Who you're bringing to Homecoming? CJ, right?" She halts and rests her hand on her hip.

"Gabby?"

"Huh?"

"You're bringing CJ to Homecoming?"

Why does she care? "I don't know."

"Don't know what?" Madison shuffles down the hill to join Caitlin.

Oh, joy. It's my lucky day. Like I don't get enough of these two in English.

"Nothing." I stand and step away from the bench. "See ya, Taylor. I gotta go."

Taylor stands. "Yeah, me too. The second half's probably starting." She waves and walks away.

Madison's gaze is like a laser boring into me. "What are you guys talking about? Your boyfriend?" She folds her arms.

What's it to you anyway? I yank on the door handle. I gotta find Asha. What's taking her so long, anyway?

Madison stalks over to me, the staccato clack of her boot heels on the walkway exacerbating my irritation. She rests a hand on her hip. Damn, I wasn't quick enough.

She swings her long dark hair over her shoulders. "Didn't you ever wonder why he asked you out?" Her mouth twitches at the corners.

Gripping the door handle, I turn to her. "What do you mean?"

"I mean, don't you think it's odd you met in a store, and he asked you out? Like that?" She snaps her fingers.

I should've known better than to tell Caitlin how CJ and I met. "What does that have to do with anything?" My jaw clenches.

She juts out her chin. "Doesn't seem like your *m.o.*, Gabby."

My heart thumps. I grip the handle tighter. "My 'm.o.'? What's that supposed to mean?"

She examines me, a smirk parting her glossy red lips. "Maybe he wants to get in your pants. Your skinny little pants. *Maybe...*" She pauses for effect. "He already has."

I let the door close and face her. "You're full of crap."

I usually don't clap back, but my heart is about to smash through my ribs. Madison's touched a nerve, and I can't stand here, silent, and take it like I usually do. My response though, seems to encourage her.

"Or maybe, in addition to getting some, he might have been looking for someone to snoop around about his sister's death." She bites her bottom lip. "Aiden said it was all over the junior class last year, CJ telling his friends he didn't believe it was suicide. Until he left school because he couldn't hack it." She snorts. "I'm sure he's told you the same, hoping you'd feel sorry for him. Hoping you'll put out."

I ball my hands into fists, my nails digging into my palms. "Shut up!"

"C'mon, you know as well as I do. Hailey Jarvis committed suicide. She had issues. Everyone knew about her eating disorder. Apparently, her brother can't face the truth." Madison pauses then flicks her hand forward, examining her nails.

Eating disorder? Panic grips my chest. Is that what Taylor meant when she said Hailey was finally 'healthy'? Had she recovered from an eating disorder at the time of her death? Blood pounds in my temples as everything spins around me. CJ never told me Hailey had an eating disorder.

The notebook.

Those pages of food lists. The ones I couldn't decipher. It's what she ate in a day. It wasn't much if her journal was any indication. Of course. Why didn't I see that? CJ's worried what happened to his sister will happen to me. That's ridiculous, I don't have a food journal. I don't document everything I eat. Not on paper, anyway.

Bile rises in my throat. CJ said Hailey was fine at the time of her death. Blissfully happy. Did her eating disorder have something to do with her death? Maybe he *can't* face the truth. Maybe she struggled so much she couldn't take it anymore... Maybe...

What else hasn't he told me?

"I guess when you walked into the music store, *voilà*!" Madison snaps her fingers and her mouth eases into a wicked grin. "Everything fell into place." She tilts her head. "I heard he's homeschooled now. You would know. Is that what he's doing?"

The ache in my chest deepens. "Use me? Right. He had no idea who I was. No idea what school I went to."

Wait.

I swallow. The day we met, I walked into Larry's after cross-country practice wearing running shorts with 'West Penn' on them. CJ knew right away where I went to school. He asked me about it. Nausea rolls my stomach. What if Madison's right? What if he's using me for information? Or flat out *using* me? No, he tried to persuade me not to look into his sister's death. He's been adamant about it. He only gave me the names of his sister's friends after I made a deal with him. Pleaded with him. It can't be an act, can it? And if not, what does he want from me?

The air slowly leaks out. I can't breathe.

Memories from last Saturday rush through me, the way we kissed in my room. Touched. The way I craved more. As if we meant something to each other. What is it, then? Is CJ using me, or does he pity me and think he can somehow 'fix' me? Neither is reassuring.

Asha steps through the doorway. "Hey, sorry I took so long. I bumped into Ella in the hall." Her gaze flits to Madison then me. "Gabs, what's going on?"

I grasp Asha's arm and lead her away, not looking back. "Nothing."

"Don't take it too hard, Gabby," Madison calls after me. "Even if the information you're feeding him is useless, I'm sure he's thrilled with what he gets in return."

As I pick up the pace, I want to turn around and

scream 'You're wrong!', but what if she's not. What if everything she said is the truth?

Asha stops and whirls on me. "Gabby, tell me. What the heck's going on?"

My head pounds. Tears prick my eyes, but they're not going to fall. "Nothing." I can't let Asha know she was right when she suspected something was off about CJ when we first met. When I should've listened to her. "Madison being Madison."

He's using me. Maybe he could get information about his sister's death or maybe sympathy. Maybe he could 'save me'. Or as Madison said, he could get 'something on the side'. One look into those pale gray eyes and I was hooked.

What a fool I've been.

Chapter Twenty-One

My phone vibrates and I flip it over on my bed.

—*Where are u? I've texted and called a ton of times. Thought we were hanging out tonight?* —

Ugh. I shut off my phone and bury my head in my pillows. *Where am I?* I'm sulking in my room while Liam and Asha are at the Homecoming Dance. I told them CJ was coming over to watch a movie with me. A big fat lie because the truth hurts too much.

Lola leaps onto the bed and snuggles against me. I smooth the fur on her head before grabbing my book from my nightstand. I'm sure Asha and Liam are having a blast right now. Asha's already texted a bunch of pictures, the two of them all smiles, looking like the happiest couple. At least someone's having fun.

I'm three pages into my latest novel when Lola's bark shatters the quiet. She bolts upright, her ears piqued and does that little head tilt thing.

"What is it, girl?" My pounding heart echoes in my ears before a knock at the front door makes me practically leap off the bed.

I fly downstairs and place my eye to the peep hole. Bile rises in my throat. I pull on the door handle and take a step back. "What are you doing here?"

"Oh hey, Gabby, nice to see you, too." CJ folds his arms over his chest. "What's going on? You don't respond to my texts or calls. You haven't even tried to talk to me for the last two days."

"I'm sorry, but—"

"You're sorry? I thought you were sick or something, but you would've texted me. At least I would hope so. That's what boyfriends and *girlfriends* normally do, so the other person won't freak out with worry." His stormy gray gaze searches my face. "I'm *assuming* you're still my girlfriend."

I glance past him into the darkness, avoiding his pointed glare, an ache throbbing in my chest.

CJ takes a step closer. "Can I come in? Please? Maybe you can tell me what's going on."

My parents are out to dinner and a play at the local theatre, so I've got no excuses. Stuck here, just the two of us. Wow, did I really think that? A week ago, I would've been totally psyched for the two of us to have the house to ourselves. Now?

Am I really going to let Madison destroy our relationship? At the very least, I need to address it with him. And since he's standing on my doorstop, I guess I'm doing it now.

"Um, yeah, sure."

I lead him into the family room and take a seat on the sofa. CJ shrugs off his coat and sits on the chair across from me, resting his elbows on his knees.

"Talk to me. Why are you shutting me out all of the sudden? I thought everything was good between us. You're not still upset I talked to Asha last week after your race, are you? C'mon, we talked about that. I thought everything was good."

I shake my head. "It's not that." But isn't it? I choke down the bile rising in my throat.

CJ looks me in the eye. "Then, what? Was it..." He

pauses, pursing his lips. "...what happened later, in your room? I thought you felt the same and..." He rubs the back of his neck. "I couldn't get it...*you* out of my head all day. And I didn't want to. Was it too much? Gabby, I wish you would've said something, told me if I was out of line. I don't want to do that to you. Ever."

Tears spring to my eyes. Something on the side. That's what Madison said. Getting into my pants. But CJ's been nothing but respectful, a total gentleman. He's never pushed me to do anything I was uncomfortable with. Maybe he's a good actor?

Before I have the chance to stop myself, I blurt out, "Are you sure it hasn't all been an act?"

CJ's eyes widen. "An act?" He leans back and rakes his hands through his hair. "I couldn't keep my hands off you." His face flushes. "*Every* time we're together. Even if it's just to hold your hand."

That was low of me. Accusing him of something I know isn't true.

He glances away. "An act," he repeats, his voice faltering. "How can you say that? I love being with you, hanging out, talking, listening to music, *talking* about music—we're supposed to see that music festival in Philadelphia next month. I wanted to see you run at Districts. I was disappointed when you didn't tell me about it, the fact I had to find out by myself. You can't be serious, Gabby. C'mon, what gives? What's this really about? Why are you pushing me away? Did someone say something to you? Something to make you doubt me? I know people can be hurtful, and no offense, but girls can be downright cruel."

My chest squeezes, the ache throbbing deep inside me, all the way to my core. "Why did you ask for my number the day I met you?"

CJ's brows jump. "What?"

"Why did you ask for my number when I bumped into you that night in the woods?" I fold my arms across my chest, to keep my heart from bursting out.

"Gabby, I told you, I wanted to follow you out of Larry's when we first met. I almost did. I had a good vibe about you. We hit it off. You seemed really nice, and it was so cool you were into music like me. I never met anyone like you. We had a connection. C'mon, tell me you didn't feel it."

Of course I did. I didn't want to leave Larry's that day. But I shrug.

He bites his lip. "Okay, I was also attracted to you, thought you were cute...*hot*," he says, his cheeks pinking. "The way you walked in, your running stuff on, hair in a ponytail..."

"I was sweaty and gross, CJ. Most people find that offensive."

"Guess I like that." He lifts a shoulder. "It's you, who you are. You're *real*."

No. No. No. I ball my hands into fists, my nails digging into my skin. I can't hold it in any longer. "And you thought maybe you could *fix* me?"

CJ jerks up his chin. "What? Fix you?"

"CJ, I trusted you. I totally fell for you. You're the first guy I've actually gone out with on more than one date and..." I sigh, my anger building. "Why didn't you tell me about Hailey, the fact she had an eating disorder?" My voice shakes. "Why did you hide it from me? You said you trusted me, that you could talk to me about anything. How come you never told me?"

CJ stands, takes two steps and drops onto the sofa.

He wraps his arm around me. "I'm sorry. I didn't think it mattered. She got better. About six months before she died, she started going to a therapist and a nutritionist. She'd gained weight. She was writing songs again. She was totally psyched about rehearsing our sets." He bites his bottom lip. "And I think she was seeing someone. I don't know who it was or if it was serious. She didn't talk to me about it. But I could tell she was happy, because..." He lowers his eyes, his blond lashes dusting his cheeks. "...she walked around with this goofy grin on her face, kinda like me, ever since I met you."

Wait, that's what Taylor said. That she thought Hailey was seeing someone. Drew.

CJ brushes a strand of hair off my face, tucking it behind my ear. "When I realized something was going on with you, it brought back everything with Hailey." He pauses. "It scared me, Gabby. I didn't know what to say to you. I wanted to tell you about her, what she went through, but I didn't want you to think I was interfering. I mean, I tried to talk to you, but you shrugged it off. It's why I talked to Asha. Is that what this is about?"

"You think there's a connection, CJ, me and your sister. You're afraid to say anything for fear of offending me, but I'm fine and I don't want our relationship to be about you trying to save me."

"What? Gabby, that's crazy." He pauses, taking a second to compose himself. "I'm not going to lie, though. I've been really worried about you. The reason you passed out at Districts? I tried to talk to you about it, but you kept changing the subject. Asha said you fainted in gym class a few days earlier. She said you've lost a *lot* of weight since the beginning of the season."

He takes a deep breath. "I've noticed too. But I didn't know how to talk to you about it." His voice is low and gravelly. "Not without sounding preachy." CJ takes my hand and squeezes it. "I think *that's* why Hailey came to you. *That's* why you keep hearing that song. She wanted you to help me figure out what happened to her, but she also wanted to help *you*. Make sure you didn't go through what she did. I can understand a little what you're dealing with, Gabby, because of Hailey. Not everything. But I'm a great listener."

The hairs on my neck stand on end.

The song. The notebook with a daily log of what she ate. Why didn't I make the connection? Is that the reason Hailey came to me? Is CJ right? I swallow the boulder in my throat before irritation bubbles to the surface.

CJ wraps his arm around me. "Can you talk to me about it?"

"There's nothing to talk about, CJ. I'm fine. I don't have *issues* with food. Asha shouldn't have said anything to you."

"She said something because she's your best friend and she cares, that's why."

"I don't want you trying to save me, CJ. Pitying me. I thought we were together because we liked hanging out with each other. Not so I can be some kind of charity project for you. Someone for you to save, now that your sister is gone."

CJ's brows jump. "Ouch! I can't believe you said that. But, yeah, you're right, I didn't save Hailey." He lowers his chin. "I think about that *every* day. But her death had nothing to do with her anorexia. She was healthy when she died. Happy." Emotions choke his words, and he scrubs his hand over his face. "Maybe you think I'm in denial like my parents, but I'm not and I don't believe it was suicide."

"I'm sorry, CJ, I didn't mean it was your fault. I feel terrible about what happened with Hailey. And I can't imagine what it must be like for you and your parents. The fact she's gone and not knowing the truth, but," I pause, trying to gather the thoughts churning through my head. "I don't know what to feel right now or how I fit in with you. *If* I fit at all."

"You fit perfectly. Right here," he says, tapping his chest. "Gabby, what do I have to say to convince you?" His voice breaks. "I asked you out because I really liked you and that feeling has grown the longer we've been together. I've fallen for you. Hard. I thought you felt the same." He exhales a long breath. "Did you think what happened Saturday was 'pretending'? Or any time we've been together? I'm a terrible actor and I couldn't fake my feelings for you."

"Maybe."

"No, not maybe. It's the truth. You said a minute ago, I was the first guy you've gone out with more than once. It's pretty much the same for me. I've had a few girlfriends, but nothing serious. You were...*are*, my first serious relationship."

I swallow around the dryness in my throat. "I don't know what to think, CJ."

"What you need to know is I love being with you. He grasps my hand and squeezes it, massaging my fingers with his thumb. "Kissing you. Holding you. Just sitting around talking. I told you my doubts, my theory about Hailey's death, because I needed to tell somebody. And I trust you," he says, his voice low.

"More than anything. I knew that from the first time we met. I felt comfortable talking to you. I never wanted our relationship to be about Hailey, even though you were so eager to help me. And I know you don't believe me, but I haven't stuck around to 'fix' or 'save' you like you said. I worry because I care about you. A lot."

An ache throbs in my chest. CJ scoots close and pulls me to him.

Let go. Give in. But I can't. Doubt still gnaws at me. Because that's the way I am.

I draw away and lean against the arm of the sofa. "I need time, CJ." Time to figure out the mess in my head. The hollowness inside.

CJ nods. "Okay. Take as long as you need." He walks to the door and turns to look me in the eye. "I would never hurt you. Never."

I watch the door as it closes with a thud. I pull my knees to my chest and sink into the sofa, the air rushing out of me. What did I do?

****

"Hey, thanks for agreeing to this. I really need to talk to you," I say, tucking my gloves into my sleeves as I run into the café's parking lot the following morning.

Low-hanging gray clouds mottle the October sky. A brisk wind churns the air and nips at my skin.

"Anytime, but what's up?" says Asha. "You only want to discuss something over a run if it's serious. Something happen with CJ?" She shoots me an inquisitive glance. "You guys hung out at your house last night, right?"

"You could say that."

We start to run in tandem and after a few steps, fall

into a comfortable pace. I don't say any more until we turn the corner onto Cherry Street, away from the bustle of Saturday morning shoppers and diners on Main.

"Ash, be honest with me, do you think CJ's using me, or, only sticking around because he's 'worried' about me? For no reason, of course."

Asha whips her head around so fast, her ponytail smacks her in the face. "What? Absolutely not. Gabs, where's this coming from?"

I stretch my neck muscles, shifting my head from side to side. "Madison said—"

"Stop. Right. There. Any sentence that begins with 'Madison said' can't be good. Or contain an ounce of truth." She glances at me and I look away. "Does this have something to do with the other day after practice? What exactly did she say to you? You were pretty upset, but you wouldn't tell me what was wrong."

"She said CJ was using me to find out what happened the night his sister died. I didn't really believe it, because like I told you, he's tried to discourage me from poking around about that night. But then..." I pause. "She told me Hailey had an eating disorder." I turn to Asha. "Did you know about that?"

"What?" Asha keeps her gaze forward, refusing to look in my direction.

"That Hailey Jarvis was anorexic."

"No. I didn't know Hailey. You know that."

"Mm. When I asked CJ about it, about why he never mentioned anything, he said he didn't think it was important because she was recovering at the time. And because he was afraid I'd think he was interfering. Why would he think that? I mean, why would his sister's eating disorder have *anything* to do with me? Huh, why

Ash?"

Asha turns her head slightly and shrugs. "I dunno."

"Maybe because you talked to him, told him there's something wrong with me? Maybe the two of you have been plotting how to 'fix Gabby'."

Asha snorts. "Nobody's plotting anything. Or trying to *fix* you. But when you passed out at the finish line at Districts, CJ asked me if something was going on, and I told him the truth. I said I was worried you were training too hard, not eating right. That's all. *He's* the one who mentioned how much weight you'd lost since he met you. And that he was worried."

"Right and you didn't try and discourage him, did you? You didn't tell him he was overreacting?"

"Because he wasn't."

I sigh and race ahead of Asha.

"Gabs, come on." She pulls even with me. "He obviously cares about you, but if you think he's faking it..." She sighs. "Let's see, he asks for your number after you've met and bonded over music, *eighties* music, which you know, *everyone's* into."

I don't look at her, but the eye roll is in her voice.

"Begins a relationship with you, goes to cross-country meets, something most guys wouldn't set foot near, goes to dinner with your friends he doesn't know, meets your parents, invites you to his house, makes plans to go to a concert together in November, kisses you *passionately*... He does all that because he thinks you need help, and oh, maybe you could shed some light on how his sister really died? Don't go there. Plus, you said he didn't want you asking around school about Hailey. He wanted you to let it go, right?"

"Maybe."

"C'mon, Gabs, you're a good judge of character. Scratch that. *Great.* You said so yourself when you first met CJ. I thought he was a little sketchy, the way he always wanted to be alone, hung out in the woods, until we found out about his sister and that's his way of grieving, of remembering her. He's a great guy. He drove up to Lehigh for Districts. He's totally into you." She looks side to side as we cross the street and head into the park. She's not finished.

"And about his sister's eating disorder? You think he's trying to 'save you' because he couldn't save her, you couldn't be more wrong."

"He went behind my back, Ash, talked to you about me. *As if* something's wrong." I sigh. "There's nothing wrong. I'm fine. You shouldn't have told him about my face plant in gym. It was nothing."

Asha clucks her tongue. "It's not nothing." She flashes a steely glare. "Do you realize how scared he was when you passed out at Districts? If you had seen the look on his face." She shakes her head. "He was so worried about you. *That's* why he talked to me." She stretches her arms overhead and blows out a breath. "You need to talk to someone, maybe Coach, maybe a nutritionist or something. I don't know. But right now, we need to discuss your relationship with CJ and how you're crazy if you break up with him."

I look at Ash and she nods. "Yes, I think you're crazy if you do. Truthfully, I think he's in love with you. You remember the night at Lucia's, when I gave you a hard time after you bailed on karaoke? It was written all over his face. He couldn't wait to get out of there, have you to himself. That's not someone who's *faking* it. C'mon, you're doubting your relationship with CJ because *Madison* said something. She's trying to get under your skin. Like always. Why does she care who you're seeing? It's none of her business."

"*Was* seeing."

"I don't want to tell you what to do, Gabs but, don't break up with him."

I swipe my forehead with the back of my hand. "I dunno. But thanks for listening."

"At least talk to him."

"We'll see. Hey, what's wrong with me? How was Homecoming? Your dress was gorgeous. You looked awesome in purple. Liam didn't look too bad either. I think it's the first time I've ever seen him in a suit. Thanks for texting pictures."

"Absolutely. It was fun. Weird, you know, going with Liam as my date, a *real* date. We went to so many things as friends, the three of us. But it was nice." A rosy glow settles in Asha's cheeks.

"That's great. I'm happy for you two. Do you remember that dance in middle school when Samantha Riley asked Liam to go with her?"

"Ugh! Yes. She totally had the hots for him, and he was all into her. *At first.* But at least he came to his senses, realized how superficial she was."

"He realized what he wanted was right there by his side all along," I say in a singsong manner. "Ooh, I think that's when I last saw Liam wear a suit."

Asha gives me an eyeroll. "Right. You sound like you're describing a cheesy movie."

"Sorry, not sorry. I always knew you guys should be together." An ache pulses in my chest. Even if I miss our trio, the way we were before everything changed the night of Liam's party. Before Asha and Liam kissed. Before I went all in for a guy I met at Larry's. I speed up and race ahead. Asha catches me and we fall into stride for the last mile before we go our separate ways at the café.

Asha's words race around my head as I run home, cruising along, breathing in the crisp autumn air, until the woods loom in front of me. My heart thumps in my chest. How did I get here? I didn't mean to take the shortcut, but I did. Like I was drawn here. Weird. Okay, I'm freaking myself out. I wasn't paying attention and ran the shorter route. That's all. There's no supernatural force pulling me to this spot. Right?

Today's the first time through these woods since my argument with CJ. Since I accused him of using me. Pitying me. I don't have to run through. I can turn around, take the long way home. No, there's nothing to worry about. It's only Hailey. And I still haven't done anything to help her. Except talk to her two friends, which led me nowhere.

I continue to run. My heartrate accelerates as I jog along the path that takes me deeper into the woods. Closer to the spot where Hailey died. Dried fallen leaves cover the ground, crunching under foot. The path narrows as the clearing looms before me. No more stalling.

Keep running, Gabby.

I jog into the clearing and halfway across, a gentle breeze caresses my face. Warms me to my toes. Like a comforting hug. I wait for it to change and intensify, to whip up into a blustery wind. For the music to start playing. Instead, a Monarch butterfly floats around my head as a faint voice is carried on the wind and into my ears.

"Trust your instincts. Be yourself."

My gaze is riveted to the butterfly's orange and black wings gliding through the air, fluttering about then gliding again, like they're in perpetual motion. I'm unable to tear away from the display of beauty and artistry. Butterflies have always fascinated me, but this one, like the one before in the woods, seems... Nah, it can't be. But it's like it's following me, seeking me out, almost...*watching* me.

And then, like that, it zooms skyward and disappears into the trees. I stand there, waiting for it to return. It doesn't. I continue across the clearing until I reach the other side.

Am I wrong about CJ? Is that what Hailey's trying to tell me? Trust my instincts? Trust CJ? Is Hailey really communicating with me? I've never believed in spirits before.

Ugh, there's a dull ache in my chest that's been there since that night. The night I sent CJ away.

Asha says I'm a great judge of character. From the first time I met CJ, I felt something. Not only a physical attraction, but a connection at a deeper level. A sense he was kind, gentle, genuine. Am I wrong?

I run again, quickening my steps along the narrow path out of the woods and sprint the rest of the way home.

Chapter Twenty-Two

I do my best to avoid Caitlin and Madison the following week, arriving to English at the last second so there's less chance for Madison to insult me. Taunt me about CJ.

Ash is right. I have to talk to CJ. Apologize. But Regionals are Saturday and that's my focus. I can't let anything or anyone get me off track until after my race.

On Thursday after gym, after everyone's left the locker room, I pull on my boots and head for the door. For some reason, I can't seem to get moving today. I was like a slug during yoga and asked for two bathroom breaks so I wouldn't have a repeat of a few weeks ago. Mrs. Allen readily agreed to my requests.

What the heck is wrong with me? I should be geared up, excited about Saturday, instead I'm listless with no motivation. And not because I'm restricting my food intake, like CJ said. My mom makes certain of that. As much as she can, anyway. She's not at school. Not there to make sure I eat my whole lunch. But it's not that kind of fatigue. It's CJ. As much as I'm trying to avoid distractions before Saturday, I can't get him out of my head.

I shut my locker door, grab my bags and walk around the corner.

And slam on the brakes.

Hushed whispers spill over the bank of lockers.

Madison and Caitlin. I'm so used to the two of their voices in class, how could I miss them? I crouch down and brace my hand against a locker.

"You need to stop. Stop harassing her, Madison. Leave her alone. Especially if she's still seeing CJ. She's persistent, that one. She's gonna figure things out. And that's the last thing we need. It's almost a year. People are starting to forget."

Figure what out? What is Caitlin talking about?

My stomach clenches. Almost a year, she said. No, it can't be. Are they referring to Hailey's death?

"Nobody knows but you and me," says Madison. "As long as *you* keep your mouth shut."

"It's not me you have to worry about," Caitlin says. "Drew was talking to Gabby in class about CJ. About Hailey. He was in love with her. As difficult as that is for you to hear. If he continues to talk to Gabby—"

"He won't. I won't say another word to her." She sighs. "Of all the people to date, though, how in the world did Gabby Patterson wind up with Cal Jarvis?"

"I don't know, but it sounds like they have a lot in common."

"Whatever. We should go. C'mon. Isn't Alex giving us a ride home?"

"Yes, but go ahead, I'm going to use the bathroom first."

"Okay, see you by the car."

Madison shuffles out the door and I release a huge breath. I have to find out what they know. This is my chance.

If I can break Caitlin.

I wait for her to leave the stall and wash her hands.

"Caitlin." I approach her by the sink.

She whirls around. Her eyes widen. "You're still here? How long have you been there?"

"Long enough. What are you two hiding? What did you mean when you said I'm going to figure things out? Figure *what* out?"

Caitlin shifts her feet around. She scans the locker room.

"There's no one here. Tell me. What are you two keeping quiet about? Does it have something to do with Hailey Jarvis' death? I know it happened about a year ago." I cluck my tongue. "And for the record, no one is beginning to *forget*. And especially not her family."

Caitlin purses her lips together and glances around. She's stalling. But she's not leaving here without coughing up information.

"I can wait all day," I say, tapping my foot on the floor.

"Fine. I can't believe I'm telling you this. She warned me not to say anything, that the story would 'go away' eventually. That everyone would forget. But you're right, they haven't. *I* haven't. It will never go away. I can't stop thinking about her, about *that night*..."

My stomach lurches. I swallow the boulder in my throat. "Go on."

"Madison and I were meeting Drew and Alex in the woods that night." She looks me in the eye. "The night Hailey died, we were just going to hang out. Alex's older brother, Nick, sometimes got us beer for the weekend. He works at that craft brewery on the outskirts of the borough." She pauses and lowers herself to the bench against the wall. "Drew didn't want to go. He and Madison were fighting, having issues.

Probably because he was seeing Hailey behind her back." She shakes her head. "Not that I blame him. Madison didn't treat him well. She didn't deserve him. But he should've broken up with Madison first."

Hailey *was* seeing Drew.

"But Alex convinced him to go with them that night," Caitlin continues. "He said Drew was going to talk to Madison afterward, tell her they were done. Madison knew about Hailey. She wasn't stupid." Caitlin pulls at her sweater. "But that night, we left Madison's car and walked into the woods. On our way, Madison said she forgot her phone and for me to go ahead, that she would catch up." Caitlin purses her lips. "She didn't forget her phone. She saw Hailey sitting by a tree, writing in a notebook. Using her phone for light."

Notebook? Of course.

Wait. She wrote something in the beginning about someone harassing her, before her writing turned to an obsessive accounting of what she ate. Is that what drove her to an eating disorder? Was she harassed? Bullied? Was it Madison who bullied her? Hailey probably shoved the notebook under the leaves when Madison approached.

"Madison didn't realize I saw Hailey, too. I'd barely sat down with the guys when Madison ran into the clearing, screaming about a rabid fox. We all raced out of there, but...I had to check for myself. I ran to where I'd seen Hailey. She was gone. I panicked, not knowing if she'd ran off because of the fox or..." She pauses and her gaze drops to the ground. "Or if something else happened. I don't know why, but something made me walk to the edge of the cliff. She was lying there in the shallow creek, not moving. Her phone was on the ground, so I picked it up and dialed 911. Then I ran off to catch up with the others."

Shaking, I take a seat on the bench with Caitlin, gripping the sides of my legs. "You *left* her?" My voice echoes around me, like its an entity detached from my body, the words floating around me. Because what I'm hearing *can't* be real. "You left her there to die."

"I was scared out of my mind. I didn't know if..." She pauses and swallows. "If Madison had something to do with it or if Hailey had also run from the fox and slipped off the edge. Or something completely different."

"You mean, you didn't *want* to know."

Caitlin nods. "What would I say to the police? Lie and tell them I never saw Hailey there? Tell them Madison and I were together the whole time?" She clasps her hands together. "I panicked." She looks me in the eye. "I know it was wrong."

Numbness seeps through my body and I stare into space.

"I called 911. I said there was an accident below the cliff in the woods."

"Yeah, using *Hailey's* phone. That way they couldn't trace it to you."

Caitlin presses her lips together and glances sideways. "I'm not proud of it, okay?"

"What happened then? Had Madison left?"

"I caught up with her as she was getting into her car. The guys were parked in front of us in Drew's car and we took off at the same time. I asked Madison what happened. She was like, 'I told you, there was this rabid fox. I certainly wasn't sticking around.' When I told her

245

about Hailey, she was shocked—at least that's how she acted. She said she never saw her." Caitlin rests her elbows on her knees. "I considered that maybe she was telling the truth, but I had this sinking feeling in my gut. It's why I told her to turn around, go back. We had to do something."

"You went back?"

"I'm not totally heartless. I mean, I'd called 911, but it didn't feel right, leaving. I thought we should go back and wait for the ambulance."

"And?"

"Madison said no. She said I'd called 911, there was nothing more we could do. Plus, she said Hailey wanted to kill herself and didn't want to be saved."

Because Madison *is* heartless. "That's horrible."

"That's when I knew. I knew something happened between the two of them." Caitlin's voice is low and rough. "Hailey didn't jump off that cliff. She'd been sitting there, writing, minding her own business. It didn't fit. I was scared. I called out sick the following week of school. There was no way I could go in while everyone mourned Hailey Jarvis' death by suicide, knowing we were in the woods that night. And the feeling in the pit of my stomach that something else happened. When I finally returned, I tried to ignore Madison, but I couldn't. I had to say something. I had to make her tell me the truth."

"Which was?"

Caitlin twists her body to me. "That she saw Hailey and confronted her about Drew. Hailey ran away and Madison chased her. Her phone dropped when she was running, and she leaned down to pick it up. That's when she fell. Over the edge. That's the story Madison told me, anyway."

An accident. Which Madison did nothing about.

Bile rises in my throat as the clues, the ones I didn't pick up before, choke me. Weeks ago, just outside the gym doors, Madison argued on her phone with someone about where they were hanging out, saying, 'it wasn't their fault'. Caitlin was the person on the other end. Madison was so casual about it. As if Hailey's death was an unfortunate consequence of her recklessness. Nausea churns my stomach. *That's* why Caitlin invited herself to Liam's party that night. She didn't suddenly develop an affection for Liam. She couldn't bear to hang out where a girl slipped and fell to her death. Or was pushed. Madison had no misgivings, apparently.

That's when it hits me. The blank look on CJ's face as Caitlin walked away from us at the football game. His sudden desire to leave the stadium and the crowd. The way he flinched when I told him Caitlin was asking about our relationship.

He recognized Caitlin's voice. Because it's *her* voice on the 911 call. Why didn't he say something to me? Pain tears at my heart. "So, you believe her? That it was an accident?"

"What else could've happened?"

I stare at Caitlin.

"Wait, you think Madison pushed her?" Caitlin sits up straight, eyes wide.

"It's never crossed your mind? I mean, isn't that's why you couldn't go to school? If you believed it was an accident, why wouldn't you or Madison tell someone? Hailey's parents believe she took her own life. How could you let her parents think that when it wasn't true? Let CJ think that when it wasn't true."

"I told you, I didn't know the whole story 'til later. It wasn't until recently I found out you were seeing her brother." She sighs. "Then seeing you talk to Drew in class brought everything back. I know he's still devastated about Hailey."

"You think? Caitlin, you need to do the right thing. Regardless of what Madison says. Hopefully, she'll go with you, but you have to go to the police, tell them what you know."

"She's going to totally freak on me when she finds out I told you." She fiddles with her pocketbook strap. "But you're right, CJ and his parents need to know the truth. And Drew. I don't know how he's going to take the news."

I nod. "They do. Better late than never, I guess."

"What do you think is going to happen?"

"I don't know. It depends on what the police think after talking to you and Madison. Whether they believe you. It doesn't help that Madison left the scene. Left Hailey there instead of waiting for an ambulance. Both of you." I dig my fingers into my legs, as if I can stop my body from shaking.

Caitlin stands and swings her hair over her shoulder. "I have to go. Madison and Alex are waiting for me."

Once Caitlin leaves, I grasp my phone, my heart slamming against my ribs. My trembling fingers hover over my phone. No, I can't text CJ. This is too big. Call him?

I said a lot of things to him at my house. Rotten things. What if he doesn't want anything to do with me anymore? He may not answer if he sees it's me. If I text him, he'll at least get the message.

—*Do u have a minute to talk?*—

His response is instantaneous.

—*Of course. Do u want to stop by?*—

My pulse quickens. No, I'm not ready to see him.

—*Actually, can I call u?*—

—*Sure*—

I leave the locker room and make my way outside. I punch in his number and the second he answers, the words tumble out. "Caitlin confessed to me, CJ. About Hailey. She's going to the police. She told me what happened that night. It was an accident. Madison chased Hailey, harassing her about seeing Drew. She and Caitlin were there with Drew and Alex that night. But it was Madison who chased her, causing her to slip and fall over the edge." My voice cracks, but I continue. "I wanted to tell you before the police contact your parents. You were right. Hailey didn't die by suicide. Hopefully, you'll get more answers when you talk to the police."

Silence on the other end.

"Gabby, are you serious?"

"Yes. I still can't believe it, but I had to call you immediately."

"I'll go tell my parents. Wait, do you believe it was an accident?"

"CJ, I—"

"You told me you weren't friends with either of them, that Caitlin invited herself to Liam's party, that—"

"Yes, CJ, you're right. Neither of them are my friends, but to think Madison could commit murder?"

CJ exhales a long sigh. "I don't know, but I should

249

go. I need to tell my parents. Thanks for letting me know. I'll talk to you later."

"Okay."

I should be relieved. CJ finally knows the truth. And he was right, his sister didn't die by suicide. But he thinks Caitlin could be lying. Is she? Damn, what if that's the sinking feeling in my gut? What if it wasn't an accident? But then, why tell me if she suspects it wasn't an accident? Madison is her best friend.

There's nothing I can do. It's in police hands now. They'll have to decide if Madison is telling the truth.

I walk to my locker, the chaos of dismissal swirling around me. My feet won't move fast enough out of this school, away from the secrets and lies within these walls.

"Hey, I have the car today. Need a ride home?"

The voice yanks me from my thoughts.

"Gabby? You okay?" Liam taps my hand.

"Yeah, fine. I'm sorry, what did you say?"

"Ride?" He jangles his keys. "Asha's meeting me at the car. She had to drop off something to Guidance. It's the one day you guys don't have practice. How about we grab some lattes at Buddy's?"

I smile. "Thanks, but I'm not really in the—"

"C'mon, the last time the three of us hung out was at the end of the summer."

"Seriously?"

Liam lifts a brow. "Gabs, you're killing me. Have you forgotten us already?" He places his hand over his heart in mock indignation.

I've been so caught up with CJ—*ruining* things with CJ—and playing detective, I've neglected Liam. Ash, too. The friends I accused of ignoring me. Maybe

I've been the one ignoring them.

But I'm a mess right now. I can't go hang out like everything's fine. Normal. I can't think of anything but what Caitlin told me. Hailey didn't die by suicide. My chest squeezes.

"Thanks for the offer, but I'm going to pass. Tell Ash I'll talk to her later."

"You sure?" Liam's bright blue eyes search my face. "Is everything okay?" He tilts his head. "Wanna talk about it?"

"No, but thanks. I appreciate the offer. I'll catch you guys later. I promise."

"Okay, I'm holding you to it." He grins and I return a small smile.

The crisp autumn air nips my face as I walk along the sidewalk. CJ was right the whole time. Of course he was. Because he wasn't just her brother. He was her best friend. Which is why my stomach is in knots, my head feeling like it's filled with cotton. My heart thumping.

I should be with him right now. To comfort him. Listen to him. Help him through this. But I screwed things up. I believed Madison over him. Where did that get me?

I head into the woods on my way home, the place that started all this, but where I've always felt at home, at peace. Where I can block out the rest of the world.

Shuffling along through the trees, absorbed in my thoughts, I'm jolted backward when someone runs up behind me and yanks my hoodie, almost strangling me.

"What is your problem?" I yell and spin around. "Madison! Did you follow me from school?"

Her breathing labored, she rests her hands on her

knees and looks up at me. "What did she say to you? Caitlin. What did she tell you back at school just now?"

I shake her off and proceed along the path. I glance over my shoulder. "She told me what you should have told the police almost a year ago. And isn't that where you should be right now?"

Madison catches up to me and runs along, keeping up with my long strides. "She's lying."

"No, for once, I believe she's telling the truth." I stop in my tracks and face her. "How could you do that? Because you were jealous of Hailey? You chased her through the woods and over that cliff because Drew liked her? And he was gonna break up with you?"

"You don't know the whole story. He felt sorry for her, that's all. Always off by herself, supposedly writing songs, like some kind of loner. Not to mention, starving herself. He pitied her. That's the way Drew is."

"What, kind and caring? Someone who sees the good in people?" Ugh, I could go off right now, but I'm so done with everything. "I have to get home. Make sure you tell the police everything. If you don't, I'm sure Caitlin will."

I run away from her and never look back.

****

After dinner I head to my bedroom to start my homework. Fatigue sinks into my bones, pulling at me. The moment I plop onto my bed and open my books, my eyelids lower, and sleep claims me. An hour later I wake to a text on my phone.

—*Just got back from the police station. Everyone was there. Want to tell u all about it, in person, but I don't know if u want to talk to me. Sorry if I snapped at u on the phone earlier. It's a lot to process. Hope we can talk soon. Miss u, Gabby—*

It's followed by a sad-faced emoji. And a heart.

My own beating heart cracks in two and I pull my knees to my chest, wrapping my arms around my legs.

I miss you too, CJ.

He doesn't know if I want to talk to him? Why would he think that? I'm the one who said all those awful things. He shouldn't want to talk to me. But I'm glad he does. And how could I blame him for his reaction. I'm not entirely sure what to believe either.

I grab my phone.

—How about later on Saturday or Sunday? I have Regionals Saturday morning—

Wait, that's selfish. Like I can't concentrate on anything but that race. What if CJ wants to talk now? It's a silly cross-country race. CJ's dealing with major news about his sister's death.

—But we can talk before then if you want. Whatever you need—

That is, *if* he wants to talk to me.

—OMG! I almost forgot. Regionals. No, let me know afterward, when you have time—

—I'll be thinking of u at your race. Good luck. Not like u need it. LOL—

I breathe a sigh of relief. He wants to talk. Maybe I haven't ruined everything.

I slog through my homework before calling it quits at nine-thirty. When I wake the following morning, the uneasiness is back, swirling in my gut. For the first time in a while, it's not about CJ, but Madison and Caitlin. How can I look at either of them again?

Maybe they won't be there. CJ didn't go into detail about what happened at the police station, but there's a good chance they're suspended. Still, I can't go into school today.

My pulse spikes. No, I have to go. If I miss school, I'm ineligible to run tomorrow at Regionals. At least I think that's the case. But I can't risk it. I'll go in late, blame a stomach ache—I feel one coming on now. At least then I'll miss first period English with Caitlin and Madison. *If* they're in school.

"You don't look so hot, Gabby. Are you feeling okay?" my mom asks as I round the corner into the kitchen.

I guess I don't need to pretend. "My stomach's...off. I don't know if it's something I ate yesterday or some kind of bug. Do you think it's okay if I go in late? Give it a chance to settle down?"

My mom lays her hand on my forehead. "Mm, you're not hot. Still, you are a bit pale. Why don't you take some ginger ale then lie down? I'll call, tell the school you'll be out today."

"But then I won't be able to run tomorrow. Regionals, Mom. Kind of a big deal."

Hand on hip, my mom paces. She puckers her mouth, and her gaze bounces around the kitchen. "I know, but if they were today, you wouldn't be able to participate if you weren't in school. Since they're tomorrow, you'll be fine." She halts and looks me in the eye. "As long as you *are* fine. Gabby, I don't want to see you rundown, have you pass out again. You've been eating better, but—"

A wave of nausea passes through me, and I wrap my arm around my stomach. I have to be okay by tomorrow. It's what I've worked for all season. "Mom, I'm fine. I'll definitely be better by tomorrow."

Mom scrutinizes me. "Are you sure, Gabby? Like I said, you're eating better, but," She bites her lip. "Is Coach working you harder at practice, having you run more than usual?"

Crap, she's not letting this go.

"Why?"

"I don't know. You...well, you're still so skinny." She scrunches up her face.

I roll my eyes. "Mom, I run cross country. I'm not a tackle for the football team. Lean and fast." I grab a bottle of ginger ale from the fridge and turn to go.

"I know, but..."

"I'm fine, Mom."

She crosses her arms. "Okay. Sip on that then get some rest. I'll call the school."

"Okay." I pause halfway up the stairs. "You don't have to stay home with me, you know. I'll be fine." I don't need Mom hovering all day, making sure I'm eating, when the last thing I can think about is food. I just want to chill.

"I know, but I don't have much going on at work today. I'll let them know I won't be in, but I do need a few things at the store. If I'm not here when you wake up, that's where I'll be. Okay?"

Worry tinges her voice. Worry I've heard many times. Does she have any idea what's going on with me and CJ or is she concerned with what I'm eating? How much I'm training?

"Sure."

"Gabby?"

"Yeah, Mom?"

"Is everything okay with you and CJ? You two haven't gone out in a while."

What, can she read my mind now?

"He's been busy, that's all." I race the rest of the way up the steps.

Sleep claims me the moment my head hits the pillow. I don't wake for two hours, until bright sunlight streams through my curtains and tickles my eyelids. Guess I needed the rest.

There are two texts on my phone. The first is from my mom.

—*Went to the supermarket, post office. Be back shortly. Call if you need me*—

The time is stamped fifteen minutes ago. The second is from Asha.

—*Where are you? OMG, the whole school's freaking out over the news. How the police believe Madison had something to do with Hailey's death. Do u know anything about this? I'm thinking you do.*—

—*Sorta. Can u stop by after school? I'm home sick*—

—*Sick??? What about tomorrow? Can u run? I can't carry the team on my own. LOL! Seriously, Gabs, are u okay?*—

—*Yes. Just an upset stomach. Probably related to what's going on. Caitlin spilled everything to me yesterday when I cornered her in the locker room. And Madison tried to get me to keep quiet when she learned what Caitlin told me*—

—*Should've known. I'll see u after school.*—

****

I jump in the shower then check my school intranet for homework assignments. I might as well make use of my time. I'll be gone all day tomorrow at Regionals and depending on the outcome, I may not be motivated to do any work on Sunday.

By the time my mom returns, all my homework is done and the grumbling in my stomach has reached epic proportions.

"Glad to see you're feeling better," my mom says as I pop the last bit of my turkey sandwich in my mouth.

It's the first thing I've eaten today, and I inhaled it, along with a handful of salt-n-vinegar chips and the rest of my ginger ale. Guilt riddles me for eating every last morsel, but I didn't eat breakfast—something that eluded my mom's hawk eye. I also didn't run this morning—there's no way I could, the way I felt. That makes it even, I guess. CJ's words intrude on my thoughts— *You're going to get accepted to plenty of schools. You don't need to starve yourself to do it.*

But I'm not starving and there's so much more than being accepted to the best schools. The best track and cross-country programs. There's always been more to it. More than fast times and top finishes. Something deeper. Or maybe, something more superficial. A 'look'. A look I'm never going to attain because let's face it, I'm not built that way. Not like Breanna. Not like Katie Watson. I have almost a foot on both of them. I should be happy with who I am.

Yeah, right.

"You sure you're good to run tomorrow, Gabriela?" my mom asks, rousing me. "You know it's not the end of the world if you don't run in Regionals. You still have your finish at Districts—"

"Mom!" I lift my hand, palm outward. "I'm fine. Seriously. It was an upset stomach." I *have* to run tomorrow. "I've worked all season for this. All

257

summer. You know Asha made it too, right? She's really psyched."

My mom pulls me into a hug. "Yes, I know. That's wonderful. I'm glad you have each other for support."

"Me too."

Two hours later, Asha drops herself into the chair by my bedroom window. "So, tell me *everything*," she says, leaning forward. "All anyone knows is that Madison and Caitlin were at the police station last night and it had to do with Hailey Jarvis' death. C'mon, what did Caitlin say?"

I sit on my bed and draw my leg up. "First, were they in school today, Caitlin and Madison? What about Alex and Drew?"

"Madison and Caitlin were both out." Asha scoots forward and rests her chin in her hands. "Why Alex and Drew?"

"They were there, too. In the woods that night. But they had no idea what happened." I pull up my other leg. "According to Caitlin, anyway. If what she told me is the truth."

"Seriously? C'mon, tell me everything."

I lean against my pillows and do just that.

"Oh my God, are you serious?" Asha's brow jumps. "Do you believe her? That it was an accident?"

"I don't know what to believe. And if it was an accident, how can Madison live with herself? Why wouldn't *she* have called 911? Instead, she left her there to die."

"You could say the same about Caitlin. After she called, she should've waited for the ambulance even if Madison left without her."

"But then she would've had to tell the EMTs what

happened. Or what she *thought* happened. Which meant giving up her bestie. *That* only took about a year."

"Ash, did you ever see Madison or Caitlin talking to Hailey before, like in a *not nice* way?"

"What do you mean, like bullying her?"

I nod.

"No, I don't think I ever saw them together. It sounds like Madison was jealous of what was going on between Drew and Hailey."

"That's what I think, too. And I let Madison know that yesterday when she accosted me walking home from school."

But what about those first few pages in Hailey's notebook? Hailey wondered why some girl treated her the way she did. Like she was being bullied. Was it Madison? Her name wasn't in the notebook.

"But you were right, Gabs."

"About what?"

"Hailey wanted your help. She knew you could figure this out."

"But I didn't do anything, Ash. Not really. Caitlin caved pretty quickly when I confronted her. And I *was dating* CJ. No more."

"What?" Asha jumps off the chair and catapults onto my bed. "Have you talked to him yet?" She nudges my leg with hers. "Because you need to talk to him. You can't let this go on."

"Only to tell him what Caitlin told me. I had to let him know that the police would be contacting his parents." I finger a thread on my jeans. "He texted me when they got back from the station, thanking me. He wants to talk." I worry at my lip. "We're gonna try and talk this weekend, after our meet, but I don't know. He must hate me."

Asha pulls her legs up on the bed and twists to me. "Gabs, how can he hate you? Madison messed with your head, made you doubt CJ. She manipulated you. She didn't want you digging around, trying to uncover stuff about the night Hailey died." Asha leans back on her hands. "When she saw you taking to Drew, then talking to one of Hailey's friends, she freaked. C'mon," she says, crossing her arms. "Don't let her ruin things between you and CJ."

"I don't know." Will he even take me back?

"I do. You're going to talk to him, work things out."

I sigh. "I guess. I was rotten to him, Ash. I said some awful things when he was here last time."

"You were upset. People say things when they're upset. Tell him you're *incredibly* sorry you believed Madison over him," she says, her voice dripping with sarcasm.

"Thanks. I already feel terrible."

Asha pulls me into a hug. "I'm sorry. I don't want you to feel terrible. You two need to talk. He'll understand. He's a good guy."

"I know."

"Please, don't let Madison ruin this for you two. She wants to ruin her own life, fine."

****

That night I toss and turn, getting barely a wink of sleep when I need it most. The night before Regionals.

Usually, the night before a big race I run the course in my head. A hundred times. Strategizing, plotting each segment of the course, my weaknesses, my strengths. Sprinting through the finishers' chute.

Breaking the tape. Not tonight.

Tonight, the only thing running through my thoughts is CJ.

Chapter Twenty-Three

Sleep-deprived and running on adrenaline, I race up the hill like someone possessed. The forest looms ahead as I crest the hill behind two other girls, loop around them and push into the woods. I pound the path, strewn with twigs, gaining speed with each harried step. I may have gone out too fast at the start, but right now there's fire blazing in my veins.

Where is Katie Watson? She was at the start. Eh, I can't worry about her. There are plenty of other girls as fast or faster here at Regionals, most of them ahead of me right now.

Stay focused, Gabby.

I can't have a disastrous finish like two weeks ago on this course. No collapsing at the finish line. I'm a well-oiled machine, moving seamlessly, effortlessly. Weightless. I have to ride this for as long as I can. Hopefully, straight to the finish line.

My focus jumps to CJ. How am I going to face him today? Apologize and beg for mercy. That's how. Ugh, why am I thinking about him? I have a race to run. The biggest race of my junior year...unless my time is so good, I make States. Hah!

Concentrate, Gabby.

I push out of the woods and continue my steady pace, crossing the dirt path onto the grass.

"C'mon Gabby, looking good!" Leah, one of the

assistant coaches, stands off the path, clapping. "How are you feeling? Okay?"

She scrutinizes me, my face, my form. No need. I'm kicking butt. I nod.

"No dizziness?"

Of course she asks me that after what happened at Districts. I'd never passed out like that before. I'd been dizzy once or twice from the heat, but that was the first time I collapsed. Our head coach, Coach Caroline, asked me twice before the start this morning if I was okay. What a mess I've become. Not today. I'm killing it out here.

If only I could get CJ out of my head.

I don't want him out of my head. I don't want him out of my life. There's a void inside me that only he can fill. Will he forgive me? Still want *me* in *his* life?

I shake myself out of my thoughts. There are four girls between me and the finish line. Turning it up a notch, I pound the dirt path along the baseball fields, steadying my breathing as I zero in on the leaders. One of them lags, struggling to keep the insane pace set from the start. I pass her, keeping my focus forward.

Three girls to catch, but the finish is only a quarter mile away. Digging deeper, I pump my arms, my breaths coming quick. And pass another girl.

The two girls left in front of me are too far ahead, but I glance at my watch. I'm on pace to set a personal best. To qualify for States in Hershey. Yes!

I gut out the last 400 meters, my quads burning from the effort. Cheers and whistles ring out from the crowd. Pain shoots through my chest as I gasp for air, stretching across the finish line in third place. Exhaustion slams me. Everything's hazy as I sway then pitch forward, but I regain my balance and walk it off.

Coach Caroline races to me and places her arm across my shoulder as I rest my hands on my legs, sucking in air. "Awesome race, Gabby. How are you? Doing okay?"

I exhale and wipe my hands, slick with sweat, on my tights. "Good. I'm good," I pant out. My throat is dry and chalky, but a smile eases across my lips. I didn't pass out and I set a personal best. An enormous sense of joy swells my chest. I didn't make a fool of myself.

Coach taps me on the arm. "States. Two weeks. You qualified."

"Yes!" Excitement flutters in my stomach. I'm so caught up in the news I almost miss Asha racing through the finisher's chute. I run and greet her at the finish line.

"Hey, nice job out there." I pat Asha on the back as she rests her hands on her knees, trying to catch her breath.

"Thanks. You? As usual I didn't see you come in, you were so far ahead."

"Nah, not that far ahead."

"Sooo?"

"What?"

"Did you qualify for States?" A smile quickens her lips, and she tilts her head to the side. Like she already knows.

I don't want to make a big deal, since I don't think she qualified, but I can't stop the big, stupid grin that breaks out on my face.

She pulls me into a hug. "That's awesome. I'm so happy for you."

"Thanks."

"Hey, nice going out there, you two."

Liam squeezes between us and we all hug. One giant, wonderful hug. Like nothing has changed between the three of us. And right now, it feels like it hasn't. My heart swells and I draw my friends closer.

"Thanks, guys. I'm so glad I have you two."

"Aww, c'mon, of course, Gabs," Liam says.

"Hey nice racing girls."

My and Asha's parents join us in walking to the team tent.

"You dropped your time again, didn't you?" I nudge Asha's shoulder.

"Yeah, not enough to qualify for States, like *some* of us," she says, arching a brow. "But it's a PR. I'll take it."

"Did you say *States*? Gabby, that's wonderful," my dad says, tapping my shoulder. "I knew you could do it."

"Thanks, Dad."

"Honey, that's great," my mom says, pulling me into a side hug as we walk. "You were okay out there today? No dizziness or feeling faint?"

"No, I felt great."

Even if I did choke down that bagel with preserves this morning. Mom made sure of it. Surprisingly, it didn't weigh me down.

"Gabby?"

"Yeah, Dad?"

"I think someone wants to congratulate you."

I follow his gaze to the line of tents stretching out beyond ours where a lone figure stands behind a crimson burning bush shrub, the same color as my face.

His hands are crammed in his pockets, his baseball cap, pulled low over his face, concealing his eyes. My heart pounds.

"Be right back."

"Take your time," my mom says.

"Be nice to him," Asha yells between glugs from her water bottle.

It's like I'm walking in slow motion as I pass the team tents, girls stretching, cooling down, celebrating with friends and family. Excited chatter fills the air. But it's all background noise. I'm hyper-focused on one thing. One person. He came. He actually came.

Breathe, Gabby.

"Hey Gabby, congrats on your finish and making States," someone yells, piercing my bubble. It's Katie Watson. "You killed it out there," she says, as she stretches on her mat.

I halt at the South tent. "Thanks. How'd you finish?"

"Dropped five seconds from Districts." She sighs. "Missed States, though. Always next year, right."

Next year. "Oh, I'm sorry, but yeah, next year."

I should stay and chat. Katie's been nothing but gracious, even if she is my biggest competition in the district and I idolize her. But I'm on a mission. To the last tent. To CJ.

"Thanks again."

My heart pounds as I walk away, the adrenaline pumping in my veins. I will my legs to move faster, not even conscious of my feet hitting the ground. Breathing heavily, I arrive at the last team tent. Gear and water bottles, sports drinks and sweats litter the grass. Their school must be lining up for the next race. I wipe my hands, slick with sweat, on my tights, and glance around.

He's gone.

Panic tightens my chest. Where'd he go? I pace around the tent and scan the row of bushes that line the field. Two girls shuffle along the grass to the parking lot. But no CJ.

Tears spring to my eyes. CJ doesn't want to see me or talk to me. I shouldn't be surprised. I treated him horribly. A tear slips down my cheek and I swipe it away with my trembling fingers. Damn, I can't help it. I'm letting some guy ruin what should be a happy occasion. States. I made States! Only he's not *some guy*. And I'd be a lot happier if I could share this moment with him. But he said he wanted to talk.

My euphoria of making States, of possibly earning a trip to Nationals in San Diego to race against the best in the country, has disintegrated into disappointment.

Why did he come if he was going to walk away? Drive all the way here then leave before I could talk to him?

"Hey, where's CJ?" asks Asha when I shuffle into our tent minutes later.

"He left."

"What? No, he was right there. I saw him. We all saw him."

"Guess he took off once he realized I wanted to talk to him." I fold my arms. "Don't worry about it. I'm gonna take a walk."

"Do you want company?"

"No, I'm fine, but thanks."

As I leave, my phone buzzes. It's a text from CJ. My pulse quickens.

—Congratulations on a great race. OMG! U qualified for States. That's wonderful! I saw u run and your awesome finish, but I didn't want to upset u by hanging around. Thanks too for everything u did with Hailey. You don't know how much it means to me and my parents. Hopefully, we can talk sometime this weekend.—

Blood throbs in my temples. He didn't want to upset me? Wait, how did he know I qualified for States? He'd have to know what qualifying times were. Of course he does. He makes it his business to be informed about everything I do. He's thoughtful that way. And I shred his heart into bits.

My body shakes and I hug myself, as if I can stop the heartache that threatens to bring me to my knees. I'm horrible. I judged CJ too harshly, thinking the worst of him. All because of what Madison said. He is the real deal. I only hope he'll listen to me when we talk later.

My parents avoid any talk of CJ on the way home and instead chatter nonstop about States and the possibility of going to Nationals, how excited they'd be to be going to San Diego for the National Cross-Country Championships. For *all* of us to be going. Both my parents have frequent flier miles from business travel, and it'll cost next to nothing for them to fly out with me. The weather in San Diego is beautiful, my mom says. We can visit the zoo. The beach.

They prattle on and on and I don't give a crap. I should be thrilled. I have a chance to run at the biggest, most important high school cross country meet in the country. College recruiters will be there. Lots of them.

That doesn't matter right now. I've wrecked things

with CJ, and I have to fix them. I consider for a second, calling him when we pull into the driveway, but I'm slammed.

Maybe tomorrow.

Chapter Twenty-Four

The following morning, I sit on my bed with my laptop, writing the same sentence five different times. Trying to write a paper for my American Government class. Every five seconds I glance at my phone. Ugh! My thoughts fly all over the place. I swipe the app on my phone and the music streams out. The same song that was on that night at CJ's house when we hung out. Kissed. Totally made out. When he told me he was falling for me. When I knew I felt the same.

My phone buzzes and I practically jump out of my skin.

Liam? What could he want?

—Hey, have a minute this afternoon? I need to talk to u bout something.—

Time is all I have. CJ hasn't called and I haven't worked up the nerve to call him. Are Liam and Ash having problems already? Asha didn't say anything to me when we talked last night. She invited me to a Diwali celebration at her house tonight. I told her I didn't want to ruin the party with my sucky mood, but she said there's no way I could do that, and I'd better come. And bring CJ. Right. How could I have ever doubted her or Liam? Because the two of them are a couple? At least I think they still are. No, she would've said something. So, what's so important Liam can't talk to me on the phone about it?

—Sure, no problem. Writing a paper (trying to anyway) for AG. right now. How about 1 pm? —

—Awesome. Thx!—

It's followed by two smiley face emojis.

I glance at my paper, at my opening paragraph, which is all I've managed, before my attention drifts to my nightstand. It's useless writing this paper now. Maybe I can make sense of some of those pages in the notebook.

The book has finally dried out, the pages brittle and crinkly in my fingers as I flip through what I now know was Hailey's food diary. Until I get to the last handful of pages which instead of lists of food, are copiously filled with her thoughts, albeit smudged and indecipherable.

Almost.

I don't care anymore what they think or say to me. Z told me it's jealousy, that they're trying to feel good about themselves by bringing me down. Maybe, but guess what? It doesn't matter. I'm writing a ton now, putting all my thoughts to words, to music, and I can't wait to show it to the guys, especially D.

Drew? And who's Z? The therapist she was seeing?

Physically, I feel better, even if I'm tempted to count the numbers like before. But I promised Z I would try and I'm doing good. Actually, really good. I'm being myself, like Z told me.

I'm meeting D later tonight. I'm going to sing that new song I wrote for him. I hope he likes it. I'm a little nervous. No, a lot nervous!

D is Drew.

Hailey wrote that page the day she died. She

wanted to sing to him a song she'd written for him. She never got the chance.

The last two pages are a washout. Literally. All the black ink smudged, rendering the pages illegible. But it doesn't matter. I've read enough. CJ was right. According to her journal, Hailey *was* happy at the time of her death.

****

I've finished my paper for American Government by the time Liam stops by at one, but it's garbage. I'll have to revise it later when my mind isn't clouded by CJ. Like that's going to happen.

"Hey, congrats again," Liam says as I lead him into the family room. "Are your parents out?"

"Yeah, they left about a half hour ago to do some shopping."

Liam takes a seat on the sofa and rakes his hand through his hair. "I haven't been over here in a while, Gabs." Glancing around, he pushes up the sleeves on his hoodie and rests his elbows on his knees.

"Yeah, I know. Now that you and Ash are a thing…" I meet his gaze. "You two are still 'a thing', right?"

A line creases Liam's brow and he stretches his arms above his head. "Why wouldn't we be?"

"Just checking. So, that's not why you're here. I thought maybe something was going on with you two. Although, Ash didn't say anything when we talked last night."

A smile twitches at the corners of Liam's mouth. "No, everything's great with us. And yes, Asha would've said something if it wasn't. It's…" He presses his lips together. "It's about CJ."

I grip the sides of my jeans, digging my fingers into my thighs. "Oh. What about him?"

"He stopped by my house yesterday." My stomach squeezes as Liam rests his forearms on his legs and hits me with those intense blue eyes. "The guy's a wreck, Gabs. A freaking mess. I know it's not my place to say anything, but you should talk to him."

I draw my legs up and hug them to my chest. "Of course it's your place. You're one of my best friends, Liam. And I want to talk to him. I just don't know if I can. I was horrible to him. I'm glad he and his parents finally know the truth about his sister's death, but I don't know. Will I make things worse if I talk to him, try to get back in his life?"

"He wants you in his life. Why do you think he talked to me? He asked what he could do to fix things. I didn't know what to say because all he told me is that he screwed things up with you and he needed to fix it. I told him you two need to talk."

How *he* can fix things? I'm the one who ruined everything. And with the new information about Hailey's death, how can even think about me?

"I doubted him. I accused him of using me, of going out with me to get info on his sister. He never believed she died by suicide, something he confided in me after we went out a few times. Because he trusted me." I lower my gaze. "I wanted to help him so badly, too. And at first, he was all into it, you know, me helping. I said I would ask around school, try to see if I could find something out. But then he totally changed his mind, said he didn't want to involve me." I pause. "I never told you, but that's what that chill in the woods was all about. Hailey, Liam. She wanted my help."

Liam furrows his brow. "Wait, what?"

"Remember that day at the movies, at the end of the summer? Ash said it was a ghost in the woods who 'had a thing' for me? She was only messing around, but…well, it turned out to be true."

He furrows his brow. "Whaddya mean?"

"I felt this chill in the woods, in a clearing off the path that overlooks the stream." I clear my throat. "Where Hailey died. It's like she was trying to tell me something. Or, get my attention, anyway."

"Oh wow. Mind blown, Gabs. So, you think she was trying to send you a message, like how she really died?" He snags his bottom lip in his teeth. "Like, my all-time favorite movie? Directed by you-know-who? C'mon, you know what I'm talking about."

"Okay, you're getting a little too excited about this, and yes, I know what you're talking about. But, it's different than that. I think. I never 'saw' Hailey. And she didn't exactly show or tell me what happened. It was more…subtle." Like a feeling. Like the wings of a butterfly.

Liam's eyes sparkle with wonderment. "Wow, so it's real. Ghosts are real. I guess you weren't surprised last week with the news about Madison and Caitlin then."

"Yes and no. I knew something else must've happened to Hailey, especially after my experiences in the woods and then when CJ said he didn't believe it was suicide." I give a slight shake to my head. "But I never imagined Madison or Caitlin were involved. Like, *ever*. Plus, you and Ash are the ones fascinated with all that supernatural stuff. Not me. I try to avoid it, remember?"

"Yeah, I know."

I laugh. "But there was no other explanation for what happened, Liam, why I kept feeling cold in that spot. CJ was right. Something else happened that night. I had to help him figure it out. I didn't learn about Madison chasing her to her death until I forced it out of Caitlin last week."

"Whoa."

"I know. Right? I can't believe we haven't discussed this before now, you know, the chill in the woods. And Ash, she never said anything?" I tilt my head. "Especially the two of you being into all that stuff?"

"Nope. Not a word. C'mon, Gabs, you girls still have your secrets. She probably figured you didn't want anyone else to know." He lifts his hands in a shrugging motion.

"You're not *just* anyone, Liam."

"I know." He laughs, but then his mouth tightens, and he taps me on the leg. "So, what happened between you and CJ?"

"Me and CJ." I sigh and recline into the sofa cushions, keeping my arms wrapped around my legs. "Before I got Caitlin to talk, Madison came to me one day after practice and said all this stuff about how CJ was using me to snoop around for him, make me feel sorry for him and..." I draw in a breath, hesitating.

"What?" Liam tilts his head.

"And 'to maybe get something on the side'." My face flushes and I hug my legs tighter. "I can't believe I told you that."

Liam tips his head back and laughs, a deep rumble in his chest that rocks his whole body.

"I didn't think it was *that* funny. Is it so hard to believe a guy would want to 'have a good time' with me? CJ was pretty ticked when I told him that. Obviously, I wouldn't want that to be the sole reason, and I'd hope he'd get to know me before he thought about that and—"

"Gabby, stop. I wasn't laughing at you. I was laughing because I can't believe she'd say something like that."

"It's Madison."

"Right." He clasps his hands together. "I don't want to embarrass you, but any guy would love to be with you. And certainly not *just* for those reasons, but because of who you are. You're kind and funny, fun to be around, a great friend. You have your quirky music tastes, passionate about running. And you're beautiful. What guy wouldn't want you as his girlfriend?"

My heart swells. "Aww, thanks, you're too nice. You're always too nice to me."

"I'm not *being* nice. It's true. Jake's been trying to get you to go out with him forever. I thought at my party you'd finally decided to give him a chance. You know, you two have the whole running thing going on. You're both diehards. You seem to get along well."

"We do, but I don't want to be his 'second choice', after Breanna broke up with him. If he had his way, he'd still be going out with her."

Liam's brows pinch together. "Uh, no. *He* broke up with her. I thought you knew that." He pauses then looks me in the eye. "No, of course you didn't. Don't tell him I told you, but he broke up with Breanna because, as much as he liked her *as a friend*, he really liked—*likes*—you."

My stomach squeezes. "Oh. Well, now I feel like total crap. I've managed to wreck two guys' lives at the same time. Never thought I'd be saying that."

"No, you haven't. Jake will be fine and CJ? You two need to talk. It was a misunderstanding."

That's putting it mildly.

"I believed her, Liam. Everything Madison said. I doubted his reasons for going out with me, because that's the way I am. She only cared about saving her own neck. Making sure no one asked around about Hailey, no one, meaning *me*," I tap my chest. "She was so worried I'd discover the truth and tell CJ. I had no idea she was involved until I overheard her and Caitlin whispering in the locker room and then forced Caitlin to tell me everything. Of course, Madison tried to stop me from saying anything afterward when she found out Caitlin told me."

Liam scoots over and pulls me into a hug. "I'm sure CJ will understand when you explain it to him."

"I don't know. He must hate me now."

"He doesn't, Gabby." Liam draws away. "That's what I've been trying to tell you. You can't give up on him." He smiles and I can't help but smile back. I mean, it's Liam.

"Thanks. You're a good friend."

"I know. That's why I'm here." He purses his lips, like he has more to say but is restraining himself.

"What? Out with it."

"I remember when you first introduced me to CJ, I just stared at him. Or maybe, *glared* is a better word." He snorts. "I had to make sure he was treating you right. That he was a gentleman. You and Ash are my best friends, and I can't let you go out with just anybody." He wiggles a brow.

"That's sweet of you." I nod. "How can I forget that day? You and Ash had your arms around each other. *In public*. It was weird." I shake my head. "No, not weird, *awesome*. Hard to believe I was really seeing it. I've always known you two belong together. You've never been very good at hiding your feelings."

Liam flushes. "Yeah, I know."

"So, what about now?"

"What?"

"What's the verdict? Did CJ 'pass the test'?"

Liam laughs this deep rumbly laugh. "Absolutely. It didn't take me long to figure it out. Even that day, I could see how he was totally into you. He didn't take his eyes off you the whole time." He clears his throat. "Except for when I kinda stared him down. Guess I was acting all dad-like, but I realized there's nothing to worry about. He really cares about you."

"Yeah, I know. I'm realizing that myself now. But, if he wants to talk, why did he leave yesterday? You saw me walk over to him after our race. He bolted. I was ready and willing." I pick at a thread on the sofa arm. "Well, as ready as possible, but I forced myself to walk over and then he was gone."

"Honestly, he didn't want to upset you, but he wanted to see your race. That's what he said to me yesterday."

"Mm, he texted me afterward." I take a deep breath, but it doesn't ease the ache in my chest, the pain ripping my heart in two. What a jerk I've been to CJ.

"Talk to him, Gabby. He could use your support next week when Madison and Caitlin have to appear at a hearing."

My shoulders sag. "Right. I forgot about that. That's going to be tough on him. His parents, too. I don't know where to begin, Liam. I said some awful things to him."

"You'll figure it out. Tell him what you told me." Liam stands and I walk him to the door. "Tell him you want to talk. Don't drive yourself crazy anymore." He pulls me into a hug. "And I expect to see you at Asha's tonight."

"I dunno. I told her I didn't want to ruin the party, but—"

"But nothing, you better come." He arches his brows.

"We'll see. Isn't Diwali the celebration of light over darkness? I'm like a dark cloud right now. I don't want to rain on everyone's party."

"Stop. You're coming?"

"Maybe."

An hour after Liam leaves, I pace my bedroom floor, my gaze bouncing between my window to the phone on my bed. Yes, I should go to Asha's. It's a big party at her house, a big deal. But first...

Dammit, Gabby, call him. At least, text him.

No, I can't do this with a text. Or with a phone call. It has to be in person. My hand trembles. I start to type:

—*Do u have time today to talk?* —

My heart pounds as I hit Send.

Ten seconds later, my phone buzzes.

—*Yes. When?* —

—*Now? Unless you're busy?* —

Now? Geez, that's not too desperate, is it?

Sounding desperate is the least of my worries. I have to do this ASAP or I'm going to jump out of my skin.

—Be there in ten—

Ten minutes. Yikes! I can do this.

I have to.

Chapter Twenty-Five

A car pulls into the driveway and the engine shuts off.

I glance out the window. My parents are home. Ugh! I can't talk to CJ with my parents here. Maybe he'll want to take a walk. It's a nice day.

But first, I grab the notebook and stuff it in my hoodie pocket. It's time to share it with CJ.

I race down the steps as my mom comes through the door with an armload of groceries. "Can I help?"

"Sure. Unless your dad has the rest."

I walk outside and halt. CJ pulls to the curb and kills the engine. Ten minutes? That was like, two and a half. Tops.

"Need help, Dad?"

My dad shuts the car door with his foot, glances at CJ's car then at me. "Nope. I've got it under control." He smiles and taps me on the shoulder. "Looks like you have a guest. Go talk to him."

Hmm. My dad's face is unreadable. Neither he nor my mom have said a word about CJ since he disappeared yesterday after my race. Do they know what's going on?

"Okay."

My dad heads into the house and I shuffle a few steps down the path, a few steps that might as well be a thousand. My heart beats double time as CJ climbs out of his car. I walk around to the driver's side, clenching and unclenching my hands.

"Hey." CJ leans against the car door and rests his hands inside his burgundy hoodie pocket.

"Hey." My gaze drops to the ground before I lift my chin and look him in the eye. "Do you mind if we take a walk?"

"Nope. It's beautiful out today."

We step away from his car. He's not reaching for my hand. That's gotta be a bad sign. He always held my hand before. He even told me how much he enjoyed it. Ugh, where do I begin? What do I say?

C'mon, Gabby. Say something. Anything.

I stop mid-stride and turn to him. "CJ, I'm sorry. I never should have said those things to you, treated you the way I did. I never should've listened to Madison. I don't blame you if you hate me."

CJ grasps my hand. God, it feels good to hold his hand again. Warm. Safe. He looks me in the eye. "It's okay, Gabby. I understand. And I don't hate you."

"But it's not okay. I said all that stuff to you because I was upset, because I believed Madison—who's not and never has been my friend—over you. I insinuated you were using me for information and—" My throat is like sandpaper. The words won't come.

"And maybe it was all an act being with you. I think those were your *exact* words."

Flames engulf my face. *Ouch.* I did say that. The words shred my insides, having CJ throw them back at me now.

"It hurt, Gabby, saying I was using you. First, I would never, *ever*, do something like that. Second, I couldn't have faked my feelings for you if I tried. Do you understand how you make me feel when we're together? When we're not together and I constantly think about you? When I know I'm going to see you?"

My heart splinters, deepening the ache in my chest. The giant hole that's been there ever since I sent him away that night at my house.

"I'm sorry. I was upset and confused. As much as I didn't want to, I believed Madison. I know now she was only trying to cover her butt, keep me away from you. Prevent you from discovering the truth about the night Hailey died." I exhale a giant sigh, after getting it all off my chest.

CJ closes the gap between us and winds his arms around me. "I don't want to be kept away from you." He rests his face against my neck. "And as for the *other* thing you accused me of, I wasn't trying to 'make up' for my sister by helping you. I was worried about you, about the weight you lost. I wanted you—*want* you—to be okay."

The scent of fresh soap and coconut overwhelms me. I breathe it in, breathe CJ in. My knees wobble. I missed him so much. Missed the way his skin feels against mine. The way his scent fills me up and exhilarates me. The way being with him melts my insides. I wrap my arms around him.

"I just want to be with you, Gabby. I hope you feel the same," he whispers against my hair.

"More than you can imagine."

"Before I forget, you were freaking awesome at Regionals." His warm breath sends shivers across my skin. "I wanted so badly to congratulate you, hug you, when you finished yesterday. When you made States. As hard as it was for me to leave, I had to. I didn't want to distract you, or worse, upset you. It was your moment to enjoy. You didn't need me messing that up."

My heart squeezes. "Thanks, but you wouldn't have messed it up. I screwed up, not you." I pause and lower my gaze. "I wanted to see you, too, CJ. Especially now, with everything that's come out." I draw away and grasp his hand. "How are you doing?"

"I'm okay, thanks. Still trying to process everything."

"I'm sure. Hey, do you want to take a walk through the woods?" I raise my brow.

"Mm, the way you say it, it sounds dirty. *Indecent*." The muscle in his jaw jumps and he grins, stirring something low in my stomach. "I would *love* to take a walk through the woods with you."

Liquid heat scalds my veins. Indecent?

"I have some things to tell you."

"Sure. I want to talk to you, too." He squeezes my hand, and we continue walking.

"First, I have to ask: you knew and didn't say anything to me, didn't you? At the football game, when Caitlin walked by, blabbing to Liam about another party. You recognized her voice. It's why you wanted to leave the game, wasn't it? You recognized her voice from the 911 call."

CJ's hand goes rigid in mine. "I didn't think you noticed." He meets my gaze. "I didn't say anything because I wasn't a hundred percent sure, which is why I didn't confront her. I had to be certain, Gabby. I wasn't. I knew though, if I said something to you, you'd ask her a bunch of questions, trying to get answers. Trying to do everything to help me. I don't know her—well, I know her enough *now*—but I had a sense of the way she was. Especially after you told me she invited herself to Liam's party." He shakes his head.

"You're a good judge of character, CJ."

He studies me for a moment and his mouth quirks up to one side. "Yeah, I am. I still can't believe she gave her friend up. I mean, I'm glad she did. After the football game, I drove myself nuts, trying to figure out if it was her voice on the tape. If it wasn't and I accused her, I'd feel horrible. But as it turns out, she confessed to you. You got me off the hook."

"I wished you had said something to me."

"I couldn't. Like I said, what if I was wrong? I can only imagine what kinda crap she'd give you for accusing her of anything. It was my problem to deal with." He drops his gaze to the sidewalk and halts.

My heart breaks for him.

I place my hands on his chest. "I am so sorry, CJ." A tear slips out of my eye.

He wraps his arms around me and pulls me against him, his heart thrumming beneath his hoodie, matching the furious beat of my own. "Hey, it's okay," he whispers in my ear. "Stop beating yourself up. Everything worked out in the end, right?"

I'm here with CJ. The truth is finally out about his sister's death. Everything *did* work out.

"Yes. I hope you know how sorry I am."

"I do. Let's not talk about it anymore for now. Aren't we supposed to be taking a walk in the woods?" He draws away, flashes those beautiful gray eyes at me and bites his bottom lip, making my heart race.

"Yes, we are."

As we approach the entrance to the woods, CJ hooks his fingers in my belt loops. "Gabby, it's my turn to apologize."

"Huh? What are you talking about?"

"I'm sorry I never told you about Hailey's eating disorder. It didn't seem important." He pauses. "At first." He splays his hands over my waist, sending goosebumps across my skin.

"It's okay. You don't have to talk about it."

"No, I want to. I should've told you. When I noticed something going on with you, it scared me."

He holds my gaze, almost daring me to challenge him, dispute his characterization of 'something going on'. But I go silent, letting those pale gray eyes hypnotize me.

"That's when it came together for me. Why Hailey appeared to you in the woods. I didn't realize it at first. I couldn't figure out the song reference." He pauses. "Then I did. It wasn't only to help me figure out the truth, but to help *you*. She didn't want you to go through what she had."

My mouth goes dry. "There's nothing going on with me, CJ. I'm fine. C'mon, you were at Regionals. I had a great race."

"I know you did and I'm so happy for you. But, Gabby, you can't honestly tell me you haven't been losing weight—weight you can't afford to lose. I wanted to tell you about Hailey, the way she struggled and fought so hard, torturing herself when it came to food."

Is now the time to bring up the notebook?

"And eventually, how she got better. But I didn't know how to talk to you about it. I tried once or twice, but ended up sounding judgey. That's why I talked to Asha. She knows you better than anyone else—her and

Liam." He slides his arms around me and rests his head on my shoulder. "I'm sorry. I didn't mean to go behind your back. But I only wanted to help."

"I know, but seriously, I'm fine. I passed out that one time at Districts, probably because I hadn't eaten enough that morning." I stare at my feet. "But it was one time. I'm fine. I swear."

"You say that, but—"

"But nothing." My agitation bubbles over. "What about you, CJ? Let's talk about you for a minute. You didn't let me help you. Ugh! Here, I need to show you something." I draw the notebook out.

"What's this?"

"You don't recognize it?"

"No, should I?"

"It was Hailey's."

CJ squeezes his eyes shut. "What? Where did you get it?"

"In a tree stump in the clearing, buried under a mound of wet leaves. I found it a few weeks ago, but I didn't realize it was Hailey's until that day Madison confronted me. That's when it all came together."

CJ turns away as if trying to process what I'm saying.

"Here." I hand him the book, opened to the middle, where she kept a daily account of her food intake, after the first few pages where she seemed to be trying to fit in, be accepted for who she was.

"Oh. Wow. I never knew she kept this." He flips through the dry, brittle pages. "I knew she wrote her songs in a book, but I didn't realize she kept something like this, an account of everything she ate." He sighs. "That's what this is, isn't it?"

287

I nod.

"I can see why you doubted me when I told you she was happy. You probably thought she was struggling with this and—"

"*And* I should've read to the end. You were right. She *was* happy, incredibly happy when she died. She'd written a new song, wanted to sing it for Drew." I cast my gaze to the ground. "She never got the chance."

"Huh?"

I take the book from his hands and flip to the end. "The last few pages, I couldn't read them at first. They were all stuck together, like the rest of the pages, from the weather. But once they dried out and I got the courage to keep reading, I saw you were right."

CJ examines the pages, before a tear slides down his cheek and I wrap my arms around him.

"Thanks," he says, pulling in a deep breath. "Can I keep this?"

"It wouldn't be right if you didn't. It was Hailey's. She'd want you to have it, CJ."

"Thanks. We talked a little at the station last week, Drew and me. He took it hard, thinking she died by suicide. Now he knows the truth, like the rest of us. I'm glad I got to talk to him. He seems like a decent guy." He laughs. "I would've approved. I wish she would've told me about him." He playfully pokes me in the side. "Hey, even though her eating disorder had nothing to do with her death, I still think it's the reason she came to you. She doesn't want you to suffer the way she did. *I* don't want you to suffer. Seriously, Gabby, she was miserable until she got help. Music was a big part of her healing. Not that everything was suddenly better, but it was a start. As you saw." He taps the notebook, which he slides into his pocket. "Like she wrote here, she totally threw herself into her songwriting. And apparently, she had a boyfriend." A large grin breaks out across his face.

CJ's so close, his breath warm on my face, his body pressed against mine. "I'm so sorry, C.J, about everything. But don't worry about me. I'm not miserable. I'm not keeping food diaries. I'm fine."

CJ sighs and draws away. "All I could think about the whole time you were running your race yesterday was if you were okay. How you were feeling. If you were going to make it to the finish line without collapsing. "I was so relieved when you didn't." His voice trembles. He rests his chin on my shoulder, wrapping me tighter in his arms. "I was so freakin' worried about you. And before you say anything, it's not why I came to your meet. I wanted to see you run, kill it out there like you usually do—before you started restricting food."

"I'm not restricting anything, and you don't have to worry about me. Trust me, my mom makes sure I eat, ever since Districts when the doctor talked to her and my dad. She's a bit overbearing, actually." I don't mention the extra miles my mom *doesn't* know about.

"Only because she doesn't want to see you pass out again, like you did at Districts. You know, make sure you're not starving yourself. End up requiring professional treatment like Hailey," he says, his voice low.

"CJ, I'm sorry about Hailey, that she went through that, but I'm fine. I eat enough. I do."

As if by repeating that mantra will convince him I'm fine. CJ searches my face, lingering on my lips, before a smile eases across his face.

"Okay, if you say so." His gaze stirs something wild inside me. What did he say a few minutes ago? Indecent thoughts?

He grasps my hand. "C'mon, let's walk."

We follow the dirt path into the woods. The trees, with their brilliant red and orange leaves, form a seamless canopy above our heads as we push into the heart of the forest. The path starts to narrow, and my pulse quickens as the tinkling of the stream below fills my ears. I keep my eyes straight ahead, not letting them wander as CJ grips my hand and squeezes it. The path widens again, hooking to the right and away from the cliff and the long drop to the water.

"I know you said you're eating more, but you're still really skinny," CJ says. "Are you running more at practice? Coach Caroline having you do double miles to get ready for Regionals?"

Crap.

I pull away slightly but CJ tugs me back. "No. Do you and my mom talk on a daily basis?"

CJ laughs. "No, why?"

"No reason."

"But you didn't answer me."

"What?"

"Are you running more?"

"Maybe a *teensy* bit more." I swallow the lump in my throat. Good thing we're moving. I have a really bad poker face.

CJ stops and turns to me. "C'mon, I can tell when you're lying, or *stretching* the truth. Are you running on your own, in addition to practice?"

So much for that.

"I thought we were taking a walk."

"Gabby?"

"Maybe."

"Maybe?" CJ looks me in the eye. "Come here." He wraps his arms around me and whispers in my ear, "What am I going to do with you?"

His warm breath tickles my skin and sends a wave of goosebumps across it.

"This is pretty nice."

"Heck, yeah. I missed this, Gabby. Missed seeing you, touching you, everything, when you weren't speaking to me."

We stand there under the trees, as a smattering of crimson leaves float to the ground. How great would it be to stay like this? I don't want to let him go. If only *he'd* let go of his needless worrying about me.

"I never want you to go through what Hailey did...even if you already have to some extent. But I'm here for you, whatever you need."

"Thank you."

CJ shakes his head, laughing.

"What?"

"To think I didn't follow you out of Larry's that day. I wanted to so badly, but..." He takes a deep breath. "I was scared. Scared because I was attracted to you. And I didn't know if I could handle it. Or, if I was even ready to talk to someone. If I hadn't bumped into you later that night, I would have kept going back to Larry's. Every. Day." He gives me a lopsided grin. "Yes, stalked you, until you showed up again. Because I couldn't get you out of my head."

My heart swells. That makes two of us.

He leans his face into my neck, touching his lips to

my skin, kissing the spot on my neck right below my ear. The blood hums in my veins.

"You know, I believe we meet people in life for a reason, not fate, but there's a reason we cross paths with others.

"Maybe."

"Hey," CJ draws back and places his hand on my face, tucking a strand of hair behind my ear. "What do I have to do to convince you I've totally fallen for you? And kinda hoping the feeling is mutual."

"Of course it is. You haven't figured that out yet?"

"I dunno. You're rather mysterious." A smile eases across his lips. "C'mon."

We continue along the path and when we reach the clearing, I stop and gaze around. The air stills around me.

"You know, we never came here together after you told me about feeling cold here, hearing the music," CJ says.

I tilt my head. "Yeah, why is that?"

"Um, you never asked, and I guess I never offered because I was afraid."

"You, afraid?"

"I told you Gabby, I felt Hailey's presence here because it's where she wrote her music, but I was a little freaked out when you told me what happened to you. I didn't know what to think." A grin tugs at his lips. "Until you convinced me she had a message and that was she wanted you to help me." CJ lifts his gaze to the trees then lowers them to the ground. "Well, there were two messages. I think she's at peace now. She doesn't need to linger here anymore. We know the truth about that night." He squeezes my hand. "*And* she knows you're not going to starve yourself or train excessively because *I* won't let you." He bites his bottom lip. "You don't need to be like Katie or Breanna or anyone else."

"What? How do you know about—"

"I know all about your 'rivals' and I know there's *no* comparison. None."

Heat flushes my cheeks and I lean into him. "You're just being nice."

"I'm being honest." He rubs my back. "You want to know why Hailey developed an eating disorder? At least the way I understand it?"

I nod.

"It started freshman year. She didn't say anything, not until I kinda figured it out, but she was being bullied. Then her grades slipped, which was totally out of character. She always had straight As. Unlike me."

A stray thought nags my brain. "Was it Madison and Caitlin?"

"Huh?"

"The ones who bullied her."

CJ sighs. "She never said. My mom tried to pry it out of her, but Hailey didn't budge, except to say some girls were saying stuff to her. I tried to talk to her, to get her to open up to me, but she said it was nothing. Nothing to worry about. She probably thought I'd confront them."

I arch my brow. "Would you?"

CJ sighs. "No. Okay, maybe I would've, but only to make them stop. Hailey and I were always close, and I felt completely useless, not being able to help her."

"You can't blame yourself, CJ. Hailey probably wanted to deal with it her own way."

"*Her* way of dealing with it was to not eat. Food was something she could control, something she had power over. But it got so bad she passed out a few times…" He pauses and looks at me, his gaze lingering.

"Go on."

"My mom was so worried, she took her to the doctor. Hailey didn't want to go. She kept saying she was fine, but she finally had no choice one day when she fainted again. She saw a doctor who deals exclusively with eating disorders. After that she started seeing a counselor. It was around that time, she totally threw herself into her music. It helped a lot. At least that's how it seemed to me. She was different. Happy. She was still seeing a therapist when she…" CJ hesitates, the words seemingly stuck in his throat. "When she died. It's why it didn't make sense, her dying by suicide."

"I'm sorry, CJ. I never knew."

"Don't be. But when I noticed you not eating or eating a little and then passing out, it brought it all back, the pain she went through, the way she tortured herself by starving, I don't want you to go through that. And you run so much, Gabby. All those grueling practices. You must burn through so many calories, you need to eat. Like, *extra* slices from Lucia's. Not fewer." He nudges my neck with his face.

I can't help but crack a smile.

"And that goes for overtraining. You can't push yourself to exhaustion. It's like you compensate for eating a sandwich—*one whole sandwich*—by running an extra five miles. Maybe you don't keep a food diary like Hailey, but you're doing the same thing."

I pull away. "Not true."

He tugs me back to him. "Isn't it? You say you need to run so much so you'll finish well, impress college coaches, get a scholarship, but..." He whispers in my ear, "It's more than that. You have to stop trying to *look* like someone else. *Be* someone else. You are absolutely beautiful and perfect the way you are. I think I've already told you that."

My heart trips in my chest. This 'talk' wasn't supposed to be about me. It's supposed to be about CJ. About me apologizing for being a jerk to him. How did I let him work it around to me and my supposed problem?

"So, how are your parents doing?" I grasp his hand and nudge him to continue walking.

We shoulder our way under low hanging branches, the wayward twigs catching on my hoodie. CJ leads me along a narrow path, further away from the clearing. I've never been this way before. Where is he taking me?

"They're okay. In one way, it's a relief, knowing my sister didn't die by suicide, that she wasn't so distraught she couldn't talk to anyone and decided to end her life. But she's gone and nothing will bring her back." He sighs. "Yeah, it's been hard on them, especially my mom. All the details about that night being dredged up and rehashed. They're reliving it all over again." CJ squeezes my hand. "I think it's gonna take a while. But at least she knows the truth. We all do. Thanks to you."

We shimmy between two pine trees and emerge into another clearing, this one smaller and more private than the other. CJ leads me to a large oak, and we sit on the grass, a scattering of reddish- brown leaves all around us. The other trees—all pines—form a circular wall of green, giving the feel of a secret clubhouse, like the spot Asha, Liam and I hung out when we were younger. In fact...

Excitement flutters in my stomach as I glance around, familiarity flooding me, the memories rushing back like it was yesterday. After school in sixth and seventh grade. Our own secret hideout. I didn't realize this place was still here. Then again, why wouldn't it be?

"What is it? Did you come here with an ex-boyfriend?" He nudges me. "Secret spot in the woods?"

I almost choke on my laughter. "Ex-boyfriend? Uh, no. Actually, Liam, Ash and I hung out here in middle school. We found it one day walking to my house and it became 'our spot'. We hung out, talked about our secret crushes." I flush. "Don't judge. We were like twelve, thirteen years old. I knew Liam was lying when he told us his was Hannah Reed. I knew back then it was Ash. It's always been Ash. He wasn't very good at hiding the truth."

CJ laughs then gets this serious look on his face, tilting his head. "And you? Who was your crush?"

"I didn't have any. Not back then." I purse my lips, stifling a grin.

"What about Jake?"

I whirl on him. "Jake? Who told you?"

"Ah, so it's true, then." A hint of concern creeps into his voice even as a small grin plays across his lips.

"Jake and I are friends, that's all. Training partners for cross-country."

"That's not what Asha said. She said he's hot for you. Has been for a while. And since you go to the same school, you're both runners…"

I place my hand on CJ's sweatshirt. "I'm here with you. So, who do you think *I* have a crush on? And back to what you said before we got off track about crushes. Why are you thanking me, CJ? I know I cornered Caitlin and forced the truth out of her, but I think she would've eventually confessed. The guilt was too much for her. She told me herself that seeing me with you brought everything back. It weighed on her." I laugh, recalling how pissed I was she kept asking me about CJ. I had no clue what she knew. I lean into CJ. "Do you have any idea what's going to happen to them?"

"No." He grasps my hand and rests it on his leg. "If only Caitlin had stayed until the ambulance came. Of course, if Madison hadn't chased her in the first place, we wouldn't be having this discussion. All they had to do was wait there with her. Instead, they left, like cowards."

"I know. I'm so sorry."

"Don't be. You helped figure it out for me. For my parents." I start to protest but he places a finger to my lips. "Shh, don't argue."

A glimmer simmers in his eyes, and he twists his body to me, slides his hand around to the nape of my neck and kisses me, brushing his thumb along my jaw. With his other arm, he lowers me to the grass, his mouth never leaving mine. He kisses me slow and deep, a kiss that sets fire to my veins, liquefying my insides and curling my toes.

I wrap my arms around him as adrenaline races through me. Careful not to lean all of his weight on me, he shifts onto his hip, draping his leg across mine. He trails his fingers along the hem of my shirt, flirting with the bare skin of my stomach. His whisper touch sends a wave of warm shivers rippling across my skin.

His heart thrums against the fluttering beat of my own. Like there's nothing separating us. And right now, there's not much. He trails his fingers up the line in my stomach, raising every hair. I want him to keep going. To keep kissing me this way. Touching me like this. To not stop. But he does.

"What's wrong?"

He draws his hand away then props himself on his elbow. "You've lost a lot of weight."

Not what I expected.

Worry darkens his eyes. "Trust me, I can tell. I've memorized the way you feel. The way you smell. Everything about you, Gabby. I missed 'everything' this past week." He holds my gaze and my face flushes in response.

I draw myself into a sitting position and lean against the tree. "Oh. I thought maybe—" I shake my head. "Never mind."

"What?" CJ sits and slides his arm around me. "You think I want to stop?"

"Forget it."

"No. Can't we talk about this? Don't you trust me enough to talk about it with me?"

My jaw clenches. "There's nothing to talk about."

"Gabby, you said you weren't starving yourself anymore. Tell me the truth." He squeezes my hand. "Talk to me."

"States are important, CJ. I can qualify for Nationals if I run well. Do you know what that means?"

He lifts his head. "Yeah, I think I have an idea. I know how important it is to you. I do. But you can't kill yourself to do it. It's not worth it. You know I'm right. And after everything I told you about Hailey? You keep telling me you're fine. Are you?" He levels a steely gaze at me, his pale gray eyes turning the shade of the November sky. I can't look away. "At least, promise me you're gonna try."

My gaze drops to the ground. "Okay."

CJ lifts my chin with his finger. "Come here."

I scoot closer and look him in the eye. "Seriously, you *noticed*?"

His jaw flexes and the spark in his eye flares into a blaze. "Absolutely." His low, rough voice sends a wave of warm shivers across my skin. A grin pulls at his lips. "Maybe I should make sure?" He winds his arms around me, and his mouth is on mine before I can respond.

He gently grasps my hips as his lips move over mine. He tugs at my bottom lip with his teeth and the fireworks go off. I wrap my arms around his neck, twining my fingers in the soft locks of his hair, inhaling his coconut shampoo. "So?" I whisper against his lips.

Without a word, he takes my hands and places them under his shirt, directly on his stomach. His hard, flat stomach. Encouraging me to touch him. Like I need encouragement. I explore the flat planes of his chest and stomach, his hard muscles flexing and quivering under my hands. I can't believe I have this effect on him, but glad I do.

Breathless, he draws away and a grin plays at the corners of his mouth. "Absolutely sure," he says, before his smile fades. "Gabby, I don't want you to faint anymore, to drag yourself to the end of the race because of exhaustion." His lips pull into a tight line. "Promise me you won't overdo it."

I nod and CJ's mouth is on mine again. He lowers us to the ground, dried leaves and twigs crunching beneath us. He trails his lips along my collarbone, lingering at the hollow in my neck, thrilling every inch of me. His hands, like his lips, are hungry, intense, moving without any restraint and driving me absolutely crazy. He slides his hand to my thigh and stops.

"Is this okay?" he whispers.

Is this okay? It's better than okay.

"Yes," I whisper, and he moves his hands across my hipbones, brushing his fingers along my stomach. Breathing hard, I place my hands on his chest. "It's okay, but I think we need to stop."

He looks me in the eye. "I'm sorry, is it too much?"

"Maybe." I pause. "No. I don't know."

What am I doing?

He pulls me up with him to sit against the tree and twines his fingers with mine. "I'm sorry."

"Don't be, but we're out here in the woods, even if this spot is totally secluded. Plus, there's this." I laugh as I grab a handful of leaves from my hoodie and toss them on the ground.

Laughter escapes his mouth, and he brushes off my sweatshirt. "I'm sorry. I was preoccupied."

"Me too."

CJ slides his arm around me and pulls me to him. "Outside of that, *is* it too much? Tell me the truth, Gabby."

I bite my lip and meet CJ's gaze. Can I really talk about *this*? Talk about how wonderful he feels. How he makes me feel. How I don't want to stop what we're doing, but I'm not ready to go any further. No, I can't say that. Can I?

"Are you uncomfortable with this, with the way things are between us? Please tell me. I don't want to do that."

"Do I look uncomfortable? It's not that, it's—"

"You're not ready for things to go any further." Can he totally read my mind?

"It's not that I don't *want* to, it's…yes, you're right, I'm not ready. But I like things the way they are now."

Flames engulf my face. I can't believe I'm having a conversation with him about this. About sex. Or not having sex. Is that what we're even talking about? Duh, of course it is. No, maybe not. My heart's thumping so loud I can't think straight. The only thing I know is I don't want to lose CJ.

CJ takes my face in his hands and looks me in the eye. "Gabby, I would love to keep things the way they are. As long as you're comfortable, I'm good. I've already told you you're the first serious girlfriend I've had. I don't want to rush things with you. I've never *been* with anyone else, so we're kinda in the same boat here."

My body relaxes and I lean into him. "Really? So, you're still a—"

"A virgin. Yes."

Yes, we are talking about sex.

He leans into my ear and whispers, "But I'd love for you to be the one to change that. *Someday*." He kisses the spot on my neck right below my ear. "And you don't know how much I want to be that person for you."

301

Heat races across my skin. Holy crap, how do I respond to that?

I bury my head in CJ's sweatshirt and breathe him in. "Thank you."

"Don't thank me. You don't realize how unbelievably freaking happy I've been since I met you. I wish we'd never had the misunderstanding between us. It made me realize when I didn't talk to you or see you, when I thought I could lose you, how much you mean to me. I love being with you, whatever we're doing. Even if we're hanging out at my house listening to music, watching a game." He laughs. "Obviously, *this* is pretty cool…" He lifts my chin with his finger. "No, it's incredible." His gaze locks with mine and my heart trips. "But I don't want to do anything you're not ready to." He places his lips to my ear. "I love you."

"I love you, too, CJ."

It rolls off my tongue. Because it's true. The whole time we were apart it was true, too.

I told a guy I loved him. Well, a guy other than Liam, one of my best friends. But it's not *just* a guy. It's CJ. I only wish it didn't take me so long to figure that out.

He wraps me in his arms and for the first time in a long while it's like everything's okay. In the silence, I sink into him, let everything go until reality intrudes on my thoughts.

"So, when's the hearing for Madison and Caitlin? This week, right?"

"Tuesday. Do you think you'll come?"

"If you want me to."

"I'd love it if you could come. It would mean a lot to me." CJ sighs. "Oh, but it's at nine in the morning.

You have school."

I tap him on the chest. "Seriously, I think I can afford to miss school for something this important. To support you and your parents. How could I not?"

"Thank you. Will your parents be okay with it?"

"Absolutely. They'll be happy I'm going with you. They like you. A lot." I suppress a giggle. "In case you haven't noticed."

"Really?"

"Yes, but don't let it go to your head."

"Nah, never."

"Maybe we should start back. It's getting cold, now that the sun's going down." Shivering, I stand and hug myself.

CJ wraps his arms around me. "We could always go back to my house. My parents aren't home."

His face is hidden from me, but the flirtation is in his voice and my stomach jumps. It wouldn't take much to convince me to go back with him.

"I should get back. I told my parents I was going for a walk. If I'm gone too long, they may come looking for me."

"Text them. I'm not ready to let you go yet," he whispers against my hair.

My heart skips a beat. "Me neither, but..." I look him in the eye. "Hey, how about coming with me to Ash's tonight? For her Diwali celebration? Her family always has a big party at her house."

"She won't mind if I come?"

"Mind? She told me to bring you. Thought you could use some fun after the week you've had. The *year* you've had."

"Yeah, absolutely."

Chapter Twenty-Six

A cold, steady rain falls outside my window as I stand in front of my closet. Black pants or black pencil skirt? Either goes with my black wedge-heel boots and burgundy sweater draped across my arm. My usual jeans and hoodie won't cut it today. Neither Madison nor Caitlin have been to school since Caitlin confessed almost two weeks ago. It's going to be a little weird seeing them in a courtroom. A lot weird.

I settle on the pencil skirt and close my closet doors.

"Are you almost ready?" my mom calls from downstairs. "CJ and his parents will be here in fifteen minutes, and you haven't eaten yet."

"Five minutes, Mom."

You haven't eaten yet.

That's all my mom worries about. I have to eat, or she won't let me out of the house. No biggie. She and Dad have no clue I slipped out early this morning to do a five mile tempo run before they were even awake. And Lola won't tell. She enjoyed every second of our run.

I don't like sneaking around, keeping secrets from them, but they'll worry if they think I'm overdoing it. Like CJ. I'm only doing what's necessary to keep pace with all those little skinny girls.

"Okay," I set my bag on the floor and grab the box

of cereal from the cabinet. "Do you think this will take long? More than an hour?"

My mom turns to me, her hand wrapped around a steaming mug of espresso and sighs. "I don't know. Depends, I guess, if they plead guilty." She studies me before a smile parts her lips. "You look nice. Change from your usual jeans and sweatshirt."

"Thanks. I didn't want the judge to throw me out for not being dressed properly." I laugh as I pour the cereal into a bowl.

"Are you going to be okay going back to school, Gabby? You don't have to go, you know. These things can be draining, *emotionally* draining." She squeezes my shoulder. "You may not want to go sit in school the rest of the day. I'd understand if you didn't."

"Um, I should be fine. I have practice, anyway. States are less than a week and a half away. Coach has sprint work planned for today. I can't miss."

My mom swallows a mouthful of coffee. "Mm, well, don't push yourself too hard. I don't want a repeat of Districts." She arches her brow.

"I know."

I lower my gaze to the newspaper on the table and there in black and white is the story. Local Teens' Hearing on Death of Hailey Jarvis Today. My chest tightens.

Front page news.

It's still surreal, the way it was when she died last year. Only now, I'm much closer, *connected*, to the situation. Dating CJ changed things.

A knock at the door rouses me from my thoughts.

"They're here," my mom calls from the hall.

"Okay, coming."

I rinse out my cereal bowl—I gulped a few spoonfuls—and grab my bag off the floor. My mom stands with my coat in her hand at the front door. I shrug it on, and she pulls me into a hug.

"Did you even eat anything?"

"Yeah, of course."

Her gaze flits over my face. "Okay. I hope everything goes well. I'll be at work, but if you need me, call. Okay?"

I nod.

"Hey, Mrs. Patterson," CJ says when my mom opens the door.

"Hi CJ. Good luck today with everything. I'll be thinking of you and your parents." She waves to his parents in the car.

"Thanks."

"Don't you look all dressed up?"

I finger the sleeve of CJ's black suit. No, not dressed up. *Totally hot!* Definitely a good look on him.

CJ takes my hand and studies me, lingering on my legs. "You don't look too bad either. You are totally rocking those boots with that hot skirt." He flashes me a crooked grin, leans close and whispers into my ear, "I'd like to spend some time taking it off. Later?"

Flames lick my face, and I meet his gaze. "CJ, your parents are right there in the car. My mom's behind us," I say through clenched teeth.

"Nah, they didn't hear a thing."

He chuckles and ushers me into the car. If only he hadn't said that. I'm going to a courthouse hearing to determine responsibility for his sister's death and all I can think of is CJ's hands on me, taking off—

"Good morning, Gabby."

"Oh. Good morning Mrs. Jarvis, Mr. Jarvis." I swallow the lump in my throat and smooth out my skirt. CJ squeezes my hand.

Breathe, Gabby.

"Sorry, not sorry," he mouths, his jaw muscle jumping around. A glimmer sparks in his eye. "Later?" he mouths.

He doesn't know when to quit. I like that about him.

"We appreciate you coming," says Mrs. Jarvis. She has CJ's coloring, golden blonde hair, which falls to her shoulders in waves, and pale gray eyes, eyes that I'm sure have done tons of crying since his sister died. And this past week when she had to rehash it all over again with Caitlin's confession. I can't imagine. "I know CJ does too. Are you sure you're okay with missing school this morning?"

"Oh, absolutely. My mom e-mailed school last night. Everything's good."

The drive to the courthouse normally should take minutes, but it's rush hour and the sidewalks are filled with people hurrying to work, running against the lights, disrupting the flow of traffic. Still, we pull into the parking garage at a quarter to nine.

CJ grasps my hand tightly as we take the elevator to the seventh floor. The air is close and stuffy. I lean my head against the wall and breathe in through my nose.

"You okay?" he asks.

I nod, but I'm suddenly lightheaded, overcome by a gargantuan wave of heat. The kind of heat that muddles my senses, sweat drenching my skin and as I step off the elevator, blackness engulfs me.

"Gabby? Gabby? Are you okay?" His voice echoes around me. Gentle hands warm my clammy face.

My eyelids flutter open. "What? What happ—" Cold dread sinks in the pit of my stomach.

Not again.

This can't be happening. Not today. I ate right before I came. Well, a few spoonfuls of cereal. Still...

"Oh my gosh, are you alright?" CJ squeezes my hand as a crowd gathers.

"Give her space, people." It's a security guard and he parts the curious, gawking crowd, pushing everyone away except for CJ who kneels by my head, and his parents who stand behind him, their faces pinched with worry. "Did you hit your head, miss?"

"No, just my butt," I mumble. I go to stand, but CJ rests his hand on my shoulder. "Not so fast. Here." He hooks his arm with mine and slowly helps me to my feet.

"If I could sit for a sec, I'll be fine. I tripped on my own feet getting off the elevator, that's all."

Both CJ and the guard help me to the wooden bench a few feet away. I slump to the wall. "Thank you."

"Are you sure you're okay, miss?" asks the guard. "I can call for help."

"No, I'm fine. Thank you."

"Did you eat this morning?" CJ asks. He takes my hand and rubs his thumb across my palm. "Tell me the truth."

"A little."

"A little." CJ blows out a breath and glances at his parents who stand a few feet away, in hushed conversation, his mom's gaze darting from us to the courtroom door. "Go ahead, Mom, Dad. I'll be in in a minute. I want to make sure Gabby's okay."

"I'm fine, CJ. You need to be in there with your parents." I keep my voice to a whisper. "You're not missing a second of this because of me. Please go. I'll meet you in there."

"No rush, you two. We'll be right back," Mrs. Jarvis says.

I guess my whisper wasn't much of a whisper.

"There's a café down the hall, Gabby," she says. "I'll get you something to drink."

Before I can protest, CJ's parents leave. The crowd that had gathered to gawk at the stupid girl passed out on the floor has dispersed, hurrying off to their offices, courtrooms or wherever else they need to be. It's just me and CJ. And an awkward silence hanging in the air.

CJ massages my hand with his thumb. "Did you run this morning?"

I keep my gaze on my lap. His soft touch soothes and comforts me. Breaks me.

I nod.

"Gabby? How much?"

The hearing is only minutes away. Why is he worried about me? This day is supposed to be about justice for his sister. But I should've figured out by now, CJ cares too much. And I can't hide it from him.

"Five miles," I whisper.

"What?" CJ straightens. "Like, is this an *every* day thing, even with practice in the afternoon?"

I nod.

"Gabby, you promised." His voice cracks and he leans close, winding his arms around me and placing his lips to my ear. "I love you and I can't watch you do this to yourself. You don't want me to have a conversation with your mom, do you?"

Panic strikes my chest. My mom. No. She thinks I'm doing well. She has no idea I go out every morning to run. Then run *again* at practice. He wouldn't do that to me, would he?

"CJ, you can't. You wouldn't. How could you betray me?"

"I'm not betraying you. You have to stop this. It's screwing up your health." He flashes his steely eyes and my heart races. Why does he do that to me? "I love you." He places his hand on the side of my face and strokes my chin with his thumb before kissing me. "But you're going to kill yourself."

The sadness in his eyes breaks my heart. It's not fair to keep doing this to him. To worry him with my stupid issues when he has so much more going on.

"Here you are, Gabby." Mrs. Jarvis approaches and hands me a bottle of juice, along with a protein bar. "Is this okay? I didn't know what to get, but juice has sugar and—"

"This is great, Mrs. Jarvis. Thank you so much. I was just clumsy, though."

It's obvious where CJ's kind, caring nature comes from.

"CJ, we'll see you in there. Don't rush. They said the D.A. is running ten minutes late, so we have some time. Make sure Gabby's okay first."

"Absolutely." CJ stands and hugs his mom. He nods to his dad before his parents slip in the door to courtroom 16. He sits and grasps my free hand, as I chug the juice with my other, the cold fruity liquid rushing into my throat. "Are you okay to go in there?"

"Yes. I'm so sorry. I didn't mean to cause a scene. I'm the last person you should be worrying about, CJ. Today's about Hailey."

"Wrong. You're the first person I worry about." He presses his lips together and glances away. "But I don't want to have to worry about you like this. You're so smart, Gabby, but not when it comes to this. You made States. You had some of the fastest times in cross-country this year. Yeah, I know. I checked," he says when my mouth falls open. "What more is there to prove? You don't need to look or *be* like anyone else. Be yourself, Gabby."

I jerk my head up. "What?"

"Be yourself," he repeats, using the words that echoed in my head the other day. The same words from Hailey's notebook, when she was recovering from her eating disorder. "You're unique. You're you. I know it sounds corny, but it's true. I love you because of who you are. Asha and Liam love you because of who you are." He pauses. "I don't want to date Breanna. Or Katie. Or any other girl on the planet. I want you, Gabby."

My heart swells.

"I guess I can't help it."

"You have to try. You need to tell yourself you're okay the way you are. Better than okay. Great. Because you are." He nudges my arm. "C'mon, do we have a deal?" He grins and tilts his head. I can't help but smile. "Gabby?"

"I guess so. As long as you promise never to date Breanna or Katie."

CJ pulls me into a hug. "No chance. Ever." He places his lips to my ear. "And you, Jake."

"No way."

Warmth fills my chest and I want to believe what I'm saying. But it's not that easy. How do I go from always measuring myself against others, always falling short, to saying, 'I'm okay with me?'

"Once you're ready, we can go in."

"Huh? Oh, right."

"Are you sure you're okay?"

"Yes, absolutely." I smile and squeeze his hand.

"I can wait," he says, nodding to the bar gripped in my hand.

"Oh, of course. I scarf down the protein bar, drain the rest of the juice and then it's time.

Time to go into courtroom 16 and get justice for Hailey.

****

Two hours and two verdicts later, we leave the courthouse and step into the dazzling late afternoon sunshine. Mr. and Mrs. Jarvis, their hands twined together stroll a few paces ahead of us. The judge decreed Madison guilty of negligence. She believed when Madison testified it was an accident and didn't push Hailey to her death, but her actions caused Hailey to slip and fall off the cliff. A tragic accident, in which Madison should have called for help. For her inaction and failure to go to the police with the truth, she was negligent. She will be doing community service, the location and duration yet to be determined.

Caitlin fared slightly better since she called 911 but should have waited for the ambulance. Alex and Drew, who were called as witnesses, were deemed innocent and unaware of what happened, until this week.

CJ is silent as we walk across the street to the

parking lot. I can't imagine what's going through his head now, but if he wants to talk, I'm here. If he doesn't, I'm here, too. He's been there for me every time I needed him.

"Do you mind if we walk?" CJ turns to me. "We can head in the direction of your house if you'd like."

"Sure, whatever you want. I'd planned on going back to school, but…" I chew my lip. "There's no way I can focus right now. Not after sitting through that. My mom was right."

We catch CJ's parents at the streetlight. "I'm gonna hang out with Gabby a little bit. I'll be home later, okay?"

"No rush, take your time," Mrs. Jarvis says. "Gabby, thank you again for coming. We appreciate it." She nods to CJ. "And I know CJ does."

"You're welcome. I wanted to be here. Sorry for the drama earlier."

"Oh my goodness, don't worry about it. Are you feeling better?"

"Yes, much. Thank you."

Mr. and Mrs. Jarvis head for the parking garage as CJ and I walk in the direction of my house, shouldering our way through the crowd on the sidewalk.

"Are you sure you don't want to be with your parents right now? I can go home by myself. I know the way." I laugh and elbow him.

A grin eases across his face. "Nah, the parents are fine. They can use some alone time. I'm glad it's over and it was the best outcome we could've hoped for." He sighs. "It'll never be the same without Hailey, but at least my parents know the truth now. Even if it took almost a year. My mom meant it when she said they appreciated you coming. It means a lot to both of them."

"CJ, I wanted to come. It meant a lot to me, too. I wanted to be here to support you and your family."

Just not make a spectacle of myself beforehand.

Silence echoes around us as we step inside my house and shut the door behind us. Both my parents are at work. It's eerily silent until Lola races down the steps and pounces on me. Her greetings never get old.

That's when it hits me. Everything. The photographs presented at the hearing today, the ones of Hailey looking sick and emaciated. The ones of her looking healthy and happy. The latter taken right before her death. She was happy then. Me, passing out in the courthouse and almost ruining the day for CJ and his parents. CJ telling me I was his top priority. How can that be?

I can't do this anymore. I can't screw up his life with my fainting, passing out. Him constantly worrying about me. He's been through so much already. And I can't keep ruining my own life. Collapsing at the end of a race. Lying to my mom. I have to get hold of things before they spiral out of control. Well, *really* out of control.

"Hey, what's up? You okay?" CJ slides his hands up and down my arms before wrapping his arms around my waist and pulling me to him.

"I'm fine."

"Seriously, Gabby, what's wrong?"

"It's nothing." Nothing to burden you with now. "Can we chill for a while?"

"I can't think of anything I'd rather do," he says, leading me to the sofa.

About an hour later, CJ leaves. I pull my phone from my back pocket and stare at the screen.

C'mon, you have to do this.

I take a deep breath and punch in Coach Caroline's phone number. She's at lunch right now at school. She said if I ever needed to talk, if I ever needed help... Well, I need help.

"Hello? Caroline Wilson speaking."

"Hi Coach, it's me, Gabby. I'm not going to be at practice today. I was at the courthouse with CJ and his family, so I won't be at school, but..." I pause, my heart thumping. "I wanted to talk to you about something. Do you have a minute?"

"Absolutely. Go ahead."

Chapter Twenty-Seven

My heart thuds, waiting for our cue, as the air around me crackles with electricity. I'm really doing this. How could I not? How could I refuse CJ?

Moisture slicks my hands and I wipe them on my pants. That's when a pair of arms close around my waist from behind and fold me into a warm solid chest. CJ. His clean, fresh scent envelops me and a warm tingle rushes through my veins. Oh my God, he smells good.

"You're gonna be awesome," he whispers in my ear. "Just like you will be next week, at States."

States? No, this is nothing like that. I've trained hard—not starving or overtraining, either. I'm keeping my promise. And seeing a counselor and a nutritionist once a week. To deal with my eating disorder.

Yes, I have an eating disorder and as difficult as it was to admit, it's been freeing. Finally admitting I have a problem, and that I need help. And there are so many people who want to help. Apparently, it's not uncommon for girls my age, and for female athletes, in particular. Coach Caroline has been nothing but supportive. Not to mention my two besties, Liam and Ash. And CJ? I can't even begin to thank him for his patience, understanding and flat out putting up with me.

But this, right now? Standing on stage with hundreds of people on the other side of the curtain, waiting for it to rise? To hear us perform? *Me* perform? This is helping a friend. Two friends, actually. Even though both CJ and Liam are much more than friends. How could I say no to either of them?

CJ's lips on my neck sends shivers across my skin. I wrap my arms around his and breathe deeply.

"I don't know about awesome, but I'm here, so there's that. I know how important this benefit is. Promise you won't be too hard on me if I screw up, forget the words because I'm nervous as hell."

"You're going to do fine. Better than fine."

I turn around and wrap my arms around him. "I don't want to ruin it for you. I'm not Hailey. I don't want you to think I'm replacing her. I could never, *ever* do that."

"You're not replacing her, Gabby. I asked you because you have an amazing voice. We've rehearsed for the last two weeks. We're ready and you're going to be great." He smiles and shakes his head. "I could've told you that the day I met you, when I heard you sing in Larry's."

"You mean when I embarrassed myself in public?"

A glimmer flickers deep in his pale gray eyes. "If not for that, we never would've met."

I purse my lips. "I don't know about that."

"I do." His eyes scrutinize me. "You okay? You're trembling. Nothing to be nervous about. Just like we practiced, okay?"

"Easy for you to say. I've never done anything like this. Asha and me goofing off at karaoke at Lucia's is the most 'performing' I've ever done. And that's when the place was empty. The entire school is out there tonight."

"Relax. I'm here with you." CJ turns to Nate behind the drums. "Ready?"

Nate nods as the curtain goes up and the lights come on. With his arms still around me CJ steals a kiss. One last, lingering kiss that promises more for later. For tonight. Tomorrow. And the day after that. Whistles and cheers rent the air as CJ releases me and takes his position to my left. Nerves churn my stomach, but I shake out my hands and breathe deeply. CJ smiles and mouths 'You've got this. I love you.' And I melt right there on stage.

As soon as his fingers start strumming, I wait for the note that's my cue and then I'm all in. The music takes hold of me as I close my eyes and sing, become one with the music, like I did that day I met CJ in the music store. Like I did when Hailey's song hit me in the woods. Blocking out the audience. The hundreds of people in the audience.

Twenty minutes and four songs later, the curtain drops. I'm drenched in sweat, but euphoric. We did it. I sang four songs with CJ and Nate and didn't hurl from a massive case of nerves. Or forget the words. CJ sets down his guitar and crushes me in a hug.

"You were awesome. Unbelievably, freaking awesome. Thank you so much," he whispers against my neck.

"Thank you for letting me sing with you guys. I'm glad I didn't embarrass you."

"Nah, Gabby, you were great," says Nate as he disassembles his drum set. "Seriously, CJ's right; you were awesome."

"Thanks. You're too kind."

"Did you say, 'embarrass us'?" C.J. asks. He looks

me in the eye. "You killed it. You nailed *every* song. You know what this means, right?"

I shake my head. "No way. This was a favor. A *one*-time favor. To you and Liam. For this benefit. I need to concentrate on running, now." Staying healthy.

"I know you do. I don't mean *right* now. I know States are next week. But after that? Come on, what do I have to do to convince you?" He nuzzles his face in my neck as he tightens his embrace. That's a start…

"Hey, awesome job you guys!" Asha slips behind the curtain and throws me a massive smile.

"Hey, Asha," CJ says, before pressing his lips to my ear. "Later, I'll find a way to convince you." He steps away. "Yeah, I will," he says when I shake my head. "I have to go say hi to someone. Don't go anywhere without me."

"Take your time. You have a lot to catch up on, I'm sure." And I'm not leaving without you.

CJ mentioned Kyle, one of his best friends, someone he hadn't talked to since last year would be here. In fact, it was CJ who asked him to come. First Nate. Now Kyle. CJ's starting to come around.

I smile as he heads out to the audience and realize maybe I am too.

A word about the author…

I'm a lifelong lover of books and storytelling and hold an M.A. in Applied Math, a subject which finds its way into many of my stories.

I live in Bucks County, Pennsylvania with my husband, two sons and two dogs. I gather story ideas as I run in the early mornings with my dogs. Running is the perfect environment for me to think and create.

****

If you enjoyed this story, leaving a review at your favorite book retailer or reader website would be much appreciated. Thank you!

Thank you for purchasing
this publication of The Wild Rose Press, Inc.

For questions or more information
contact us at
info@thewildrosepress.com.

The Wild Rose Press, Inc.
www.thewildrosepress.com